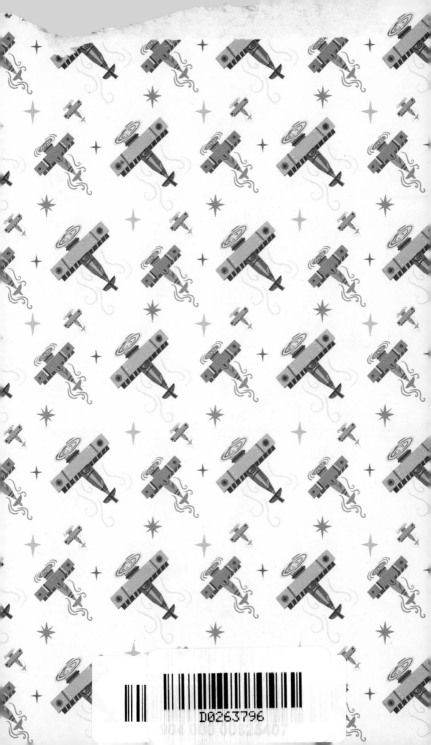

Also by Katherine Woodfine

The Sinclair's Mysteries

The Clockwork Sparrow
The Jewelled Moth
The Painted Dragon
The Midnight Peacock

TAYLOR & ROSE
Secret Agents

PERIL IN PARIS

KATHERINE WOODFINE

Illustrated by Karl James Mountford

EGMONT

EGMONT

We bring stories to life

First published in Great Britain 2018
by Egmont UK Limited
The Yellow Building, 1 Nicholas Road, London W11 4AN

Text copyright © 2018 Katherine Woodfine
Illustrations copyright © 2018 Karl James Mountford

978 1 4052 8704 3
67186/001

A CIP catalogue record for this title is available from the British Library

Typeset by Avon DataSet Ltd, Bidford-on-Avon, Warwickshire
Printed and bound in Great Britain by the CPI Group

To all the readers who asked
for more of Sophie and Lil

LAPLAND

SIBERIA

FINLAND

U R A L M O U N T A I N S

BALTIC SEA

ST PETERSBURG

R U S S I

EMPIRE

WARSAW

POLAND

VIENNA

STRIA - HUNGARY

RoMANIA

BLACK SEA

BULGARIA

TURKEY

TIC S

PART I

'Arnovia is as pretty as a picture postcard. It feels rather like we have gone back in time to another century. We arrived yesterday by train, travelling through a tunnel that cuts through the mountains: Papa told me it is the longest railway tunnel in Europe.

Arnovia itself is a tiny country, sandwiched in between Germany, Switzerland and Austria-Hungary. We are staying in the capital, Elffburg, on the banks of the River Elff, in lodgings close to the Royal Palace. This morning we saw the Royal Family drive out in their carriage – quite a spectacle!

Papa says that his business here will be complete in three days, and then he has promised me a trip into Arnovia's wild countryside. Until then I believe I shall be perfectly happy trying all the cakes in the city's wonderful cake shops, which are as famous as the glorious mountains I can see in the distance . . .'

– From the diary of Alice Grayson

NO8921　　　**NORTON NEWSPAPERS**　　　ONE HALF-PENNY

THE DAILY PICTURE

10th June 1911

FIRST GRAND AERIAL TOUR OF EUROPE ANNOUNCED

LONDON

prepares for Coronation celebrations.

Preparations are well on the way as the entire capital is gearing up for the grand day in our Royal history. Gladis May Berkshop of East Clapham speaks of the excitement,'We're planning a street party, with lots of cake & songs we're all very much looking forward to celebrating our new King. Continues p5.

INTERNATIONAL NEWS

British scholar killed in Paris burglary

Mysterious death of scholar. FULL investigation to be carried out by officials. More details on this tragic news continues on page 12.

PILOTS PREPARING FOR RACE

INTERNATIONAL NEWS: TENSIONS MOUNT IN ARNOVIA

Unsurprisingly the frictions in Arnovia are coming to a boil. Continue reading the full report on page 10 by our own foreign affairs reporter Richard Gleeson.

Norton Newspapers are proud to announce the inaugural GRAND AERIAL TOUR OF EUROPE – an air race in ten stages, with a prize of £10,000. Sir Chester Norton is personally offering this astonishing prize for the pilot who completes the race in first place. Our correspondent Miss R. Russell reports from Paris, where the race will commence (continued p4)

Worth appointed new Commissioner of Scotland Yard - p19

SOCIETY PAGES

Meet the Season's loveliest debutantes! - p25

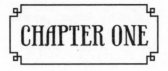

CHAPTER ONE

Wilderstein Castle, Arnovia

Anna knew that there was something strange about the new governess.

She'd had the odd feeling that something wasn't quite right about Miss Carter from the first day she'd arrived in the schoolroom. She'd been dressed exactly as you'd expect a governess to be: spectacles, sensible shoes, hair in a neat bun. But as she'd glanced around, taking them all in – the Countess, her pouchy face patched scarlet with rouge and white with powder, the Count with his bristling moustache and his head as pink and shiny as a boiled ham, and of course, herself and Alex – Anna had thought at once that she didn't really seem like a governess at all.

To begin with, Miss Carter was young and pretty. Their last governess had seemed at least a hundred years old. She'd had grey hair and a bonnet with a drooping black feather in it, and Alex had made up stories about how she was really a wicked witch, who lived in a cottage in the

3

woods and kidnapped little children. But Miss Carter did not look like a witch, or not that kind of witch, anyway. Her clothes were neat and plain, but there was a sort of glamour about her. Her voice was smooth as cream as she held out a hand in the English way and said: 'You must be Princess Anna. How do you do?'

Anna winced as she shook hands. Miss Carter had begun all wrong: she ought to have addressed Anna as 'Your Highness' but, more importantly, she ought to have greeted Alex first. Anna might be the eldest, but royal etiquette dictated that Alex came first in everything. The Countess pursed her lips, already displeased, but of course Alex didn't care a bit, he just smiled and shook Miss Carter's hand too. The new governess smiled back at him, and for a brief, flashing moment, she seemed somehow familiar. Then the moment was gone and Miss Carter was a stranger again, smiling a rather too-wide, too-white smile. It was a Cheshire Cat grin, all sugar and charm, whilst her dark eyes flitted about the room as though she was looking for something.

'Rather a peculiar choice, isn't she?' Anna overheard the Count say to the Countess later. They were in their private sitting room, but his voice rumbled out of the open window, on to the terrace where Anna could hear every word.

'Hmmm,' said the Countess. It was amazing how she could fill such a small sound with so much disapproval,

4

Anna thought. 'You know what Leopold is like. But she does at least come with solid *academic* qualifications.' There was the rustling of paper – that must be the letter that Grandfather had sent about Miss Carter. 'He says that she speaks German, French and Italian. And she knows all the best English schools. I suppose he thinks she will help to *prepare* Alexander.'

The Count grunted in reluctant agreement, but her words made Anna feel cold inside. Alex was eleven now, and she knew that very soon he would be sent away to boarding school in England. Going away to school was what boys in their family always did: it was what their father had done, and Grandfather before him, and no doubt *his* father and grandfather before that. The Countess said that English schools were the best, and of course Alex must have the best of everything. For he was the Crown Prince of Arnovia, next in line to the throne after Grandfather, and that meant that one day he would be King.

Anna, on the other hand, would not be going away to school. Not to England, nor to anywhere else for that matter. Although she was thirteen – two whole years older than Alex – in Arnovia, girls could not inherit the throne. It was always the eldest *boy* who was Crown Prince, and heir to the kingdom. Anna was a princess, but a princess's education was not considered to be very important. When Alex went away to school, she would be left here. Left *behind*, she thought now, with nothing but more coaching from the

5

Countess in deportment and etiquette, to prepare her for a future of attending balls and making polite conversation, which was all that anyone expected of a princess.

That was what the Countess meant now, when she said: 'Leopold says that the governess is musical, and can dance. That could be useful to Anna.'

'But she's so young!' protested the Count. 'She must be scarcely out of the schoolroom herself!'

The pages rustled again, and then the Countess said: 'Well perhaps that is no bad thing, Rudolf.' Her voice was as precise as the tick of the ancient clock that had been passed down from generations of long-ago Wildersteins. 'Considering everything, a *young* girl may be easier to manage . . .' Then her voice dropped lower, and Anna could hear no more.

She walked slowly back along the terrace, taking care that her feet did not make more than the quietest scrunching sound on the gravel. Anna knew that princesses were not supposed to listen in at windows, or to eavesdrop on private conversations, or to do what Alex affectionately called *sticking their noses where they didn't belong*. If she were caught by the Countess, Anna knew she would be sentenced to even more time sitting at the hard back-board, embroidering the crest of the Royal House of Wilderstein on yet another handkerchief. There were few things Anna hated more than embroidery; and worse still, while she sewed, she'd have to listen to one of the Countess's lectures about their family's proud history. Though, of course, the Countess didn't think the lecture was a punishment. In fact, she probably thought she was giving Anna a delightful treat.

'The Royal House of Wilderstein has a most distinguished heritage,' she would begin grandly. Her jewellery would tinkle as she moved to and fro in a waft of lavender water and scented face-powder, the train of her brocade gown trailing across the floor. 'Our family dates back to 1314, with the heroic King Otto the Wise of Arnovia . . .' Anna had heard the lectures so many times she thought she could probably quote them in her sleep.

Family history and tradition were impossible to escape here. In the ballroom, generations of her own ancestors seemed to watch her from the oil paintings that hung on the walls. There was King Otto the Wise himself, shown in a dramatic battle scene, brandishing his sword aloft. There was the Count, in full military dress, wearing a helmet with spikes on it and holding a sabre. There was the Countess as a young woman, in a vast, fearsomely ruffled gown.

Anna's own face was amongst them too. On Alex's last birthday, Grandfather had sent a photographer to the castle to take portraits of each of them, which now hung side by side in small oval frames. But they were not very good pictures; somehow the photographer had managed to make them both look even smaller and paler than they actually were. Alex did not look at all like a future King:

7

instead he was mouse-like, blinking short-sighted dark eyes, a rogue tuft of hair sticking up at the back of his head. As for herself, while princesses in fairy tales were usually radiantly beautiful, she was anything but. Instead she looked uncomfortable in the formal black velvet frock with the stiff collar that the Countess liked, her hair hanging straight and smooth over her shoulders, very dark against the white of her cheeks.

Their photographs hung beside the vast framed portrait of their mother and father, which was surrounded by sombre black curtains. Until Anna was four, the children had lived with their parents and Grandfather in the Royal Palace in Elffburg – but then their parents had died.

Assassination was the proper word for what had happened to them. It hissed like a snake, tracing along her spine.

An *assassination*, Grandfather said, was when someone – often a royal someone – was murdered in a sudden or secret way, for political reasons. In this case, some people who opposed the monarchy had thrown a bomb at their parents' carriage when they had been travelling home from the opera. They had both been killed at once.

The assassination had caused an uproar, with riots on the city streets. The children had been whisked away to safety in the mountains, under the careful supervision of the King's cousin, the Count von Wilderstein and his wife, the Countess. Even when the danger had passed, they had remained at Wilderstein Castle. The air was supposed

8

to be healthier for Alex, who had asthma and suffered from fits of wheezing. 'Up here, I know you are safe,' said Grandfather.

His eyes were heavy when he talked about their parents, his voice husky and sad. People whispered about what had happened in hushed voices, saying it was *a terrible tragedy*. But the truth was that Anna and Alex didn't really miss their mother and father because they couldn't really remember them. Anna sometimes stood and looked at their portrait, but even when she searched her memory, willing herself to conjure them to life in her mind, she couldn't. They were strangers: just paint and canvas. No more than an old portrait in a tarnished gold frame.

Grandfather, on the other hand, was very real indeed. He spent most of his time in Elffburg, busy with his royal duties, but once or twice a year, he'd arrange for them to visit him. These trips seemed to Anna to belong to a different world, in which she wore a white dress with a green sash and Alex a smart uniform. Grandfather would take them out on official visits all around the city: they'd go to the huge old cathedral dedicated to St Anna, the patron saint of Arnovia for whom Anna herself was named. They'd take a boat trip along the River Elff, or drive in the royal carriage down the narrow streets of colourful houses, where the warm smell of chocolate would drift from the open door of a little *konditorei* selling delicious cakes. In Elffburg the sky always seemed to be blue, and wherever

9

they went, people smiled and waved the green-and-white Arnovian flag; officials bowed low; the head *konditor* rushed out to present them with the speciality of the house. It was wonderful and strange, like being in a dream.

Anna sometimes let herself imagine what it would be like if they lived in Elffburg with Grandfather all the time. But she knew that wouldn't happen, at least not until they were quite grown up. Grandfather was much too busy to have time for them; he preferred to keep them here, in the mountains, under the Countess's watchful eye.

At least he visited them often. Whenever he came, he'd bring presents – boxes of chocolates tied with ribbons, or sometimes things for them to read. For Alex, he'd bring magazines about theatre stars, or programmes from the latest production at Arnovia's Royal Theatre. For Anna, he'd bring storybooks, most especially English school stories. Ever since she'd read *The Fortunes of Beryl*, a splendid story about a girl who travelled from South America to England, to go to a wonderful boarding school, she'd been entranced by these kinds of books. She might not be able to go away to school herself, but at least she could get lost in marvellous tales of bold schoolgirls who played hockey and tennis, and had all kinds of thrilling adventures, which usually ended in them becoming Head Girl, or at the very least the heroine of the Fourth Form.

The Countess did not really approve of Anna's storybooks, which she considered unsuitable reading for a princess; nor of Alex's magazines, which she said were 'inappropriate' and 'frivolous'. Unlike the Countess though, the new governess didn't seem to mind in the least what they read. She'd grinned at the sight of *The Fortunes of Beryl* and Anna had even seen her flicking through Alex's theatre magazines herself, once or twice, when she thought that nobody else was watching. It was almost as though Miss Carter didn't really care about what was appropriate for a princess and the future King of Arnovia, Anna thought with a frown.

What was even more puzzling, although she was supposed to be preparing Alex for school, she didn't seem to care very much about lessons either. She had a habit of letting them slide: 'That's enough arithmetic for one day,' she'd say, pushing the textbook away as if she was as bored of it as they were. Instead, she'd let them act out plays, which Alex loved more than anything else. She helped them rehearse some scenes from Shakespeare's *The Tempest* to perform for the Count and Countess, even making them costumes – sticking silver-paper stars on to an old curtain so that Alex could dress as the magician, Prospero, and carefully cutting wings out of cardboard for Anna to wear to play the part of his magical servant, Ariel. She seemed to understand what acting meant to Alex, who was quite different when he was performing, or making up a story. He could roar and rant as the mighty Prospero in a way he never could as his ordinary, timid self.

Other times she'd read aloud, or play games with them – Hide-and-Seek, or Stuck-in-the-Mud, or their favourite, Murder in the Dark. She played just as enthusiastically as Alex and Anna did themselves: when it was her turn to be 'murdered' she died with such horrifying groans and moans that even Alex was impressed.

It ought to have been fun, but there was something about it all that made Anna feel uneasy. She didn't like the way that Miss Carter always seemed to be *there*. Their previous governesses had been attentive, but Miss Carter never left them alone for so much as a moment. For Anna, who was used to being able to slip about the castle by herself, it felt stifling to have the governess always with them, suggesting she read them a story or that they all played a jolly game. After all, Anna was thirteen years old, not a child to be coddled and amused.

Alex, on the other hand, seemed to relish Miss Carter's company. He spent hours listening to her talk about the school he'd be going to in the autumn. 'My brother went to the same school, and he told me all about it,' she'd begin, before embarking on complicated explanations of what the boys ate, their games, their lessons and the pranks they played on the schoolmasters. Alex hung on to every word whilst Anna fidgeted resentfully beside him. It was bad enough that Alex would get to go away and live in the wonderful world of school she'd read about – that enchanted realm of satchels and swimming baths, and delightful unknown things like 'chemistry labs' and 'gymnasiums' – without having to hear every detail of his new life, before he was even gone.

'I don't know why you're being so funny about her,' Alex said, on a rare moment when they were alone. They were in the castle grounds, throwing a ball for the Count's dog, a rather sorrowful-looking long-haired dachshund that Alex had nicknamed Würstchen, because he was exactly the same shape as the fat sausages the Count always ate for breakfast. 'I thought you loved all that boarding-school stuff. Besides, I think Miss Carter's marvellous. She's by far the best governess we've ever had.'

Now he was even starting to *sound* like her, thought Anna irritably. Couldn't he see that there was something odd about the way Miss Carter was always hanging around them? And what kind of governess didn't care about lessons? The only time she ever made them do any work was when the Countess appeared in the schoolroom – then suddenly it was all grammar and arithmetic and history dates. But as soon as the door had closed, she'd be back to acting out plays.

Alone with Miss Carter in the schoolroom, Anna studied the governess carefully from behind her copy of *The School by the Sea*. The two heroines, Mops and Jean, were having a most thrilling adventure in the middle of the night, but somehow she couldn't fix her attention on their exploits. Why was Miss Carter working so hard to make them like her? Why did she sometimes have that odd, wary look on her face, like a fox on the prowl?

Just then, there was a sharp tap on the school-room door and Miss Carter sat upright, suddenly alert. But it was only Karl, one of the footmen.

'A telegram for you, Miss Carter,' he announced, offering her a silver tray. Karl was one of the children's great friends, and he paused to flash Anna a quick grin before performing a bow, and withdrawing politely again.

Miss Carter had already ripped open the envelope. As she glanced at the telegram, Anna saw a frown flit over her face, but then she said cheerfully: 'Oh, how nice – a message from an old friend.' She got to her feet, pushing the telegram into her pocket and out of sight before Anna could see it. 'Excuse me for a moment – I'm going to go and telephone through a reply.'

'Is everything all right?' Anna asked at once.

'Oh, yes, of course – quite all right,' said Miss Carter blithely. But she went out of the room in a hurry, so distracted that she forgot the spectacles she always wore for reading and writing, leaving them lying beside Anna on the table. Without really thinking about what she was doing, Anna picked up the governess's spectacles and tried them on. As soon as she did so, she realised something very surprising.

They were not real spectacles.

The lenses were quite plain, ordinary glass.

She dropped the spectacles back on to the table as though they had burned her fingers. Why would a person wear pretend spectacles – spectacles that clearly they did not really need? It was as though Miss Carter were wearing a disguise, or a costume. As though she were merely *dressing up* as a governess, and acting the part.

The thought electrified her, as though a flash of something had run through her. Now she was quite sure of it. There was something very strange about the new governess, and Anna was determined that she would find out exactly what it was.

CHAPTER TWO

Victoria Station, London, England

'Read all about it! Preparations under way for the coronation of His Majesty George V! Read all about it! Arnovia faces new pressure from Germany! Grand Aerial Tour to launch in Paris! *Read all about it!*'

It was going to be another scorcher, thought the newspaper-seller, wiping his forehead with a handkerchief. It was not yet ten o'clock, but already the streets outside Victoria railway station were hot and dusty, and he was thinking longingly of a glass of cold beer. 'Thank you kindly, guv'nor,' he muttered, without really paying attention to the thin man in grey who took a copy of *The Daily Picture* and handed over a ha'penny before shuffling on in the direction of the station entrance.

The thin man's jacket was grey, his hat was grey, and the hair that could be seen beneath it was grey too. Even his face – if the newspaper-seller had noticed it – had a greyish tinge. But neither the newspaper-seller nor anyone else gave the man a second glance as he crossed the busy station concourse, heading in the direction of the Left Luggage Office. It was the grey man's special gift, his ability to move through crowds unseen.

As it happened though, there was one person at Victoria station who was looking out for the grey man. Not far away from the newspaper-seller, a girl with a blue parasol was making her way sedately into the station. The girl knew a great deal about the grey man. She knew that if anyone had asked him – that policeman over there, talking to a station porter, perhaps – he would have said his name was Dr Frederick Muller, which was the name on the identity papers he carried in the pocket of his grey jacket. She knew that those papers stated that he was a scholar from Hamburg University, who wrote learned articles about museums for a German magazine. She knew too that the papers were a clever forgery, and that the grey man had never been near Hamburg University in his life.

She watched him closely as he made his way between the people: porters sweating under the weight of heavy luggage; ladies in shady hats, up to London for a day's shopping; a huddle of tourists, poring over a *Bradshaw's Railway Guide*. Not one of them noticed the grey man, but the girl's eyes followed him keenly.

As the grey man drew near the Left Luggage Office, she went briskly in the same direction. Seeing a young lady approach, he doffed his hat with a courteous but unremarkable bow, and held the door open for her, keeping his head down. Her frilly skirt swished forward as she tip-tapped ahead of him into the office.

The Left Luggage Office was busy and the grey man slid invisibly through the hustle and bustle to join the queue behind a smart gentleman in a bowler hat. Rummaging in her handbag as if she were looking for her ticket, the girl stepped quickly into the queue behind him. He was staring down at the newspaper in his hand, as if quite absorbed in an article of the kind that would have interested Dr Muller – a write up of a new exhibit at the British Museum.

When it was his turn to approach the counter, the ruddy-faced fellow on duty barely glanced at him as he handed over the ticket. 'Right you are, sir! Just a moment!' he said cheerfully, disappearing to the shelves where the parcels were stored.

The grey man waited. His shoulders had stiffened slightly and for the first time, the girl thought she could detect signs of unease. He leaned forward, turning his grey hat over in his hands. She tried to imagine what he was thinking. Was he wondering why the fellow was taking so long? Was he wondering if his contact could be trusted – whether he had delivered the parcel as promised, or whether he'd simply taken the money and run? Was he thinking of Ziegler, watching and waiting in faraway Berlin? But then – there it was! The fellow was returning, and in his hands was a small rectangular parcel, wrapped in brown paper and tied with string.

'Here you are, sir.'

The girl's breath quickened as the parcel was placed into the grey man's hands. It looked heavy: there must be at least four of the books inside. She could not allow them to fall into Ziegler's possession.

The grey man's face did not reveal even a shadow of excitement. He remained bland and ordinary as he said a polite 'thank you', wished the fellow 'good day' and turned to go, the parcel tucked under his arm.

The girl stepped swiftly after him. She must not lose him now; she had to get her hands on that parcel. But even as she did so, the fellow on duty called out: 'Excuse me, sir, stop there!'

The grey man froze.

'Now then, sir. Don't you rush off in such a hurry. You've forgotten your hat!' said the fellow cheerfully, as he held the grey man's hat out towards him.

The grey man beamed back at him. 'So very kind,' he flustered.

How foolish, how unexpectedly *amateur* of him to have forgotten his hat like that, the girl marvelled! Yet as he set down the parcel for a moment to reach into his pocket for two-pence to press into the fellow's hand, it came to her that perhaps it was not so very stupid after all. He was playing the part of scholarly Dr Muller to perfection, she realised. Leaving his hat behind was exactly the sort of thing that a

19

man like Dr Muller would do. He would be forgetful and absent-minded, distracted by the research he was doing in London's museums. He was quite beyond suspicion – the kind of man who could not even remember his own hat.

All the same, he had played right into her hands. As the grey man bowed and smiled, she stepped forward, swept up the package from where he had set it down, and was gone in an instant, before he or anyone else had realised she was there.

The office door swung open before her. Behind, she heard a voice cry: 'My . . . my parcel!'

'Your parcel, sir?'

'It's gone!'

She did not stay to hear any more. The station concourse was large and she knew the grey man would soon be on her trail. She made her way through the crowds walking briskly, but not so fast as to draw attention to herself. She weaved between a porter with a pile of trunks and a man with a luncheon basket, making for the station exit. Behind her, she knew that the grey man was following. As she stepped outside, she dared to glance back over her shoulder: yes, there he was, speeding through the crowds. He was gaining on her, and she knew exactly what he would be thinking. She'd heard it plenty of times before. *A young girl – all alone!* He'd be certain that she'd be easy to overpower, or outwit.

'Hey, mister, watch where you're going!' she heard

20

the newspaper-seller call out indignantly as the grey man sprinted out of the railway station and down the steps behind her, shoving his way past the barrow of newspapers. He was no longer concerned about being quiet or anonymous, the shuffling Dr Muller quite forgotten now. Ziegler must want this parcel very badly indeed. She tried to hold her nerve, to keep walking, lengthening her stride, going a little faster now, but not too fast. She wanted him uncertain. She mustn't give anything away.

She moved steadily onwards, towards the row of station cabs. Behind her, the grey man dodged a delivery boy on a bicycle with an angry yell. She had stopped beside a cab; she had nodded to the driver; the door was open; she was stepping up inside –

The grey man leaped forward and just as she was about to clamber into the cab, he grabbed her by the arm and wrenched her back. His fingers bit into her skin.

She stared up at him, widening her eyes. She knew exactly what he was seeing: a young lady, daintily dressed, with white gloves and a parasol and a straw hat decorated with forget-me-nots. She let out a little gasp of alarm. 'Sir, I beg you, let go of me at once!' she cried out in a faint voice.

The cab driver had seen what was happening. 'Here, what d'you think you're playing at?' he demanded angrily. 'D'you know this fellow, miss? Leave go of her at once or I'll yell for the constable.'

But the grey man ignored him completely. 'The package . . . give me the package,' he hissed.

'The . . . the package?' she gaped back at him.

'Give it to me now! Or it will be the worse for you!'

'But . . . but I don't have a package,' she said with a confused gasp, making her eyes wide and fearful. 'I only have this.'

She thrust forward the object she was holding and the grey man gawped at it for a moment. It was not a brown-paper parcel at all, but a large blue-and-gold hat-box, marked with the name of London's most fashionable department store. Startled, he let go of her, and she took the opportunity to scramble up into the cab, taking the hat-box with her.

'You want to watch yourself, mate,' the cab driver was admonishing him. 'You can't go round accosting young ladies like that!'

But the grey man wasn't listening. She could see that he was furious with himself for chasing after a perfectly ordinary girl – a young English miss, collecting something as innocent as a new hat – whilst somehow the enemy had tricked him, swiping his precious parcel from under his nose. His face darkened with anger. He had lost the parcel he had worked so hard to obtain. He had failed Ziegler. He cursed aloud.

'That's enough of that kind of language,' the cab driver told him. He looked down at the girl: 'Don't you worry, miss. You're safe now. Just you sit tight and I'll see you home.'

He shook his head one last time as he drove away at a smart pace, leaving the grey man standing empty-handed, glaring furiously after them.

CHAPTER THREE

London

Inside the cab, the girl settled herself back comfortably against the seat.

'So . . . where to?' asked the driver, a young, good-looking fellow, with curly hair showing from beneath his cap.

'The Inns of Court,' she said, pulling the hat-box on to her knee and taking off the lid. 'I expect the Bureau will want to see this straight away.'

'All right, but let's go the long way round,' said the driver, reflectively. 'You never know. That fellow might have some pals around who could still be watching us.'

'Good scheme,' agreed his passenger. Beneath some filmy tissue paper, she had unearthed from the hat-box a small, rectangular parcel, wrapped in brown paper. She weighed it in her hands.

'What d'you reckon it is?' asked the driver.

'Probably Navy weapons manuals or signal books. Something highly confidential, at any rate.'

'Something our old friend Ziegler would very much want to get his sticky hands on?'

'Absolutely. That fellow was one of his agents. He'd paid someone in the Navy to steal these for him.'

'And I s'pose he had to give him a tidy sum to get him to do that? No wonder he looked like he'd lost a shilling and found a sixpence.' The driver grinned. 'Unlucky for him – and old Ziegler too – that we just happened to be passing through the station, Soph.'

'Oh, jolly unlucky,' she agreed, smiling cheerfully back.

Sophie Taylor knew she had plenty to be cheerful about. Their assignment had gone like clockwork; the stolen package was safe; and it was very pleasant to be driving through town with Joe on a beautiful summer morning. The London Season was in full swing and, although it was still early, the day already had an air of gaiety about it. The long period of court mourning after the sad death of King Edward VII the previous year had come to an end, and now the city had cast off its sombre greys and mauves, and burst into summer colour, just like the new Queen Mary, who had been seen strolling in Richmond Park wearing a yellow hat with blue feathers. Clerks were strolling to work in their shirt-sleeves; flower-sellers were offering baskets of summer blooms on the street corners; and even London's hansom cabs had been arrayed in brightly coloured tassels. As they drove through the park, she saw that people were reclining in the green-and-white sixpenny deckchairs, and

25

that children had taken off their shoes and stockings to paddle in the lake.

Out on to the busy streets beyond, already thronged with buses and bicycles, the air was hot and shimmering, thick with the smell of horses and hay and motor-car fumes. Some people might have found it too hot, or too loud, or too crowded, but this was Sophie's London, and she loved every buzzing, electric inch of it.

Now, she gazed out of the window as they rumbled along Piccadilly, past the Royal Academy, past the Ritz Hotel, and past the magnificent Sinclair's department store, where doors were opening to the morning's shoppers, and the uniformed doorman recognised them and tipped his hat.

Sophie knew that inside, on the first floor of the great building, the Taylor & Rose team – *her* team – would already be hard at work. Since their detective agency had first opened its doors two years ago, they had gained an excellent reputation, and were rarely short of clients. Now that they had expanded their offices and taken on more staff, Sophie could leave the others to deal with the day-to-day cases, whilst she concentrated her efforts on their most *unusual* client.

She had been working for this particular client for six months now, and she felt that she was getting rather good at intercepting telegrams, retrieving parcels and monitoring suspicious characters on their behalf. Working on assignments like this one, she felt a little thrill knowing that the people around her on London's crowded streets couldn't possibly have guessed that she was not an ordinary girl, but a government agent, doing vital work for the Secret Service Bureau.

Of course, most people didn't know that the Secret Service Bureau existed. It had been set up by senior government officials to conduct highly confidential intelligence work. It was terribly mysterious: even Sophie herself wasn't quite sure what all of the Bureau's official work involved. What she did know was that a lot of it was concerned with what she had learned to call *espionage* – in other words, *spies*.

Although everyone seemed to be talking about the growing threat from Germany, and the Kaiser's new warships, what the ordinary people around her on the streets of London didn't know was that a network of enemy agents had already been established in Britain. The brilliant German spymaster, Ziegler, had been recruiting spies whose job it was to collect secret information to pass back to the German government. It was part of the Bureau's job to stop them and, as one of their agents, that made it Sophie's job too.

She grinned to herself. Three or four years ago, even the idea of working for a living would have been impossible to imagine, never mind doing a job like this. She'd certainly come a long way from her old life of piano lessons and pretty frocks. Now she was a detective, a businesswoman, and a government secret agent. She was a girl who knew how to crack a safe and pick a lock and throw a punch; a girl who had been taught to shoot a pistol by legendary New York detective Ada Pickering. She had found a missing diamond, had recovered two priceless paintings by the famous artist Benedetto Casselli, and had even helped to foil a plot to assassinate the King. She had outwitted the notorious villain who called himself 'the Baron' and, in doing so, had saved London from disaster. Not too shabby for someone who had only just turned seventeen.

It was strange now, to look back on the person she had been when Papa had died and she'd first been alone in London. Then the city had seemed like such a vast and lonely and frightening place. Now it felt familiar and friendly, full of places and people she knew. Most of all, of course, there were her friends – Joe and Billy, and all the other members of the Loyal Order of Lions, the organisation to which her parents had once belonged. The Order were sworn to work against the Baron's sinister secret society, the *Fraternitas Draconum*, who had been responsible for the murder of both Sophie's parents. Even though they were gone, keeping the society alive made her feel closer to them. Not that the society had needed to *do* very much lately – after all, they'd heard nothing of the *Fraternitas* since the Baron's death, over a year ago. But just the same, Sophie was glad it was there. Being part of the Order felt almost like being part of a family. She was very grateful to have a circle of friends she knew she could count on, no matter what.

But as she hopped down from the cab outside the Inns of Court, she acknowledged to herself that even with the support of her friends, life wasn't always entirely straightforward. Despite the success of Taylor & Rose, there were still plenty of people who did not care for the idea of young ladies being detectives. And running the agency was jolly hard work, especially without her best friend and business partner at her side.

Nothing seemed quite right without Lil. Certainly nothing was anywhere near as much fun.

Almost as though he had read her thoughts, Joe leaned out of the cab window and asked: 'Reckon you can find out how she's getting on?'

Sophie smiled up at him. She knew that he missed Lil too. 'I'll ask,' she promised. 'I might be a while – shall I meet you back at the office later?' He nodded and she gave him a quick wave goodbye, before she turned and went under the archway and inside.

In the cool, echoing hallway, the sleepy concierge was sitting exactly as usual behind his desk. 'Mr Clarke, is it, miss?' he asked.

'Yes please.'

'Second floor and to the right,' he instructed, exactly as if he hadn't seen her here at least once a week for the last six months.

Following his instructions, Sophie made her way up the stairs. At the top was a door marked with a small printed card that read simply: *CLARKE & SONS SHIPPING AGENTS*. She knocked, and when a voice inside called out: 'Come in!' she stepped inside the headquarters of the Secret Service Bureau.

CHAPTER FOUR

Secret Service Bureau HQ, London

'**O**h, it's *you*,' said a sardonic voice.

Captain Carruthers was lounging in his chair, his shirt collar slightly open, his feet resting on the desk beside the typewriter, as he flipped through a stack of reports. 'What do you want?'

'I'm here to see the Chief,' Sophie said shortly. She usually thought of herself as rather a polite person, but Captain Carruthers was always so rude that it was difficult to be anything but rude back.

'Oh, well then, go through – you know where he is,' said Carruthers, waving her away without bothering to look up from his papers.

Swallowing down her annoyance, Sophie crossed the room to the door that led to C's office.

'C' was a code-name, of course. She didn't know what it stood for – perhaps C for Chief, as they often called him, or C for Commander, or even C for Clarke the Shipping

Agent, though that seemed unlikely. Lil sometimes joked: 'I say, I wonder what happened to A and B?' but Sophie had noticed she never said it to his face. Even Lil was rather in awe of C.

Now, as Sophie always did when she stepped into C's office, she found herself looking around, thinking of all the secret business that must take place here. Not that there was anything especially mysterious or clandestine about the room itself – in many ways, it looked exactly like the ordinary shipping agent's office it pretended to be. There was a big desk, stacked all over with piles of papers; a map of the world, dotted with pins; and a big bookcase crammed with fat leather-bound books. At the centre of it all was C himself, busily writing letters in his characteristic green-ink scrawl. To all intents and purposes, he too could have been a perfectly ordinary shipping agent. He looked like any affable older gentleman, with a gold watch chain and the traces of what Sophie suspected was his breakfast boiled egg on his shirt front.

The only thing that was unusual about C's office was that there was a very large wind-up gramophone playing on a table in the corner, and C was humming along to the melody as he worked. Sophie knew very little about C, besides the fact that he ate soft-boiled eggs for breakfast, but she did know he had a passion for music. She had grown accustomed to having a musical accompaniment to their meetings. Today, she noted, it was Mozart's Magic

Flute Overture that could be heard drifting from the gramophone.

'Ah, Miss Taylor! Delightful to see you. Well, well, and what have we here?' C rubbed his palms together in anticipation, as Sophie placed the box on the desk in front of him. 'Oh, splendid!' he said to himself as he lifted the lid, pulling away the brown paper with the air of a child with a birthday present. 'Aha! Code books . . . Signalling manual . . . Ah, yes, this one does look rather important . . . Carruthers!' he called out in a louder voice.

After a moment's pause, his assistant slouched in. He looked as surly as always, although C didn't seem to notice. 'Take these and check through them for me, there's a good fellow, and telephone through to Admiral Stevens and let him know we have them. I rather think he might be worried about what's become of them. Excellent work, Miss Taylor!'

Carruthers accepted the parcel without saying anything, tossing Sophie a bad-tempered glance as he strode back out of the room.

'Now, tell me, who was Ziegler's agent this time? The fellow calling himself Dr Muller, was he one of our old friends?'

Sophie shook her head. 'I've not come across him before.' She described the thin grey man, whilst C scribbled a few notes on the back of an envelope. 'He wasn't at all happy to have lost the parcel,' she finished up.

33

'I'm sure he wasn't,' said C, with a chuckle. 'Well, I daresay we'll meet him again before long. Now, I have a new assignment for you. Not parcels this time, but something rather different, which I think you may find interesting.'

He pushed a folder across the desk towards her, printed with the name *PROFESSOR BLAXLAND* in large black letters. Flipping it open, she saw several densely typed sheets of paper: lying on top was a photograph of a handsome, well-dressed, middle-aged man. Scribbled beneath the photograph were the words *SSB AGENT*.

'This man works for the Bureau?' she asked, picking up the photograph to look at it more closely.

'Yes, in a way. Not in the same capacity as you, Miss Taylor, but as what you might perhaps term a consultant. Professor Blaxland had a specific area of expertise that was very useful to us. He was a language specialist, teaching at the Sorbonne in Paris, with a particular interest in codes and ciphers.'

Sophie looked up from the picture. '*Was?*'

'I am sorry to say that two days ago, Professor Blaxland was murdered.' The Chief's plump, good-natured face looked sombre as he went on: 'He was shot in his apartment, in the fifth *arrondissement* of Paris. It appears to have been a burglary gone wrong – his apartment had been broken into and the intruders were going through his possessions, when he returned and surprised them. The thieves shot him and escaped. However . . .' C fell silent for a moment, leaving

34

a heavy pause hanging in the air before he continued: 'My fear is that Blaxland may have been deliberately targeted, and the murder set up to appear like a burglary.'

'But who would do that, and why?' asked Sophie.

'That is exactly what I want you to find out. I am sending you to Paris, Miss Taylor. You leave on tomorrow morning's boat-train.'

Sophie stared at him, taken aback. Paris? Following suspects; intercepting parcels; trailing Ziegler's spies through the London streets she knew – she could do all that quite easily. But investigating a murder in an unknown foreign city was something else altogether. Why would the Chief send her on an assignment like that when he had plenty of more experienced and well-travelled detectives working for him – tough former Scotland Yard men, and seasoned private investigators like her friend Mr McDermott?

But C answered her question before she had chance to ask it: 'You'll be going undercover, of course, as Miss Celia Blaxland, the Professor's niece.' He pushed another folder across the desk towards her and opened it, tapping the photograph that lay on top. Sophie leaned forward to see a portrait of a fair-haired girl of about eighteen years old. 'As you'll see from the dossier, she is rather a wealthy young lady. She hasn't seen her uncle for several years, but she is his only close living relative, so the authorities will not be at all surprised to see her – or, that is to say, to see *you*.

I'd suggest you begin by meeting with his solicitor to find out as much as you can about what happened. It would also be worth talking to his friends and colleagues at the Sorbonne.'

Sophie looked from the Chief, to the photograph, and back again. She had so many questions it was difficult to know where to start. 'But why the need to send someone undercover?' she asked at last. 'Couldn't the French authorities investigate through official channels?'

C tapped his pen thoughtfully against the desk in time to the music. 'Blaxland worked for us on the quiet, and I'd rather we kept it that way. I'd prefer our investigation to go unnoticed by either the French or the German authorities, and by the newspapers too, for that matter. With that in mind, you'll need to be discreet, Miss Taylor. Stay on your guard and, whatever you do, don't reveal who you really are.'

'What about the real Miss Blaxland, won't she turn up and give the game away?'

C shook his head. 'We'll take care of that. What I need you to do is to find out what happened to Blaxland. Did someone deliberately orchestrate his death, and if so who and why? Of course, my suspicions may be quite misplaced. It's perfectly possible that Blaxland's death was no more than the unfortunate consequence of an ordinary robbery – in which case, your job will be a straightforward one. But Blaxland was an unusual man with remarkable skills, engaged in top-secret work for our government. There is a clear possibility that his death may be the work of our enemies.' For a moment there was silence but for the crackly sound of the music coming from the gramophone – the singing of the strings and the silvery notes of the flute – then the Chief continued: 'I won't mince words with you, Miss Taylor. This could be a matter of national security. If you do find evidence that Blaxland was murdered by our enemies, you will likely be in danger yourself. In that event, you must leave Paris and return to London at once and report to me, do you understand?'

Sophie nodded, and C went on: 'Familiarise yourself with the contents of these folders. They include your instructions, and all the information you'll need. Your train leaves from Victoria first thing tomorrow morning.'

The overture came to an end with three long notes, and Sophie realised she was being dismissed. She hastily scooped up the two folders, as he added:

'Oh, one last thing. Miss Blaxland of course travels with a chaperone – normally, I believe, she has a lady's maid to accompany her. You'll need to arrange for someone to go with you in that capacity. I'm sure one of your quick-witted young ladies will do the job. Well, very best of luck. Farewell, or I suppose I ought to say *au revoir*.'

He smiled and turned away to fiddle with the gramophone, but Sophie paused at the door. She was still trying to make sense of all that C had told her, but in spite of that, she had to ask: 'I . . . I don't suppose there's any news of Lil?'

She knew she wasn't really supposed to ask. When they'd first agreed to work for the Bureau, they'd been told that their work would be top secret; and Lil's current assignment was especially confidential. Even Sophie hadn't been allowed to know where Lil was going or what she was doing. All she had been told was that Lil would be away for some weeks – perhaps months – and that she would have no way of keeping in touch. Sophie had sometimes imagined her sleeping in a tent in a desert; trekking through wild jungles; or even sunning herself on the deck of a steam-boat on a faraway ocean. Now she added, feeling rather foolish: 'I just wondered if she was all right.'

C shook his head. 'I'm afraid I can't tell you anything.' Her impatience must have showed on her face because he added more gently: 'Not because I won't, but because I can't. I haven't heard anything from her for a little while, you see. It's not always easy for her to get reports through. Though last time I did hear from her, she was perfectly well and in high spirits as usual. Your friend is a very courageous young woman.' He nodded her a brisk goodbye: '*Bon voyage*, Miss Taylor. Good hunting.'

Carruthers was typing very fast and very loudly when Sophie closed the office door behind her.

'So we're off to Paris, are we? How nice.'

'It's not a holiday,' said Sophie tightly, wishing Carruthers didn't always succeed in irritating her. 'It's an assignment.'

'Oh, I know all about it. *Someone* has to prepare all those reports and dossiers, you know. Though I must admit I couldn't quite believe it when I heard they were sending *you* undercover as Celia Blaxland.' He snorted sarcastically. 'Good luck!'

'The Chief seemed to think I'd manage perfectly well. Good morning to you, Captain,' and before he could say anything else, she swept out of the room.

She didn't have time for Carruthers now. Her mind was whirling, and she knew she had to gather herself. She had a lot to do if she was to be on a train to Paris first thing tomorrow morning.

Paris! It was a daunting thought, but there was a spark of excitement too. Her mind darted at once to thoughts of artists and writers, the sumptuous outfits created by designer César Chevalier, grand boulevards, splendid architecture, delicious food . . . She'd never travelled abroad before, although she knew that her parents had been all over the world. Paris made her think especially of her mother, who had spent time there as a young girl: Sophie had read all about it in her mother's old diaries, which she had inherited. She thought it would be rather wonderful to follow in her mother's footsteps, although of course she wouldn't have much time for sight-seeing. As she had told Carruthers, this would be no holiday: she had a murder to investigate.

The thought of that made her feel suddenly tight with nerves. She knew she was a good detective, but she'd never taken on a case like this before. If only Lil were here, she'd have made the assignment seem fun and exciting – an adventure in a foreign city. Lil was an actress, and the idea of going undercover in some extraordinary role never daunted her in the slightest. But now Lil was miles away – who-knew-where – and Sophie would have to manage this by herself.

For a moment, she saw Carruthers' sneering face again, and then heard the Chief say: '*Your friend is a very courageous young woman.*' Was the implication that she herself was not? But surely that wasn't fair: her mind flashed at once through scenes of underground passageways and rooftops and standing in an empty office, face to face with the Baron himself. But that had been different, she realised. Then she'd always had Lil by her side.

As she came out into the street and flagged down a cab, she told herself she was being silly. There was no reason at all that she couldn't handle this just as well as anyone else. She oughtn't to let Carruthers rattle her; the Chief had faith in her, or he wouldn't have given her the job.

'Sinclair's department store, please,' she said to the cab driver as she clambered inside.

'Off to do a spot of shopping, miss? And very nice too.'

Sophie didn't bother to correct him. She was fairly certain that the cab driver wouldn't believe her if she explained that she wasn't going shopping at all, but that in fact the young girl with the blue parasol was the co-proprietor of Taylor & Rose detective agency, and even now making arrangements to embark on a secret undercover mission.

A secret undercover mission! Well, there was no turning back now, she thought. She'd told the Chief she would do it, and after all, it was hardly likely that there were any other young ladies working for the Secret Service Bureau who could go undercover as Celia Blaxland.

Besides, it was not as though she'd be entirely alone, Sophie reminded herself. The Chief had said that Miss Blaxland was always accompanied by a lady's maid. Before she did anything else, she should make sure that she would be too, and luckily she knew exactly the person she wanted to help her.

CHAPTER FIVE

Taylor & Rose Detective Agency
Sinclair's Department Store, London

'No. No chance whatsoever. Absolutely not,' declared Tilly at once. 'Look around you! I'm far too busy!'

Sophie obediently glanced around Tilly's workshop, though in fact, calling it a 'workshop' made it sound a good deal grander than it actually was. In reality, the little office that Tilly had claimed at Taylor & Rose was scarcely bigger than a large cupboard. But Tilly had been adamant that she must have a place of her own to work, no matter how small it might be. She was a student at University College London, and had a passion for all things mechanical and scientific. When she wasn't studying, she provided Taylor & Rose with a good deal of technical help with everything from developing photographs to testing for fingerprints. She had even invented several useful and unusual devices to help them in their detective work.

Tilly was presently taking a course in chemistry, which

42

went some way to explaining why the table in front of her was covered with a jumble of glass bottles, jars and test tubes. Behind her, shelves were crammed with thick books, stacks of papers and a framed photograph of Madame Curie, the French scientist who was Tilly's greatest hero. In the midst of all this was Tilly herself – a tall, brown-skinned girl with a lot of curly black hair. She was wearing a large apron over her frock, and what looked like a pair of old motoring goggles on her head, and her hands were placed firmly on her hips.

'I've got an examination in two weeks. I can't just go haring off to Paris at the drop of a hat to be a *lady's maid!*' she insisted.

'I know it's rather a lot to ask. But this assignment is for the Secret Service Bureau. It's jolly important – the Chief said it could be a matter of national security.'

'Surely one of the others could go instead?'

'But no one else would be nearly as good at this assignment as you. Miss Blaxland is a terribly wealthy young lady. You know exactly what someone like her would be like – you could help me to impersonate her. And you *know* you'd be able to play the role of her lady's maid to perfection.' It was true – though Tilly was now a London student, it was not long since she'd been working as a maid in a grand country house. What was more, Sophie knew that she was practical, sensible and extremely clever – exactly the person she needed to help her solve this case.

43

'If you can't come, I suppose I'll have to ask one of the others. But I do wish you *would* come with me. It's a very important assignment, and I'd really value your help.'

Tilly's face softened a little. 'It's not that I don't *want* to help, Sophie. You know I'd do anything for Taylor & Rose. It's just . . . would I really *have* to be a lady's maid? Honestly, I can't bear the thought of going back to doing nothing but saying "yes, ma'am" and "no, ma'am" and fussing with hair and petticoats.'

'I promise you wouldn't have to think about so much as a single petticoat,' said Sophie gravely. 'You have my word on that. You'll only need to *pretend* to be a lady's maid when we're in company. The rest of the time you'll be working with me to solve the case.'

Tilly said nothing, but Sophie could see she was wavering. 'Besides, it would give you the chance to see Paris, and the Sorbonne – isn't that where Madame Curie studied?' Remembering something she'd read in the morning newspaper, she added hurriedly: 'And there's that big air race too starting in a few days, isn't there? The Grand Aerial Tour of Europe. You might be able to go and see all those new aeroplanes.' Sophie knew that Tilly was fascinated by the new flying-machine technology, though personally she couldn't think of anything worse than flying in an aeroplane. The thought of someone launching themselves into the air in a fragile-looking craft like those she'd seen in the newspapers made her feel queasy. But she knew Tilly would love to have the chance to see the latest aeroplanes up close.

'Well, all right then,' said Tilly at last. 'I suppose I could manage, as long as it really is only a few days. And as long as I can bring my chemistry books so I can prepare for my examination,' she added hastily.

Sophie grinned in relief. As far as she was concerned, Tilly could bring all the books she wanted, just as long as she'd be there to help her go undercover to investigate a murder in an unknown city.

After agreeing their plans for the following morning, she closed the door, leaving Tilly to finish her work. As she emerged into the small reception area of the Taylor & Rose office, Sophie felt a familiar glow of pride. This was their place – the place that she and Lil had built together. There were the pictures they'd chosen on the walls; a vase of Lil's favourite roses on a table; the sound of voices and the cheerful trill of a telephone bell. Two or three people were sitting waiting for appointments, whilst at the reception desk, a business-like young lady, with glossy black hair and a blouse with a neat bow at the neck sat busily typing. Mei Lim was the youngest member of the Taylor & Rose team, and acted as their receptionist. She looked up at once and smiled as Sophie came in. 'Oh, there you are. These letters have come for you.'

Sophie took the stack of letters then glanced quickly around at the people sitting fanning themselves or sipping tea. 'Come into my office for a minute,' she said in a low voice to Mei. 'I've got something to tell you.'

Mei got up at once, looking most intrigued, and followed Sophie through into the room that she and Lil used as their office. It was a very comfortable place, with a big window looking down on to the street below, and two desks positioned companionably opposite each other – Lil's currently rather bare and looking most unusually tidy.

'Did everything go well today?' asked Mei eagerly, the second that the door closed behind them.

'It did,' said Sophie, taking off her hat and hanging up the blue parasol beside it. 'Everything went very well indeed. But the Chief has given me a new assignment. I'm going away tomorrow, and Tilly's coming with me. We may be away for as much as a week.'

'A week!' exclaimed Mei, her eyes wide. 'But . . . how will we manage without you?'

'You'll be fine,' said Sophie, going over to her desk. 'Billy and Joe will be here, and I know that between you, you'll look after everything beautifully.'

'But . . . but we've got our meeting of the Order on Thursday,' Mei protested. 'It won't be right without you and Tilly, *and* without Lil.'

'It can't be helped. You'll have to have the meeting without us,' said Sophie, though she said it a little sadly. The members of the Loyal Order of Lions were all very busy, and without even the smallest glimpse of the *Fraternitas Draconum* to concern them their meetings had become increasingly few and far between. But Sophie always loved their friendly gatherings in the Lims' cosy kitchen, sitting around the big table in the glow of the lamp-light, and she would be very sorry indeed to miss this one. The Pendletons would be back from their honeymoon in Italy, she remembered, and Mei's brother Song had promised to bake a special cake to celebrate her seventeenth birthday.

But there was no time to dwell on missing the meeting now. If she was to be on the train to Paris the next morning, there were a great deal of preparations to be made. Very soon, Mei had hurried off with a long list of tasks, whilst Sophie settled down at her desk. There was plenty of urgent business to deal with – letters requiring replies, accounts to balance, and artwork to check for a new advertisement. Putting things in order was soothing, and once she'd attended to her work, and felt satisfied that everything was in place, she was ready to turn her attention to Paris.

She went in search of Billy, who she soon found at his own desk, busy with several important-looking ledgers. Like Joe, Billy Parker had been part of the Taylor & Rose team from the start, and now kept their office running in perfect order. She wasted no time in explaining her mission, and a short while later, the two of them were on their way to the Sinclair's Ladies' Fashions Department.

As usual, Sinclair's was busy with shoppers: gentlemen in white flannels and striped jackets, ladies in summer frocks, and groups lingering to listen to the band in the Entrance Hall, who were playing one of the latest Ragtime tunes. As Sophie left the office, she noticed several shoppers pausing to look curiously at the gold sign for Taylor & Rose, or even trying to peep through the glass to see what was happening in the office within. That was quite usual, of course. After all a detective agency in a department store was rather an extraordinary thing, especially one run by young ladies. But then again, Sinclair's was anything but an ordinary shop. It was a department store of dreams: a place that you could buy more or less anything, from the finest rose and violet creams, to the very latest Paris hat. You could dine on fashionable dishes like *lobster a l'americaine* or peach Melba ice-cream sundaes in the Marble Court Restaurant; you could visit the famous concierge, who would work his magic to secure you a suite at the city's best hotel, or tickets to a new West End show; or you could have your hair perfectly Marcel-waved by London's most elegant hairdresser. Was it any wonder that, if you wanted, you could hire a detective too?

Billy wasn't paying any attention to the shoppers. He was busy adding things to his carefully organised list. He had a list for every occasion, and was never very far away from a well-sharpened pencil and a notebook. 'Let's see . . . magnifying glass . . . fan . . . eau de cologne . . .' he muttered to himself, as Sophie contemplated a selection of gowns, reflecting, not for the first time, just how convenient it was to have the support and backing of the owner of Sinclair's, Mr Edward Sinclair himself. If Sinclair's was no ordinary store, then Mr Sinclair was certainly no ordinary store owner: he had himself worked undercover for both the British and American governments. He was one of the few people who knew about their work for the Secret Service Bureau, and had given them free rein to take whatever supplies they needed from Sinclair's when they were working on Bureau business.

'. . . pen-knife. Ball of string . . . oh, and mackintosh squares, of course,' Billy murmured, scribbling them all down.

Sophie grinned. 'Mackintosh squares?' she repeated. 'Don't you think that's going a bit far? We're not going into the wilderness, you know.'

'Well, it's always good to be prepared,' said Billy rather indignantly.

'Look – what do you think of this for Miss Blaxland?' asked Sophie, pointing to a grey tailor-made outfit. 'And perhaps that hat with the roses?'

Billy screwed up his face. 'No. That won't do at all. It's too plain, and besides it's last year's. Miss Blaxland is very well-off, isn't she? She's bound to have the very latest thing.' He pointed to a sumptuous midnight-blue travelling suit, new in from Maison Chevalier. '*That's* more like it. With the hat with the plumes and the net veil.'

Sophie took the hat and tried it on uncertainly. Her face in the mirror looked back at her, very small and rather doubtful. Even knowing that Tilly would be coming too, a fluttering feeling of nervousness was growing in her stomach about the new assignment.

Billy seemed to know how she felt. He gently tweaked the hat into the right position. 'There. Perfect. You can do this, Sophie,' he said quietly. 'I know you can.'

An hour or two later, the things were all packed neatly into two large trunks from the store's Luggage Department. Once Billy had checked the list twice, and then insisted on checking it just once more to be sure; and once Sophie had made certain he had everything he would need to take charge of Taylor & Rose while she was away, she was at last ready to go. It felt very peculiar to be saying goodbye to Billy and Mei, and to be closing the office door.

'Well, I suppose I'll see you next week, when you get back,' said Billy casually. He grinned at her, but then suddenly looked anxious. 'You will take care, won't you?' To Sophie's surprise, he gave her a sudden hug. 'Good luck. Be safe.' he said in a gruff voice.

'I will,' she promised him.

But as she walked out of the great doors of Sinclair's amongst the shoppers, Sophie reflected that she was not sure she really wished to be *safe* any longer. *Safe* made her think of the person she had been before – a china doll, dressed in finery and kept on the nursery shelf. Yes, she was nervous about the assignment, but there was no doubt about it, there was a smouldering feeling of excitement too.

In the carriage on the way to collect Tilly the next

morning, she took out the first volume of her mother's diaries – the notebook in which she had written about her travels in Europe, and especially her visit to Paris. She hadn't been able to resist slipping it into her pocket as she left, and now her hand closed around the well-known, worn shape of it: she remembered something that her mother had written. *I do believe I have a taste for adventure.* There it was again – that thrill of recognition. A feeling that told her this was what she was meant to do.

Fewer than twenty-four hours after she'd tricked the grey man at the Left Luggage Office, Sophie once more crossed the concourse at Victoria station. But the girl with the frilly dress and parasol had vanished. Now she was Miss Celia Blaxland, an elegant, sophisticated young lady. Her dark blue skirts swished; beneath her large plumed hat, her hair was piled high, and pearl earrings dangled from her ears. Behind her came a smart lady's maid, carefully carrying a little fur in case her mistress should feel chilly on the journey, and last of all a station porter, pushing a trolley piled high with trunks.

As she approached the first-class Pullman carriage, her heart was thumping. A uniformed attendant bowed low and extended a hand to help her inside, and Sophie was aboard the express train to Paris.

Although she didn't know it, somewhere further down the platform, a thin grey man carrying papers bearing the name of Dr Frederick Muller was getting aboard the train too.

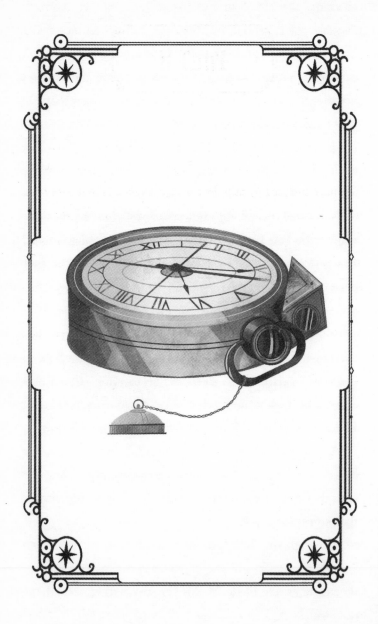

PART II

'We have travelled by ship, by carriage, by donkey and even once on the backs of camels! But my favourite journeys of all are those by train. The very smell of the smoke, the rattling of the carriage, the chatter of our fellow passengers, all seem to promise romance and adventure.'

– From the diary of Alice Grayson

CHAPTER SIX

Wilderstein Castle, Arnovia

Anna held her breath as she crept along the hall, towards the governess's bedroom. It was past midnight and the castle was whisper-quiet, the passageway made strange with shadows. In the dark, the antlers of the stuffed animal heads on the wall, the rusting suit of armour, even the painted shield with the arms of the Royal House of Wilderstein seemed to shift into new and sinister shapes.

A long, thin crack of yellow light was visible at the bedroom door and Anna moved towards it, her bare feet soft on the chilly stone flags. She felt excited. She knew that she was not supposed to be out of bed late at night, creeping around the castle, but it was rather thrilling to be slipping along the passageway in the dark in her nightgown, without even her bedroom slippers. It was absolutely the kind of thing that the heroines of the Fourth Form would do, even if it meant breaking the rules.

There were certainly plenty of rules at Wilderstein

Castle. The Countess's favourite words were *discipline* and *decorum*, and each day was the same, following an exact pattern. The day began with the ringing of the gong for breakfast at eight o'clock sharp, and ended with the chime of the bedtime bell, which meant that Alex and Anna must go to bed. Sometimes Anna felt that she was no more than a tiny cog in the Countess's giant machine: a kind of musical box, where the Countess turned the handle, and spinning on top in time to the music was Alex. Not the real Alex she knew, but the Alex who would one day become King, shining out light like a golden star.

They all moved in time to the Countess's tune: even the Count was bound by her strict timetable. Left to his own devices, Anna knew he would have been quite happy pottering about the castle, tinkering with his latest hobby – butterfly collecting, or motor cars, or more recently, his new-found passion for flying machines. Instead, the Countess insisted that each day at precisely the same time, the Count took Alex into the castle grounds for what they called 'drills' – a series of physical exercises inspired by his army training, which Alex simply loathed. This would be followed by a discussion of weapons and military strategy; the Count would give a detailed explanation of battle manoeuvres, or test Alex to see if he could correctly distinguish between a sabre and an *épee*. Alex, who couldn't care less about broadswords and battle-axes, would return to the schoolroom pink-faced and wheezing, whilst the

Count hurried back to his workshop to pore over the plans of aeroplanes.

Meanwhile, Anna's morning always began with time at the back-board to improve her posture, whilst the Countess lectured her on royal etiquette and the importance of decorum. 'As the Princess of Arnovia, you are an ambassador for your country and the House of Wilderstein wherever you go,' she proclaimed. 'You must never forget that.' The Countess had many such maxims, most of which were about what princesses did and did not do: *Princesses do not run. Princesses do not slam doors. A princess should not be inquisitive. Princesses do not lose their temper. A princess must never raise her voice.* Now, Anna added in her head: *A princess should not sneak about the castle at night in order to spy on her governess.*

One of the many things that had struck her as odd about Miss Carter was her lack of interest in rules and discipline, and what princesses did or did not do. She had no sort of a timetable: one morning she'd let them read poetry aloud, the next she'd take them into the grounds for what she called a 'nature ramble'. She hardly ever scolded them, except when she heard them speaking German. Then: 'In English, please!' she'd say at once. That made sense, Anna thought, for Miss Carter was supposed to be preparing Alex for his English school. And anyway, neither of them really minded speaking English. Although most Arnovian people spoke German, they usually spoke at least

57

one other language as well, and Grandfather had always especially liked Anna and Alex to speak English, because of the strong relationship between Arnovia and Britain, and because their own grandmother had been an English princess. What was strange though was that Miss Carter barely ever spoke a word of German herself, except for the occasional *bitte* or *danke*. Anna had heard the Countess say that Miss Carter was fluent in several languages, but when Bianca, the Countess's Italian maid, had tried to talk to her about some laundry, Anna had been certain she didn't have any idea what Bianca had said.

It was yet another puzzling thing for Anna to add to her list. She was certain that the governess was up to something, and that was why she was here, creeping towards her bedroom door at night.

Some people might have thought twice about spying, but Anna didn't. She liked to *know* things, and she had a talent for finding things out, especially the things she wasn't really supposed to know. She was the one who had discovered the old secret passage in the castle cellars that no one else knew about; and she was the one who had found out about the secret love affair going on between Bianca and the Count's valet. She had an uncomfortable suspicion that the heroines of the Fourth Form might have thought this kind of thing 'sneaking' or 'dishonourable', but she pushed that thought away as she peeped, feeling rather thrilled, through the door into Miss Carter's bedroom.

Like many of the rooms in Wilderstein Castle, the governess's bedroom was quite bare and cold. The stone walls were hung with crossed swords and tapestries of hunting or battle scenes – wild pigs being gored with pikes, and people in helmets hitting each other with swords. Miss Carter did not look like she belonged at all, sitting beneath one of the tapestries, writing a letter. The governess seemed quite different in a dressing gown, with her hair falling loose over her shoulders in long, snaking curls. She was not wearing her spectacles again, Anna realised, stepping a little closer, hardly daring to breathe.

She watched intently as Miss Carter put down her pen, tucked her letter into an envelope, and then got up and went over to the bed. Anna expected to see her turn back the covers, but instead, she bent down and reached under the bed, drawing something out from beneath it. Anna saw that it was a small leather attaché case, rather battered and stuck all over with luggage labels. As she watched, Miss Carter unlocked the case with a little key which hung on a chain around her neck.

Anna leaned forward, eager to see what was inside, but to her enormous annoyance, she could see only the back of Miss Carter's head. The governess was taking something out of the case – a small object, which she dropped into her dressing-gown pocket. Then she locked the case, pushed it back underneath the bed, and made for the door.

Almost tripping over her nightgown in her haste, Anna

scrambled back down the passage. From a safe spot behind the rusting suit of armour, she watched breathlessly as Miss Carter padded out of her room and down the hallway. Where on earth was she going at this time of night? She hurried silently after her, feeling more thrilled than ever. To her astonishment, she saw the governess's dark figure approach the door of the Count and Countess's sitting room, and then go swiftly inside.

Anna scampered quickly down the hall, creeping as close to the sitting-room door as she dared. The door had been left ajar: inside, the room was quite dark, but Miss Carter had lit a small lamp, and as Anna peered in, she saw that it had cast out a circle of light, illuminating her like an actress on a stage.

As Anna watched, she saw Miss Carter open the Count's desk, and begin rifling through his letters and papers. The governess's lips were moving as though she was muttering to herself, though Anna couldn't hear what she was saying. After a few moments she took out a single sheet of paper, and laid it flat on the desk under the light.

Anna stared and stared as the governess took out the object she'd dropped into her dressing-gown pocket. It was small and round, and looked rather like a silver watch. But as Anna watched, she held it close to the paper. There was a loud, distinct *click*. Miss Carter wound the watch and held it out again. *Click* went the watch, the mechanism loud in the night. Except it wasn't a watch at all, Anna realised.

It was a *camera*. The governess was photographing private papers from inside the Count's desk!

She let out a little gasp of surprise, and Miss Carter looked up sharply. She couldn't see Anna standing in the dark of the hallway, but at once she turned out the lamp, plunging the room into blackness. Frightened now, Anna darted as quickly as she could back along the passageway. But before she could reach the safety of her room, she collided with someone coming the other way, someone tall and solid. She looked up in alarm to see that she'd slammed into a footman, a new one, whom she'd never spoken to before. He looked down at her with an unpleasant sneer on his face.

'Why are you here, running about in the dark?' he hissed. 'You ought to be more careful by yourself at night, *Princess.*'

Anna stepped back at once, alarmed. Footmen never spoke to her like that – they always bowed respectfully and addressed her as 'Your Highness'. They certainly would never say 'Princess' in that contemptuous way. She was so surprised she couldn't say a word: meanwhile, the footman only gave a mocking little snigger.

Just then, to Anna's enormous relief, Karl appeared around a corner. 'Your Highness! What are you doing out of bed in the cold, and without any bedroom slippers? Whatever would Her Ladyship say?' he clucked. He gave the new footman a doubtful look. 'You can go – I'll take care of Her Highness,' he informed him. Then, more reassuringly to Anna: 'Come along. Back into bed for you.'

But even when Karl had brought Anna back to her own bedroom, and she was tucked up safely in her own bed again, sleep felt very far away. There was no doubt about it, she thought as she lay wide awake in the dark. There were strange things happening at Wilderstein Castle. Strangest of all, she was now quite sure that the new English governess was a spy.

CHAPTER SEVEN

The London–Paris Express

In the plush comfort of the first-class Pullman carriage, the coffee cups rattled gently as the train ran onwards through the countryside of northern France. Sophie sat back against the upholstered seat, gazing out at the landscape passing by outside the windows – French fields that were somehow a different colour from English ones, neat rows of pointed trees, a meadow strewn with red poppies, a white farmhouse. It was fascinating – but she tried not to stare too hard. All this might be new to her, but of course, Miss Blaxland would have seen it a dozen times before.

In the same way, she tried not to look around at the sumptuous interior of the carriage, with its snowy tablecloth and gleaming silverware, its lamp with the crimson shade. Miss Blaxland was an experienced traveller and would be accustomed to such luxury. Although there was no one to see her but the white-gloved waiter, she tried to look as though all this was quite normal, even the unaccustomed weight of Miss Blaxland's curls and combs and hair-pins, and the bones of her tight corset digging into her sides. She tried not to notice how the face-powder they had used to disguise the thin scar on her forehead was making her face itch.

Across the table, Tilly grinned at her. 'I must say, you look the part,' she said. 'You don't look a bit like *you* at all.'

Come to that, Tilly didn't look much like her usual self either. The apron and goggles of the previous day were gone, replaced by a smart maid's ensemble, complete with neat gloves and a lace collar. Her usually wild curls had been tamed into a prim bun. Dressed in this way, her tall figure looked somehow rather smaller than usual, and Sophie felt a stab of guilt for asking her to step back into her old role as a maid. Just the same, it was very reassuring to have her here, poring studiously over the newspaper and all the latest reports of the Paris air race.

Sophie tried to read too. The thick documents the Chief had given her had been tucked discreetly into a secret pocket in an expensive leather writing folder of the type a young lady like Miss Blaxland might use to keep her letters. Now that the waiter had left them, she took it out, and began to read once more through the dossier about Professor Blaxland, recognising the lopsided typing and occasional angry flourish of blue-black ink that indicated Carruthers' work:

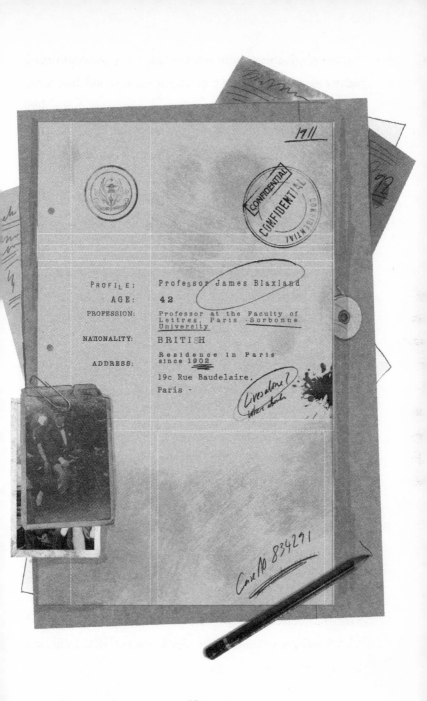

1911

PROFILE: Professor James Blaxland

AGE: 42

PROFESSION: Professor at the Faculty of Lettres, Paris -Sorbonne University

NATIONALITY: BRITISH

ADDRESS: Residence in Paris since 1902

19c Rue Baudelaire,
Paris -

Lives alone?
Where stands

Case 10 834271

65

She had learned Professor Blaxland had no living relations except for his niece, and in any case, had long been estranged from his wealthy family. *Rather the black sheep* Carruthers had scribbled in a margin. Blaxland had been unmarried and appeared well-off, living in an expensive apartment not far from the university, where he specialised in the study of ancient languages. There was a great deal of information about his career at the Sorbonne, his achievements and the books he had written, all of which Sophie thought sounded very impressive. For the past year he had been engaged in some work for the Secret Service Bureau: Carruthers did not give many specifics about his assignments, but he did note that the Professor was unusually clever in deciphering obscure codes and ciphers. Sophie read this section with particular interest: she'd had a little experience of cracking codes herself.

Next she turned to the second dossier, marked *MISS CELIA BLAXLAND*. She had to admit Carruthers had done a very thorough job – it was a thick document, full of scribbled notes and annotations. She learned that Celia Blaxland was eighteen; her parents had both died some years ago, leaving her alone in the world, and she was the heiress to an unusually large fortune, currently held in trust until she came of age at twenty-one. She was now in Northumberland, taking care of a friend who was unwell, and Sophie guessed that the Bureau would make sure she stayed there, whilst Sophie was impersonating her in Paris.

Carruthers had furnished her with lots of details about Miss Blaxland. Sophie learned that she preferred Earl Grey tea; she used rose-scented soap; she had distinctive loopy handwriting; and her dresses were generally made by the London *modiste* Henrietta Beauville. She had made her debut in society this summer; her particular friends amongst the debutantes were Diana and Violet; and she had been photographed for the society pages of *The Daily Picture* wearing what was described as 'a ravishing pink silk evening gown'.

Sophie stared at the photograph of Miss Blaxland, and Miss Blaxland stared back at her. There was certainly more than a passing resemblance between them, though it did not escape her notice that Miss Blaxland was a good deal prettier than she was. No doubt that had not escaped Carruthers, either, she thought with a bristle of irritation.

Miss Blaxland had barely known her uncle, and had not seen him since she was a child, although Sophie saw with interest that they had exchanged one or two letters in the past year. In particular, Carruthers had noted that they had corresponded about Miss Blaxland's aspiration to study at Cambridge – rather an unusual ambition for an heiress. Carruthers had scrawled something next to this in his spiky writing: Sophie had to squint to read it. *Miss Blaxland is a distinctly modern young woman. Independent and a supporter of 'women's suffrage'.* She could almost hear him saying it, with a sneer.

Sophie flicked through the pages again, frowning. Even if she did know what tea Miss Blaxland drank and what soap she liked, she wasn't sure she'd ever be able to act like her. They might be a similar age, but their lives could not have been more different. Whilst Celia Blaxland had been at her expensive finishing school, Sophie had been working as a shopgirl and renting a shabby room in a cheap boarding house. Whilst Miss Blaxland had visited friends in London and travelled in Europe, Sophie had been suspected of committing a crime and had been kidnapped by her parents' murderer. Whilst Miss Blaxland had been making plans to study at university, Sophie had discovered a talent for detective work that had taken her to London's docks, rooftops and back-streets.

But there were some things that they did have in common, Sophie thought now. They both knew what it was like to be all alone in the world, and how to be independent. The Chief evidently considered Celia Blaxland to be the sort of intrepid young lady who would undertake a journey to Paris with only a maid for company. She traced the shape of Carruthers' words *a distinctly modern young woman*. She thought suddenly that, in spite of their differences, if they were to meet, she and Miss Blaxland might get on rather well.

The white-gloved waiter opened the door to their compartment, and Sophie closed the leather folder, hiding the dossier from sight.

'More coffee, *mesdemoiselles?*'

'Earl Grey tea, if you please,' said Sophie, as the train rattled onwards towards Paris.

The Gare Du Nord was a chaos of noise and smoke, quite different from the orderly bustle of Victoria. The air seemed full of new smells – Sophie caught the scent of warm bread, the tang of garlic, a whiff of strange cigar smoke and something else, like the aroma of over-ripe fruit.

Getting through customs was more difficult than Sophie expected. She'd thought she spoke reasonable French – she certainly ought to, after all the hours she'd spent with her old governess Miss Pennyfeather, practising her French verbs. But it turned out that French in the schoolroom was quite different from French in the clang and clamour of a Paris station, as first one official then another scrutinised her papers, barked questions, and then insisted on opening and searching her trunks. They found one of Tilly's chemistry books, and there was a great deal of frowning and explaining and suspicious muttering over it. At one point it seemed that the officials would confiscate it altogether, and it had taken all of Sophie's tact to persuade them to give it back, whilst at the same time trying to prevent Tilly from losing her temper. Thank goodness for the leather folder with its clever hidden compartments concealing the secret dossiers about Professor Blaxland and his niece, she thought, as they finally made their way out of the station, and settled back against the comfortable seats of the motor car that had been engaged to take them to their hotel.

It was late, and dark was already falling, but as they drove, she caught a few tantalising glimpses of the city and remembered with a flutter of joy that they were really here, and this was Paris. Cobbled streets opening up into wide squares; shutters and chestnut trees; tall, narrow houses and ornate lamp-posts. Brightly coloured posters fluttering on a high wall; the embellished façades of grand shops – and then the motor rolled down a long, straight, tree-lined boulevard and rumbled to a halt outside the Grand Hotel Continental.

As she was helped out of the motor by a uniformed doorman, Sophie took in flags flying and the shimmer of electric light. Inside, there was a soft carpet underfoot; a piano playing; the heady scent of flowers. Beside her, she knew that Tilly was gaping around at the immense foyer, but once again, she tried hard not to stare. Miss Blaxland would not goggle, she reminded herself sternly.

Besides, there was no need to feel out of place here. Even though they were in faraway Paris, as a porter in a scarlet-and-gold uniform bowed low, and a waiter whisked by with a tray of glasses, Sophie felt on reassuringly firm ground. The Grand Hotel Continental was rather like Sinclair's – it had the same rich glow of luxury, the same sense of stepping into a busy private world, full of its own bustling activity. She nodded graciously to the smart gentleman who had come forward to greet them, imagining herself as one of the elegant ladies she had served in the Sinclair's Millinery Department not so very long ago.

'*Bonsoir, Mademoiselle Blaxland.* We are delighted to welcome you to the Grand Hotel Continental. I trust you had a pleasant journey? I am Monsieur Martin, the manager here. Your suite is waiting for you – please allow me to escort you. *Serge, Henri – les baggages!*' He clicked his fingers to two young porters in the red-and-gold livery and they sprang into action at once.

Sophie was ushered up a grand staircase, and along a carpeted hallway. Behind herself and the hotel manager came a small procession headed by Tilly, still carrying the fur and wearing her primmest expression, followed by the two porters struggling under the weight of their luggage. They passed some other guests – a middle-aged gentleman in evening attire; a lady dressed all in lace who lifted her lorgnette to look at them; a young man of fashion who gave her an inquisitive glance, but Sophie kept her chin up and ignored them all.

'I hope you will enjoy your stay at the Grand Hotel Continental, *Mademoiselle Blaxland,*' said M. Martin as they went along a corridor. 'We have many important guests here at the hotel. The King of Bergania himself stays when he is in Paris. And we have also hosted the Princess of Slavonia, and the Crown Prince of Belsornia – a most delightful gentleman! Just now we have the Countess

71

von Stubenberg staying with us. Now, here is your suite, *mademoiselle*.' He ushered them into the room with a flourish. 'All just as requested – a private sitting room *avec balcon*, and then, if you will permit me, the bed-chamber, with of course an adjoining room for your attendant, and the *salle-de-bain*.'

Sophie eased off her gloves, trying to take in her surroundings without looking unduly impressed. It was a lavish suite, sumptuously decorated with a pale-blue-and-gold silk paper on the walls and elegant, gilt-edged furniture. Draped curtains framed a magnificent view of Paris rooftops and spires: she could even see the shapes of the Eiffel Tower and the great ferris wheel, *Le Grand Roue* silhouetted against the evening sky. But what pleased her more was that the bedroom had a balcony, from which a wrought-iron spiral staircase led down into a quiet courtyard garden. She saw at once that it would be simple work to slip out without anyone knowing she was gone.

'Charming,' said Sophie with a polite smile. 'Thank you, Monsieur Martin.'

'May I send anything up for you, *mademoiselle*? You are no doubt fatigued from your so-long journey. Some *chocolat*, perhaps?'

'That would be delightful.'

When the door had closed upon M. Martin and his porters, Tilly blew out a long breath and then dropped down on to the elegant sofa. Very conscious of her tightly

72

laced corset, Sophie eased herself carefully down beside her, and they grinned at each other. She felt a sudden fizz of excitement, like bubbles bursting. They had made it this far. They had convinced the customs officials and M. Martin that they really were Miss Celia Blaxland and her lady's maid. Now they were here in a grand hotel suite in the heart of Paris.

Downstairs, M. Martin instructed a waiter to take a pot of *chocolat* up to Miss Blaxland's suite, paused to twitch a flower arrangement more correctly in position, and bowed low to the elderly lady with the lorgnette: '*Guten Abend.*'

Back at the hotel reception desk, he picked up the telephone and requested a number. His voice was low but precise as he said: '*Oui, c'est Martin. Elle est arrivée.*'

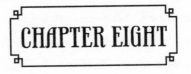

CHAPTER EIGHT

Wilderstein Castle, Arnovia

'Alex . . . Alex, do wake up!'

Alex had always been a heavy sleeper. Now he moaned and tried to pull the pillow over his head. 'What are you doing, Anna? Go away! It's too early! Leave me alone!'

'You have to wake up! It's important! It's about Miss Carter.'

'What are you babbling about?' Reluctantly, Alex struggled upright.

'Last night I followed her . . . and I saw her go creeping secretly into the Count and Countess's sitting room. She opened the Count's desk and *went through all his papers*.'

'Oh, well maybe she'd left something there – a book or something like that?' Alex shrugged. He still looked half-asleep, and his dark hair was sticking up everywhere in tufts. 'You didn't really wake me up just to tell me that, did you?'

He laughed, but Anna felt like she was going to explode. '*Alex*! Don't you understand? She was reading all the Count's private letters and papers. She had a tiny camera – it looked like a silver watch, but it wasn't. She used it to take photographs of them. She's a *spy*!'

Alex screwed up his face. 'A tiny camera that looked like a silver watch?' he repeated. 'That sounds like something from a story. I think you must've been dreaming.'

Anna felt her cheeks turn red. 'I *wasn't* dreaming! And I'm not making it up, either. Look – can't you see that Miss Carter isn't anything like a proper governess? She doesn't teach us real lessons; she doesn't really need to wear spectacles; and I'm pretty sure she can't speak German *or* Italian.' Alex's face was disbelieving, and Anna snapped out: 'She's not what she's pretending to be, and you're completely taken in by her!'

Now Alex's pale cheeks flushed too. 'Well, so what if she *isn't* a proper governess?' he snapped back. 'I don't *want* a proper governess. I couldn't care less about her spectacles, or what languages she speaks. Until she came I didn't have the first idea what going to school would be like – what to say, or what to do, or how I was supposed to manage it. I don't know anything about boys' boarding schools. I don't even *know* any other boys! I'm always just stuck here, with *you*!' Anna shrank back, hurt, as Alex went on: 'But thanks to Miss Carter, now I actually know what school will be like. You haven't the first idea how I've loathed the thought of going, but now I won't look like such a stupid fool when I get there. She's the best thing that's happened to us for ages – can't you see that?'

Anna stared at him in surprise. She'd always thought she knew everything about Alex, but she'd never had the slightest idea that he had been dreading going away to school. It struck her as so horribly unfair that Alex, who didn't want to go to school must leave; whilst she, who would have given anything for such an opportunity, must stay behind without him.

But that wasn't important now, she reminded herself in a hurry. It was what she'd discovered about Miss Carter that really mattered. 'I know you like her, Alex,' she tried to say more gently. 'But if she's sneaking around, snooping through the Count's private things, it means she's untrustworthy. She could be part of a plot! For all we know, she could be working with those people who *oppose the Crown.*'

She could not bring herself to say more, but Alex understood what she meant. 'That's an awful thing to say!' he flashed back at once. 'Whatever you may think of her, you can't accuse Miss Carter of being involved in something like what happened to our parents. She'd never hurt us! She cares about us!' He frowned, and gave her a sudden, scornful look. 'Besides, I don't see how you can criticise her for snooping when *you* were the one following her around in the middle of the night. If you ask me *you're* the one behaving like a spy.'

His voice was cold, and Anna took a step back. Alex had never looked at her like that before – as though he was staring deeply inside her, and didn't much like what he saw there. He finished: 'Now go away and let me go back to sleep!'

He rolled over and pulled up the covers, in a huff. For a moment, Anna stared at his curled-up shape under the eiderdown, and then she turned and stormed out of the room.

It was still early; not knowing quite what else to do, she went back into her own room to wait for the gong to sound for breakfast. One of the maids had already been in to make her bed and draw back the curtains: now, Anna stood restlessly, looking over the view of dark green forest, slate-grey lake and, in the distance, the chilly peaks of the mountains. It was exactly the same view as always, but everything seemed different since last night. There was something in the air, almost like the first breath of cold autumn wind, although it was only June. Or perhaps it was more like the feeling just before they went away to Elffburg, trunks packed in the hallway and carriages waiting outside. It was the feeling that *something was going to happen*. A crow was pecking at the lawn below: as she watched, it turned its head as if to look at her, and then took flight, outlined like a shadow against the sky.

She stood there looking out until she heard the sound

of the gong. As she hurried downstairs, she realised that she had to tell the Countess what she had seen. It didn't matter if she were scolded for creeping about the castle late at night, or even if Alex were furious with her for making accusations about Miss Carter. She had to let the Countess know that the governess could not be trusted. What would happen to Miss Carter, she wondered uneasily – would she be sent away in disgrace?

But when she came to the Breakfast Room, she saw to her surprise that the Countess was not there. The Countess always had breakfast with them, but today it was Miss Carter who was pouring coffee from the silver pot. Beside her, Alex was feeding Würstchen with a bit of bacon – something he loved, but was never normally allowed. Anna stopped still. 'Where's the Countess?' she blurted out.

'Good morning, Your Highness,' said Miss Carter cheerfully. 'The Count and Countess are attending to some urgent business this morning.' She patted the seat next to her. 'Come and sit down. Would you like some coffee?'

Anna stayed where she was. 'No thank you,' she said coldly.

Miss Carter looked at her in surprise. 'Is there something the matter? Are you feeling unwell?' She got up and made as if to put her hand on Anna's forehead, but Anna pulled away. She didn't want Miss Carter to touch her. She could feel Alex scowling at her and, all at once, she darted out of the room and back up the stairs, towards the Count and

Countess's sitting room.

At the door, she almost collided with Karl: 'Your Highness, where are you off to in such a hurry this morning?' he asked. Then, realising where Anna was headed: 'No . . . no . . . you mustn't disturb the Countess. Her Ladyship is very busy –'

But Anna had already burst through the sitting-room door. The Count and Countess were sitting close together, surrounded by a spill of papers and talking in urgent voices. As Anna came flying in, the Countess looked up. 'Princess Anna! What are you doing? You know you should never enter a room without knocking! You must remember that a *princess should always have perfect manners!*'

'I . . . I'm sorry, but I need to speak with you – it's important! It's about Miss Carter!' Anna blurted out. But even as she spoke, her eye was drawn to the newspapers that were spread across the Count's desk and she fell abruptly silent. The headlines screamed out at her – *ARNOVIA ON THE BRINK OF INVASION! TROOPS AT THE BORDER! NEW GERMAN THREAT!* – before the Count hurriedly whisked them out of her sight.

'Whatever it is, I'm afraid it will have to wait,' said the Countess gravely. 'We have some very important business to attend to. Now hurry along to the schoolroom.'

Too shocked by what she had seen to say anything else, Anna did as she was told.

CHAPTER NINE

Wilderstein Castle, Arnovia

The rest of the morning dragged horribly. In the schoolroom, Anna refused to meet Miss Carter's eye. Her mind kept running over everything that she had seen: the governess's hands, rifling through the Count's desk; the sneering face of the new footman; and most of all those headlines in the newspapers, sharp and shocking as the report of a gun.

She wished she could talk to Alex, but for once, Miss Carter seemed determined to keep them focused on lessons, making them draw maps of Europe and label the capital cities, and then giving them a French test. She was reading aloud to them from a book she had brought from England called *The Prisoner of Zenda* when the door opened and the Countess came in, looking unusually flustered.

'Pardon the interruption, governess. Your Highnesses, your grandfather is here to see you.'

Alex and Anna exchanged startled glances. Grandfather's visits were usually planned weeks in advance: he never arrived without warning. Why was he here so suddenly, out of the blue?

Without hesitating, they both hurried to the ballroom, where Grandfather was waiting for them. He grinned to see their astonished faces, and hugged each of them in turn. 'Well, well, Alexander! Good heavens, Anna, you have a grip like a bear! Oh, and Würstchen, old friend, you've come to greet me too? How splendid. Here we all are again. I'm afraid I can't stay very long, so we must make the most of it.'

It was so wonderful to see Grandfather that the horrid feeling in Anna's stomach began to get better at once. Everything about him was reassuring – his long, wispy white beard, the kind blue eyes with wrinkles at the corners. Grandfather always understood things. Anna knew he would listen to her, and would know what to do. But the comfortable feeling melted away almost at once, as Grandfather began to speak.

'Anna, the Countess tells me you have seen some rather alarming stories in the newspapers this morning,' He cleared his throat. 'I must tell you that unfortunately at present, our little country is under threat.

'You understand, don't you, that whilst Arnovia is only a small country, we have one asset that is of very great value – an important railway line, which connects the German

Empire and the Austria-Hungarian Empire through a tunnel cutting through the mountains? That railway line is what we call *of strategic importance*.'

'But what does that mean?' asked Anna breathlessly.

Rather to her surprise, it was Alex who answered her. 'It means that whichever country controls it will have an advantage. In a war or something like that. Lots of other powerful countries in Europe would like to have control of our railway line.'

'They would,' said Grandfather. 'The German Empire in particular. And to get it, they may try to seize control of Arnovia, or even invade us.'

Anna's stomach clenched, but Grandfather went on: 'But Arnovia has allies. Powerful friends, who we can trust to help and protect us. So whatever you may hear – or see in the newspapers – you must not worry. I will be working hard with the support of our friends to ensure this threat blows over quickly. And until then, you will be quite safe here at Wilderstein Castle.'

There was a heavy silence. Anna could hear the big old clock ticking in the stillness. Alex was frowning intently at Grandfather, and then he said: 'But what about *you*? Will you be safe?'

Grandfather looked at him for a moment, an odd expression on his face. Then he said: 'You need not fear for my safety, Alexander. All will be well. There is much work to do which will keep me occupied, so you may not see me again for a little while. That's why I wanted to come here today to see you and to tell you what was happening myself.'

Alex stared back at him unhappily, but Grandfather shook his head. 'You mustn't worry,' he said again. 'You can help me a great deal by taking good care of each other, and by doing exactly what the Count and Countess and Miss Carter tell you. I shall come back to see you again just as soon as I can.'

He got to his feet, and then said in an ordinary voice, as if this were exactly like any other visit: 'Now then, Alexander, I hear Miss Carter has been teaching you some cricket? I played for the school cricket team myself once, you know! Perhaps we can go out into the grounds and you can show me what you've learned, before I go?'

Alex got up at once, but Anna reached out and grabbed Grandfather's sleeve. 'Wait . . . wait . . . there's something I have to talk to you about,' she rushed out. 'It's about Miss Carter!'

Grandfather stopped and frowned; Alex said: 'Anna!' in a furious voice. But Anna knew she could not possibly let Grandfather go without telling him what she had learned about their governess. She was still trying to take in all that he had said, but she knew that if the country was in danger, then her discovery was more important than ever.

'I think she's a spy!' she exclaimed anxiously. 'I saw her snooping about the castle at night, and going through the

83

Count's desk! She could be plotting against us – working for the enemy!'

The words sounded wild and silly as soon as they came out of her mouth. '*Anna!*' exclaimed Alex again, but Grandfather just smiled.

'My dear Anna,' he said gently. 'Do you really think I would let *anyone* take care of you if I wasn't *certain* they could be relied upon? Miss Carter has my complete trust.'

She opened her mouth to argue, but he put a reassuring hand on her shoulder. 'I promise you, my dear, you have absolutely nothing to worry about. Don't give it another thought.' He turned back to Alex. 'Now, then, Alexander. Where do we find the cricket bat?'

'But –' Anna got to her feet, intending to say more, and to follow them outside, but Grandfather just gave her a small smile, and shook his head. Then he put his hand on Alex's shoulder and guided him out of the room.

They were gone for nearly an hour. Anna had no intention of going back to the schoolroom, so instead she loitered by herself in the ballroom, listening to the clock ticking. The eyes of the portraits on the walls seemed to watch her more closely than ever as she waited for them to return, feeling more and more anxious and lonely with every minute that passed. But when at last the door opened, she saw that it was only Karl.

'It's time for His Majesty to leave, Your Highness,' he said gently.

Outside, Grandfather hugged them both goodbye. 'Farewell,' he said. 'Remember what I said, Alexander.'

He gave Anna a tight squeeze. 'Take care of yourself, my dear, and take care of your brother too,' he whispered. 'You're a good girl, Anna. I know that I can count on you.'

She tried to blink back tears as the royal carriage drew away. Grandfather leaned out of the window to wave a hand in farewell. 'Look after yourselves, and each other!' he called, as the horses began to move, and he was carried away from them. As the carriage ran along the road and out of the castle grounds, Anna saw a flock of black crows rise up from a tree in a great flapping of wings and harsh cries.

She turned to Alex. 'What did he say to you?' she demanded.

But Alex just shook her away. 'I don't want to talk,' he said, fierce and solemn. 'Just . . . go away and play or something, can't you?'

He walked off and for the second time that day, Anna found herself staring at his back. *Go away and play?* How dare he!

Without really thinking about what she was doing, Anna turned sharply in the other direction, and walked away from him as fast as she could. Along the terrace, along the path, down the stone steps, to the secret place where she knew there was a door in the wall, half-concealed by a tangle of ivy and creepers. Of course, the children were strictly forbidden to leave the grounds, but Anna had made it her business to find out all the secret corners of the castle: the paths that were not overlooked, the hidden entrances that were not guarded. Through the hidden door she went and out, on to the hillside beyond, up along the steep rocky path. She knew she would be in trouble with the Countess if she were caught, but she felt too angry to care. In another mood she might have relished the excitement of being out on the hillside by herself, feeling the rush of wind, looking down at the expanse of forest and lake spread out below her. But now she was far too busy with her own thoughts, buzzing like a swarm of furious insects.

Arnovia was in danger. The German Empire was working to overthrow Grandfather, and to seize control of the country. People were conspiring against the King. Her breaths came quick and fast: Grandfather had said everything would be all right, that he would come to no harm, but how could he possibly be sure of that? What had he said to Alex to make him look so solemn? She hated that Alex always got to know about everything properly, just because he was a boy, and because he would be King someday.

Most of all, she hated that Grandfather had not listened to what she had told him. She kicked at a stone furiously and it went skittering away from her down the path. She knew it sounded silly, and of course she realised that he must have chosen Miss Carter with great care. But what if the governess had tricked him into thinking she could be trusted? Anna's chest tightened. If Miss Carter was a spy, then she could be working for the German Empire – for those who even now were trying to seize control of Arnovia. Perhaps she'd been sent here to spy on the royal household – to find out secret information to send back to Berlin, and to use in the plot against Grandfather?

She'd been walking so fast that she was breathless, and now she'd realised she'd come further than she'd intended: she was already halfway up the dusty path that led up the hill. Pausing to catch her breath, she stared down at Wilderstein Castle below her. From here, it looked like a fortress, with its fierce grey stone ramparts, its turrets spiked like medieval spears, the green-and-white Arnovian flag fluttering proudly against the sky. It looked like a place that could withstand anything, somewhere they would always be safe. But she knew the castle was not safe any longer. How could it be when there was a spy in their midst?

Take care of your brother, Grandfather had said. *I know that I can count on you.* But how could she look after Alex when no one would believe her about Miss Carter? She knew the Countess would not take her seriously if Grandfather had not: she could already imagine the lecture she would get about the impropriety of making wild accusations, and why princesses should not question His Majesty the King's choice of governess.

As she stood there, wrestling with her thoughts, she heard the jangle of cowbells coming closer. A moment later, a cowherd passed by on the mountain path above her, with half a dozen big brown-and-white cows. He was a tall, bronzed young man, with a feather in his hat, and he gave her a curious look before calling out the local greeting: '*Grüß Gott, Fraulein!*'

Anna blushed, realising how strange she must seem – a girl in a stiff black frock, standing halfway up the hillside all by herself. But just the same, she rather liked the thought that the cowherd had no idea who she was. He hadn't bowed or called her 'Your Highness'. He did not know she was a princess, or a member of the Royal House of Wilderstein. As far as he was concerned, she could have been anyone at all.

She waved a hand in reply. '*Grüß Gott,*' she replied, trying to sound casual, as if she greeted cowherds every day. She watched him go, leading the cows on up the path, and for a moment she longed to follow him – to walk on, up the path and over the mountain, to discover what was on the other side. Instead, she turned back towards the castle. She knew she should go back before anyone noticed she was missing.

But for a few final moments, she stood and stared out –

over the turrets of the castle, over the dark green conifers, and out to the glittering snow-capped mountains. Beyond lay the German border, where even now the troops could be mustering, making ready for an invasion. The thought of it made her shiver, but also quite sure of what she must do.

Grandfather had said they should do what the Count and Countess and Miss Carter told them, but he had also said they should *look after each other*, and that was exactly what Anna intended to do. Alex might be the Crown Prince, but *she* was his older sister. She would not let Miss Carter put him in danger. She would find a way to stop the governess and prove exactly what she was up to – before she could do anything more to help the plot against Arnovia.

She thought of the attaché case she had seen hidden beneath the governess's bed. Surely that would be where she'd find the evidence she needed? That was where Miss Carter kept her pocket-watch camera, and no doubt other secret things too; after all, there must be a reason why she kept the key so carefully, hanging around her neck. If only Anna could think of a way to get hold of that key! Then she could sneak into Miss Carter's room and unlock the box, and once she had the evidence, she would take it straight to the Count and Countess and prove that Miss Carter was plotting against them.

Anna stood shielding her eyes with her hand, feeling the wind blow her skirt against her legs and flutter in her hair.

She felt tall and strong, and full of a blazing determination. She knew she was much more than a useless princess, no matter how they treated her. She would show them. She would find out the truth about Miss Carter – whatever it took.

CHAPTER TEN

Wilderstein Castle, Arnovia

The next few days were strange ones. The castle seemed unlike its usual self. Sentries were stationed in the grounds each night: Anna knew they were there to help keep them safe, but it gave her an odd, shivery feeling to watch their shadowy figures marching up and down the paths, with their long rifles over their shoulders. The Countess did not make Anna sit at the back-board, nor correct her deportment, and the Count did not pore over plans of aeroplanes, nor did he take Alex on his morning 'drills'. Instead, they spent all their time shut up in their private sitting room, and the castle felt odd and lonely without them. From behind the sitting-room door, Anna could sometimes hear the sound of their raised voices.

Alex seemed unlike his usual self too. Although he appeared to have forgiven Anna for telling Grandfather her suspicions about Miss Carter, he was obviously uneasy: quieter than usual and distracted in the schoolroom. He didn't even seem very enthusiastic about their performance of *The Tempest*, which they gave in the ballroom as planned, although the Count and Countess were now too busy to come and see it. Instead they performed for an audience of three – Miss Carter, Karl and Würstchen. But however enthusiastically Karl clapped and Miss Carter cheered, their applause was hollow, echoing around the empty ballroom, where the portrait of their parents seemed to look on silently from the wall.

All the while, Anna was watching Miss Carter. She watched her in the ballroom, as she carefully arranged Alex's Prospero cloak; and in the schoolroom as she read aloud or gave them a spelling test. She watched her at breakfast, and while she played cricket with Alex in the garden. More and more, she suspected that Miss Carter was watching her too. Sometimes when she glanced up from her books, she'd see the governess's eyes glittering at her in a way she found disconcerting. The day that Grandfather had visited, she'd come into Anna's bedroom. 'I know you left the grounds this afternoon,' she'd said, giving Anna a piercing look. 'Don't worry. I won't tell the Countess. But really, you must be careful. Please don't go wandering off like that again. It isn't *safe*.'

Anna had stared after her as she left the room. How on earth could she have possibly known about Anna leaving the grounds? She'd been right on the other side of the castle when Anna had returned, and surely she couldn't possibly know about the hidden door? She'd only been at the castle for a few weeks. Had she been snooping around again? And what did she mean *it isn't safe?* Could she have been making some kind of threat?

All the time she was wondering how she could possibly get hold of the key to Miss Carter's attaché case. But even though she'd peeped inside the governess's room more than once, she'd never seen so much as a glimpse of it anywhere. She probably wore it around her neck at all times. She was certainly far too clever to leave it lying around. Miss Carter might seem jolly and cheerful, but more and more, Anna saw a different side of her – sharp, fox-like, secret. She thought again about how different she had looked without her spectacles, and with her long hair flowing loose – like someone else altogether. That peculiar sense that she'd once seen her somewhere before kept niggling away, as she watched Miss Carter bending over Alex's shoulder to look at something he was showing her in one of his magazines.

Magazines! It flashed into her head like a burst of bright light. Could *that* be where she had seen Miss Carter? It seemed a wild idea, but as soon as she had the chance, Anna slipped quietly along the passageway towards Alex's bedroom. Inside, she found his big stack of theatre magazines, and she sat down on the floor beside them, rapidly turning over the pages. She scanned photographs of West End leading ladies, Parisian dancers, Broadway actors, moving-picture stars – yet not one of them looked in the least bit familiar. She must have been mistaken. She had almost given up on the idea when in the middle of one of the magazines, she saw that a page had been ripped out.

She felt the rough, torn edge with her fingertips. Of course, it was perfectly possible that Alex had taken the page out himself, but Anna knew that the magazines were precious to him, so surely he would have cut it out carefully with scissors, not torn it out roughly like that? She remembered that she'd seen Miss Carter leafing through the magazines: what if *she* had found the page and ripped it out, in order to hide a photograph from Alex? After all, thought Anna, who could be better to play the part of a governess than a real-life actress?

The thought of it made her throat feel very dry, and her skin prickle. She took the magazine and slipped out of Alex's room again. A footman was standing outside the door, like a sentry on duty – she recognised him with a sudden start as the one who had caught her out of bed, the night she'd spied on Miss Carter. Now, he bowed to her and said: 'Good afternoon, Your Highness', but there was something about the way he said it that made her feel horrible. He held her gaze and smirked, as though he knew that once more he'd caught her somewhere she shouldn't be.

Anna turned her back on him and went into her

bedroom, closing the door firmly behind her. She hid the magazine carefully, sliding it inside the covers of one of the books on her shelf. She thought she might need it later, but as evidence went, a magazine with a missing page certainly wasn't enough. She had to think of a way to get into Miss Carter's attaché case, and she could not afford to wait a single minute longer.

What if she were to steal the whole case, she thought suddenly? It was not very big, and the lock did not look especially strong. Surely there must be some way she could break the suitcase open – cut the leather or smash the lock – and see what was inside? It would be a bold thing to do, but Anna was beginning to feel desperate.

She went back out of her bedroom, ignoring the footman, and down the passageway in the direction of the governess's room once more. On the way, she saw two of the new maids, coming out of the bathroom, each carrying a large empty bucket. '*Danke schön,*' she heard Miss Carter's voice say from inside, as the door closed behind them.

Anna realised at once what was happening. Wilderstein Castle had old-fashioned plumbing; there was no hot running water; so when anyone had a bath, the servants had to bring up hot water from the kitchen. Her heart quickened. If Miss Carter was taking a bath, then this would be the perfect moment to take the attaché case!

Looking quickly around her to make sure there were no maids or footmen in sight, she slid inside the governess's bedroom, pulling the door closed behind her so she would not be seen.

Peeping inside the room was one thing, but actually sneaking in was quite another. Her skin felt damp, and her hands were trembling. Even though she knew Miss Carter was safely in the bathroom, she found herself tiptoeing across the room towards the bed, hardly daring to breathe.

It was not very tidy. A gown and a couple of petticoats were tossed every which way over a chair, there was a muddle of books and papers on the table, and even a pair of stockings tangled on the floor. She crept over to the bed to find the attaché case, but then something stopped her. Lying on the messy dressing table beside a brush, a comb and a powder puff, Anna glimpsed a little key, hanging from a fine silver chain.

She almost clapped her hands in satisfaction. Of course – Miss Carter had finally taken the key off, while she had a bath! But there was no time to lose: Anna snatched it up at once, and reached beneath the bed as she'd seen Miss Carter do. Her hand closed over the shiny leather of the attaché case, which rattled intriguingly as she slid it towards her. Her hands fumbling in her haste, she fitted the little key into the lock, and then eagerly lifted the lid. Inside, she saw . . . nothing.

Nothing but some embroidered handkerchiefs and a few pairs of gloves. Was that really all that the mysterious case contained? She sat back on her heels, disappointed.

But why go to so much trouble to lock it and hide it away if all it contained were handkerchiefs, she wondered. Surely there must be more to it than that? She began feeling around inside the case, and realised to her excitement that the handkerchiefs and gloves were lying on a shallow tray, which could be lifted out. Carefully she removed it, and what she saw underneath made her gasp aloud. Underneath the layer of filmy lace and embroidery was concealed a dozen small compartments, each holding something different. A map. A fat roll of bank notes. The silver pocket-watch camera she had seen. Some folded identity papers. A little glass phial, barely bigger than her finger. A small set of field-glasses. A bundle of letters with foreign stamps.

Anna's fingers trembled. For a moment, she didn't know what to look at first. Then, she reached out, breathlessly, towards the identity papers.

'What on earth do you think you're doing?'

Anna looked up in horror. Miss Carter was standing above her. She was wearing her dressing gown; and her wet hair was hanging down her back in a long, dark waterfall. Anna pushed the case away, spilling its contents, but of course it was too late. Miss Carter had seen exactly what she was doing. She looked shocked, and for a moment an anxious expression flashed across her face. But then as quickly as it had come, the expression seemed to vanish and then her dark eyes sparked with fury.

'How dare you come into my room and go through my things! What a rotten, low-down thing to do!'

Anna took a step back. She was afraid, but she felt suddenly furious too. Her cheeks blazed red: how could Miss Carter say that Anna was *rotten* and *low-down* when *she* was the one who was a spy? She opened her mouth to retort, but Miss Carter didn't give her a chance. 'I'm not in the least bit interested to hear what you have to say for yourself. I'm very disappointed in you.'

Seizing Anna firmly by the elbow, she marched her out of the room, slamming the door on the attaché case and its contents. Anna tried to struggle, but the governess held her firm. As she marshalled her down the passage, Anna felt tears of anger and frustration starting in her eyes. She was mortified to see the footman was still standing outside her bedroom door, staring at her with insolent curiosity. For a moment his eyes met the governess's, and she gave him an imperious glance before bundling Anna inside her bedroom.

'Now, I want you to stay in here and have a very good long think about what you've done,' said Miss Carter, her voice so loud that Anna was sure half the castle would be able to hear. Her face crimson with anger and embarrassment, she made a dash for the door, but Miss Carter was too quick. Before Anna could do anything else, she had swept out of the room, closing the door firmly behind her. The key turned with a clunk in the lock, and there was a grating sound as Miss Carter took it from the keyhole, before walking rapidly away down the passage.

Anna rattled the handle, but the door didn't budge. Miss Carter had locked her in her room and taken away the key.

Anna collapsed on to the bed, a torrent of rage and indignation sweeping over her, and burst into furious tears. How dare Miss Carter lock her in her bedroom? How dare she speak to her in that rude way, as if she wasn't a princess at all, but only a naughty child? It was only the thought of that awful footman outside the door listening that forced her to calm her sobs. She scrubbed at her eyes with her handkerchief and tried to breathe, and as she did so she realised it all made a terrible kind of sense. Miss Carter was a spy, and Anna was the only one who knew it.

What would Miss Carter do now? Would she run away while she had the chance, or might she do something to try and prevent Anna telling anyone what she knew? That thought made her feel worse than ever, and she darted to the window wondering if she could try and climb out, but her bedroom was high up on the second floor, and there would be no way to get down. Then she ran to the door, thinking that she should bang and shout for help. But who would answer her? Everyone was far away: Alex would be in the schoolroom; the Count and Countess would be in their private sitting room; and she did not trust that footman in the passageway one bit. She remembered what he had said to her in the night; and she remembered too how Miss Carter had looked at him. What if he was working with her? For all she knew, he could be part of the plot too.

She sat in the middle of the bed, making herself small, tucking her knees under her chin. The courage she had felt on the mountainside just a few days ago had vanished and now she felt very small and alone.

She was still sitting there when it began to get dark. She had been sure that Alex would come and whisper to her through the door, or perhaps a maid would appear with a tray of supper, but no one came. After suppertime had come and gone, she went over to the door and cautiously called: 'Hello? Is anyone out there?' But no one answered her. Even the footman seemed to have gone away.

Wilderstein Castle was silent. No one talking. No servants going by in the passageway. Not even so much as a bark from Würstchen. She went to the window and looked into the garden, but there was no one there. All she could see was the distant figures of the guards on duty far away from her, the shape of their rifles outlined in the fading light.

Bedtime arrived and still nobody came. It was a hot night and Anna lay flat on her bed, listening. After a while among the ordinary night-time sounds – leaves rustling in the garden, a bird calling in the dark – she began to hear other things, odd little noises. First the sound of a door opening and closing softly somewhere on the floor above, then a distant low murmur of voices. Somewhere outside the quiet rumble of a motor-engine, and then once, the rapid pattering of feet in the corridor, gone before she had the chance to call out.

After she had lain awake listening for a long time, she must have fallen into an uneasy sleep, because when she woke, it was very dark. Someone was leaning over her bed, and fear jolted her awake at once. It was Miss Carter, fully dressed and holding a candle.

'Wake up, Anna,' she said in a tense, low voice. 'Get out of bed!'

'W-what?' Anna managed to stammer. 'Why? What's happening?'

The governess's face was shadowy and strange. She whispered: 'We're going to play Murder in the Dark.'

PARIS

PART III

'*Of all the cities that Papa and I have visited this year, it is Paris that still seems to me the most marvellous. Perhaps it is because it was there that we first began this great adventure.*'

– From the diary of Alice Grayson

CHAPTER ELEVEN

Paris, France

The offices of Monsieur Dupont, *Notaire*, were very dark: the blinds had been pulled closed against the glare of the summer sun. Little particles of dust floated and turned to gold in the light, as Sophie watched M. Dupont turning over papers, his gold signet ring flashing in a faint beam of sunlight.

'*Voilá, mademoiselle.* If you please, sign here. And again *here*.'

Sophie signed Celia Blaxland's name carefully. She wasn't sure whether her imitation of Miss Blaxland's loopy writing would hold up to close scrutiny, but it seemed to satisfy the Professor's solicitor.

Just the same, M. Dupont looked uneasy even as he smiled politely at her across the expanse of mahogany desk. The Chief had said that he'd be expecting Miss Blaxland, and yet he had seemed surprised by her arrival, courteously pressing her hand and expressing his great sorrow for her loss whilst at the same time, hinting delicately that she should not have come alone.

'But I am not alone. My maid is with me,' Sophie replied in a voice that sounded more haughty than her own would have done. She was beginning to feel more comfortable in the character of Miss Blaxland now. Lil had taught her something about how to play a role in the last few years, and she sat with her back very straight and her head held high as she felt sure a young lady like Miss Blaxland would do.

M. Dupont looked uncertainly over at Tilly, who was sitting on a chair by the door. He flashed her a quick, artificial smile, and Sophie knew that Tilly was fighting the desire to pull a face back.

'Of course, of course. Quite *comme-il-faut*. But perhaps a gentleman of your family would be best placed to . . .?'

'I'm afraid that there *are* no gentlemen of my family, now that my uncle is dead,' said Sophie briskly. 'But his affairs must be put in order, so here I am.'

'How delightful to meet such an independent and business-like young lady,' said M. Dupont, smiling in a way that suggested he did not find it in the least bit delightful. 'Well, naturally I am quite at your service, *mademoiselle*. Here is a copy of your uncle's will. The legal language may be difficult, so I will summarise. It is all most straightforward: his book collection has been left to the university library, but besides a few other small bequests, all his remaining property should come to you, to be held in trust until your twenty-first birthday. However . . .' The solicitor's voice trailed away and there was an awkward silence.

'Yes?' Sophie prompted him.

'It is a matter of some *delicacy*, *mademoiselle*,' muttered the solicitor, casting another uncertain glance at Tilly.

'You may speak freely before my maid,' said Sophie, haughtier than ever.

'But of course, if you wish it, *mademoiselle*. I . . . er . . . I regret to inform you that your uncle has left a number of *debts* behind him. *Considerable* debts. I am afraid that he had been living beyond his means for some time.'

Living beyond his means? Sophie listened intently as the *notaire* went on:

'Fortunately, it seems that your uncle had a significant amount of cash, in bank notes, at his apartment. Together with the proceeds from the sale of his property, it will be enough to cover his debts. But of course that means unfortunately there will be nothing left for you to inherit, *mademoiselle*.' He coughed delicately. 'Then there is also the small matter of our own account, which will need to be settled . . .'

'I see,' said Sophie. Of course it didn't matter to her whether Miss Blaxland inherited any money or not, and in fact it probably didn't matter much to the real Miss Blaxland either, since she was already so very well-off. But this discovery was certainly a rather interesting one. The Professor came from a wealthy family; he must have earned a good salary at the university; and he would also have been paid well for his work for the Secret Service Bureau. However had he managed to get himself into such financial difficulties?

'Of course, your bill will be taken care of,' she said graciously. 'May I ask if there was anything particular which caused these debts?'

But the solicitor just shrugged. 'I really could not say, *mademoiselle*.'

Sophie eyed him sceptically. She was certain he knew far more than he was admitting, but she doubted she would get much more from him on the subject. 'I would be very grateful indeed for any more information you could give me about exactly what happened to my uncle,' she said, changing the subject. 'All I know is that his apartment was burgled, and that he disturbed the thieves.'

Now M. Dupont looked alarmed. 'What happened to Professor Blaxland was a most terrible tragedy! A young lady such as yourself ought not . . . that is, I would not wish to upset or to offend your most delicate . . .' He gulped and muttered something about 'Such unpleasantness!'

'But what was stolen from him? Was it valuables? If there was a sum of money found at his apartment, then I suppose the burglars did not take everything?' Sophie pressed.

'No – his cash-box was left in his desk. It is possible the thieves were scared away before they found it. But the police have said that his safe was left open – and empty – though what he kept inside it I am afraid I do not know.'

'And the police are investigating?'

'Oh, but assuredly, *mademoiselle*,' M. Dupont was quick to tell her. 'The *Préfecture de Police* have been most helpful and attentive. Rest assured that your uncle's apartment is being examined thoroughly and every effort is being made to catch the culprits. If they did get away with any valuables, you may be confident the police will do their utmost to see them restored to you.'

'Well, I should very much like to see his apartment for myself. Would you be able to arrange for me to visit?'

The solicitor gaped at her. 'Oh no, that will not be possible, not at present. The apartment is still being studied by the police – it is the scene of a most disturbing crime.'

Sophie felt annoyance rising in her chest. 'But what about my uncle's personal belongings – his papers and letters and so on?'

'You do not need to trouble yourself with such matters, *mademoiselle*. We will of course ensure that all personal items are safely packed and sent to your home once the police have completed their work. You may count on my full assistance in this.'

'So you mean to say that . . . there is nothing for me to do?' she asked at last.

M. Dupont looked relieved. 'That is exactly it, *mademoiselle*. There is nothing for you to do! You may rest easy. Do not trouble yourself about any arrangements. If you will be kind enough to settle our account, our firm will be delighted to take care of everything. You can take your mind off these matters so unpleasant and enjoy the city. Maybe a little shopping at the *Galeries Lafayette*, or a promenade in the Bois de Boulogne?'

Sophie battled to keep her expression neutral. There was no sense in arguing or showing her frustration, she told herself: it was perfectly obvious that M. Dupont was not going to help her to examine the Professor's apartment. But there was one more thing she might try.

'What about the Sorbonne: might I see my uncle's office there?' Thinking of what Lil might have done, she introduced a tiny quiver into her voice. Since a business-like approach was not working, it was time to try a different tack. 'I should so dearly like to see where he worked, you see,' she added, taking out a lacy handkerchief and trying an experimental little sniff. 'Or perhaps to meet some of his colleagues?'

Now Monsieur Dupont beamed at her kindly. 'But of course. I am sure that his colleagues would be most happy to receive you.' He handed over a card with the address on it and made his farewells. Sophie sensed he was glad to be rid of them.

Out on the street, it was hot and bright and dusty.

The road jostled with traffic: rough horse-drawn carts mingling with motor cars and carriages and omnibuses that somehow did not look at all like English ones, bearing the names of unknown places like 'Place St Michel' or 'Avenue de Clichy'.

'Well!' said Tilly reflectively as they climbed once more into their waiting motor car. 'That wasn't quite what I was expecting.'

Sophie nodded. 'I know. There wasn't a word about the Professor's debts in the dossier. He must have kept them a secret. If only I could have got some more information out of that infuriating man – I'm certain he knew more than he was letting on.'

'But you can't really blame him,' said Tilly rationally. 'I don't expect he's used to young ladies coming to his office and demanding to know about finances and the gory details of murders.'

That was true enough, but Sophie still felt spiky and cross. The leather cushions of the motor were sticky and uncomfortable, and her skin prickled under Miss Blaxland's embellished gown, her petticoats and gloves. She felt stifled in the tight bodice and fashionably narrow 'hobble' skirt which only allowed her to take small, mincing steps. Being Celia Blaxland felt like it was hobbling her completely. 'I do wonder why the Chief thought this would work,' she mused aloud. Surely someone else could have got more out of a man like Dupont. He just isn't going to say anything useful to a girl like Miss Blaxland.'

Tilly looked thoughtful. 'Well, he must havehad his reasons. He obviously thought it would be the best approach. Otherwise, we wouldn't be here, would we?'

Sophie frowned. For a moment she found herself thinking of something Mr Sinclair had said to her once – it felt like a very long time ago now – on a cold January day with snow falling against the windows of Sinclair's: *'You showed me very clearly, Miss Taylor, that you and your friends could see things and do things that I could not.'*

Perhaps that was why the Chief had sent her. Perhaps he thought Miss Blaxland would be able to find out different kinds of information – to go to different places and find out things that might otherwise be difficult to learn. Whilst the *notaire* had not been very helpful, perhaps there were other avenues to explore. She looked down at the card she was still holding between her fingertips:

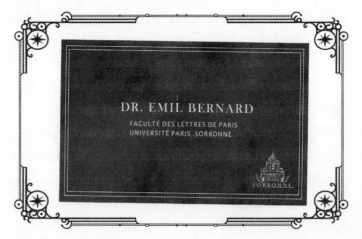

DR. EMIL BERNARD

FACULTÉ DES LETTRES DE PARIS
UNIVERSITÉ PARIS SORBONNE

'Let's try this,' she said. Leaning forward she pushed back the partition that separated them from the driver. '*La Sorbonne, s'il vous plaît.*'

CHAPTER TWELVE

Wilderstein Castle, Arnovia

'Quickly, Anna!' The governess was a silhouette, standing over her in the dark. 'We'll pretend we're playing a game. It will help Alex not to be frightened. It will make all this seem normal.'

'*Normal?*' Anna managed to gasp. Then the words came in a rush, so quickly that they caught in her throat. 'How could this possibly seem *normal*? You're a spy! You're plotting against us – working for the enemy!' She struggled away, untangling herself from the bedclothes, opening her mouth to scream for help, but the governess was as fast as a snake. Before Anna had the chance to make a sound, she had pounced and pressed a hand firmly over her mouth. 'Hush! They'll hear us! You don't understand. You're in danger! Not from me – *I'm here to protect you.*'

She was lying. Anna knew exactly what she had seen. Panic flooded through her; she struggled and fought; but Miss Carter was too strong. In wild desperation, she bit down hard on the governess's fingers. Miss Carter let out a cry of pain, and in that moment, Anna seized her chance to wriggle free. She made a mad dash for the door, but again the governess was too fast: she caught her and dragged her back, holding her so tightly that she couldn't move.

'You little beast!' she panted. But there was something almost like admiration in her voice as she said: 'Gosh! I'd never have thought you had it in you. You aren't going to make this easy for me, are you? Look, I'm awfully sorry but I don't have time to explain. The longer we take the more danger you'll be in. They're coming for you both *tonight*. We have to go!'

Still holding Anna, with one hand pressed over her mouth, Miss Carter thrust the bedroom door open with an elbow, and pushed her out into the passageway. Anna kept on struggling, but Miss Carter was tall and strong, much taller and stronger than Anna. As they stumbled together along the darkened hall, she could hear Miss Carter murmuring in her ear in a low voice: 'You've got this all muddled. I'm sorry I had to lock you in your room, but it simply couldn't be helped. I couldn't risk you giving away the whole show. Besides, I knew you'd be safe in there, as long as I had the key. If only I hadn't been so jolly stupid! I ought to have realised it was *her* idea all along. She's dragged the Count into it too of course, but I don't think he understands the half of it.' As Anna struggled against her still harder, she whispered: '*I'm not a spy*, Anna. Well actually, I suppose I am, but not in the way you think. I'm a British agent. I'm here to protect you.'

Anna knew that she was lying. She struggled harder, but all at once, Miss Carter stopped dragging her along, and froze. 'They're coming!' she hissed, and dragged her around a corner, behind the same rusting suit of armour that Anna had hidden behind not many nights before.

It was a warm night, but Anna was shivering. Miss Carter was holding her so tightly that she couldn't move or make a sound; the governess's fingers were gripping into her arms like irons. In the distance, she could hear footsteps along the stone passage and the echoing sound of the Countess's voice. She too was out of bed, in the middle of the night! Had she and the Count discovered what Miss Carter was up to? Would they be able to save her?

Then she heard the Count's voice, a little louder: 'But Maria, are you sure? Is this really the right thing –'

'Of course it's the right thing. Right for us, and more importantly, right for *Arnovia*,' cut in the Countess. 'Leopold's a fool if he thinks he can hold out against them for much longer. Do you really want to risk throwing your lot in with the losing side? We could lose everything!'

'Of course not, but –'

'Besides, if Leopold has his way, you'll be marooned here for the rest of your life – away from the Court, away from everything. Do you really want to be stuck here forever, collecting butterflies and tinkering with the workings of aeroplanes? If we do this, then *you*'ll be in charge. Once Leopold steps down, they'll make you King, Rudolf, or as good as! They've promised us that. Then you can govern Arnovia the way it *ought* to be governed. And all we have to do is hand over the children tonight.' She paused and issued a sharp order to someone, her voice as strict and precise as when she was correcting Anna's deportment: 'Fetch the prince and put him in the motor. Restrain him if you must.'

'Yes, Your Ladyship!' came the swift reply. Anna knew that voice. It was the new footman – the one who had been standing outside her bedroom door.

'But –' said the Count again.

'Oh, for pity's sake, Rudolf! Have some backbone. Are a couple of children really more important than the fate of your country? Sometimes I find it difficult to imagine how you ever won any of those medals.'

The Count gave a mournful yelp, rather like the noise Würstchen made when he got under someone's feet by mistake. But the Countess had already moved on: 'Lock the governess's door,' she instructed in the same curt voice. 'I don't want any unnecessary difficulties tonight.'

Anna heard the clunk of Miss Carter's door being locked. She could feel the governess's breaths, warm against her ear, a piece of her hair tickling her cheek. Then their footsteps and voices disappeared along the corridor and Anna let out a little strangled sob.

117

She had got it all upside down. Miss Carter had been telling the truth. She wasn't the one plotting against Grandfather. It was the *Countess* who was planning to hand over Alex and Anna to his enemies, and now she was headed straight for Alex's room in the middle of the night.

'I'm sorry, Anna,' whispered Miss Carter in her ear.

'Alex!' she managed to choke out.

'It's all right. He's not there. He's in the schoolroom waiting for us. But we should hurry.'

The schoolroom was in darkness, but Anna could see Alex straight away, looking very small and white-faced in his outdoor coat. She could hear immediately that he was struggling to breathe. 'What's happening?' he managed to choke out between wheezing breaths, whilst Anna rushed over to him and rubbed his back, wishing she could do something more to help him. 'It's part of the plot, isn't it?' he demanded.

Miss Carter let out a sigh, and with it seemed to give up any notion of games and pretence. 'Yes,' she admitted. 'They were heading to your room. They'll know any moment that you're gone.' She paced over to the window and glanced quickly out, into the darkened grounds. 'We have to get away, but they have their people everywhere. There must be at least a dozen men out there, and they're armed. We need a way out of the castle without being seen.'

Alex turned paler than ever, but the solution flashed into Anna's mind at once. 'I think I know how we can go!'

she exclaimed. 'There's a way through the castle cellars – a kind of secret passage that leads out into the grounds. Hardly anyone knows about it. Then we could go through the secret door in the wall on to the mountainside.'

What would happen to them after that she hadn't the least idea, but there was no time to wonder about that now. Miss Carter nodded at once. 'Let's go. We'll have to be quick, and stay very quiet. Anna, you lead the way.'

She grabbed her little attaché case, and put an arm round Alex. Then, almost before Anna could take in what was happening, the three of them were sneaking out of the schoolroom together, and hurrying through the darkened castle.

But it was a different castle now. Not the place they knew, but somewhere menacing, where voices and feet thrummed on the stone floors. In the distance, Anna heard Würstchen barking and then, much closer, something that sounded horribly like the rattle of a sword. With every moment that passed, she expected to see weapons flashing in the dark, to hear voices yelling: 'We've got them! They're trying to get away!' Behind her, she could hear that Alex was struggling to keep quiet, his wheezing growing louder and louder. Once he paused to try and get his breath back, but Miss Carter urged him onwards at once. 'I'm sorry, Alex. We can't risk stopping even for a moment,' Anna heard her whisper.

Then: 'Anna, wait!' came Miss Carter's voice again,

more urgently this time. 'I can hear something.'

For a moment they all froze in the shadows outside the ballroom. Now, Anna could hear it too: the sound of soft footsteps approaching. Someone was coming closer and closer towards them. Her mouth felt horribly dry; she could hear Alex doing his best to muffle his breaths, but however hard he tried, the sound of his wheezing was loud in the dark.

'Who's there?' came a tense voice.

A light flashed over them suddenly: Anna cringed back, expecting a cry of discovery. But instead there was silence. Karl was standing in front of them, holding up a light: Miss Carter stepped forward boldly, as though to shield them from its brightness. Karl stared at her for a long moment, in which there was no sound but Alex's rough breaths.

'What's happening? What are you doing?' Karl demanded at last.

'I'm doing what has to be done,' Miss Carter said. She spoke bravely, but Anna could hear a tremble in her voice. *She doesn't know if we can trust him*, Anna realised with a lurch of fear. 'I'm getting Alex and Anna safely away from here.'

Karl just stared back at her. Anna's knees felt weak. But then Alex stepped forward and managed to wheeze out: 'Karl, you'll help us, won't you?'

Karl glanced quickly behind him. Then he turned out the lamp he was carrying, plunging the passage back into darkness. 'Your Highness, I'll always help you,' he said hoarsely.

'Thank you!' whispered Miss Carter, sounding almost as giddy with relief as Anna felt herself.

'How will you get out?'

'Anna says there's a way through the cellar.'

'The secret passage – through the trapdoor,' Anna managed to whisper. 'Then we'll go out into the grounds and through the door on to the mountainside.'

'But what then?' asked Karl. 'Even if you make it on to the road, they've got men, and motor cars. They'll soon catch up with you.'

'I'm not taking them on the road. I'm going over the mountain,' said Miss Carter at once. 'We'll walk over the pass, and across the border to Switzerland.'

'But Princess Anna can't walk over the mountains, not dressed like this!' objected Karl. 'It'll be cold – she doesn't even have a coat!'

Miss Carter gaped. 'We don't have time to *fetch coats!*' she exclaimed. 'In case you haven't noticed, these children are about to be *kidnapped*.'

But Alex grabbed her arm. 'Wait – I know,' he said through a gasp. He darted quickly inside the ballroom, making Miss Carter hiss after him furiously: 'What d'you think you're doing! Come back at once!'

But a moment later he was back, and now he was carrying the velvet curtain they'd used as Prospero's cloak. 'It was

121

still in there,' he explained. Rather shakily, he unfolded it and put it round Anna's shoulders. In that moment, it felt like a hug.

Now it was Karl who led the way as they hurried onwards, to the trapdoor that led down to the cellars. He helped Miss Carter to heave it open, even as the sound of running feet drew closer.

'Look – I'll try and head them off,' said Karl. 'You go – quickly!'

'You'll be all right?' Miss Carter asked, not quite a question, nor quite a statement either.

Karl nodded. 'Goodbye, Your Highnesses,' he whispered, as he helped them one after the other down into the darkness below. 'Keep safe. Good luck.' A moment later, Miss Carter had pulled the trapdoor closed over their heads, blotting out his white, anxious face.

It was not a moment too soon. Even as they stumbled down the steps and into the cellars, Anna could hear angry voices above them.

'They went that way – upstairs!' she heard Karl say.

'Then what are you standing there for – find them!' the Countess screeched, her voice loud and harsh now, without its usual precise sound.

'*Hurry!*' whispered Miss Carter. But it was hard-going in the pitch dark of the old cellar. They had no lamp or candle; Alex's wheezing grew louder; and once Anna stumbled into an old barrel and almost cried out. For a moment she was frightened she had lost her way in the dark, but at last, after what seemed like a very long time, she managed to find the door that led out into the grounds. Thank goodness for all the hours she'd spent *putting her nose in places she wasn't supposed to*, she thought as the door creaked open, loud and alarming in the dark. A moment later they were stumbling together through the grounds, under the cover of the trees, and through the secret door in the wall that led out on to the mountain path.

It was almost dawn, and the darkness was beginning to fade into the pale light of early morning. Miss Carter would not let them rest even for a moment, but hurried them onwards, up the steep path that Anna had come just a few short days ago, stones skittering beneath their feet.

Not far up the path was a rough wooden hut that the cowherds used. Now, Anna realised that someone was standing there watching them, in the chilly grey light. A bronzed cowherd with a feather in his hat was looking down on them, as though he was not really very surprised to see them. '*Gruß Gott*,' he said cheerfully. Then, speaking in English with a British accent as crisp as Miss Carter's own: 'Well done, old thing! I wasn't sure whether you'd pull it off! And I suppose *you* must be the young prince and princess. Jolly good to meet you, chaps! Right-ho, let's get out of here, shall we?'

CHAPTER THIRTEEN

The Sorbonne, Paris

Bells were ringing out across the city, as the motor car rumbled south, carrying them over the River Seine. Sophie gazed out at the the colours of Paris – the pale yellow stone, the grey-blue slate rooftops, the vivid scarlet of a window-box full of geraniums. Outside the great church of Notre Dame, she saw that tourists were gathering: little groups clustered around a tour guide, pointing out its stone gargoyles and columns; or poring over a *Baedeker's Guide to Paris*; or photographing the view of the river with their pocket cameras. The motor rolled on, past the *bouqinistes* on the Left Bank, where people were rummaging through stalls of yellowing second-hand books; past the pavement cafés, where smart ladies and gentlemen sat under striped canopies, drinking iced drinks in tall glasses, or coffee in tiny cups.

Sophie found herself watching a girl in a beribboned hat tucking into a succulent-looking strawberry tart with something like envy. She knew that was exactly the kind of thing that her mother had done when she'd visited Paris as a girl; it was the kind of thing Sophie would have liked to do herself, if she wasn't here on the trail of a murder.

The university district was pleasant: cooler and quieter, with shady green trees clustered around stately stone buildings. Sophie thought that the Faculty of Letters looked rather forbidding, with its tall statues labelled *La Littérature* and *L'Histoire*, but as a student herself, Tilly seemed perfectly at home. 'Why don't I have a look around while you go and talk to Dr Bernard? Term will be over now, but you never know, I might be able to make the acquaintance of some of the Professor's students,' she suggested, as they walked together across a cobbled square with a fountain at its centre.

Sophie felt an unexpected stirring of envy at her confidence in these surroundings. What would it be like to study in a place like this, she wondered, as she went up some stone steps and through a great door, surrounded by immense pillars.

Inside the corridors were empty and echoing – there was only an occasional student passing by, with an armful of books or an over-stuffed satchel. A secretary helped to direct her to an office door marked *Lettres et Langues*, where a slim young man with a neat little moustache answered Sophie's knock. She had expected Dr Bernard to be older – a grey-haired man in tweeds – so she was rather surprised when he answered her in perfect English, with a charming smile: 'Yes, I am Dr Bernard. Can I be of any assistance to you, Miss . . .?'

'Miss Blaxland,' supplied Sophie promptly, and saw the young man's eyes widen in recognition at the name.

'Miss Blaxland! Then you must be the Professor's niece. I am very sorry for your loss. I'm new here this year, so I am afraid I did not have much time to get to know your uncle, but I know he is greatly missed by everyone.'

'I didn't know him very well myself,' explained Sophie. 'In fact I barely knew him – I hadn't seen him since I was a little girl.'

Dr Bernard looked surprised. 'So? But of course – I remember he once said that he did not see eye to eye with his relations. Though I know he was proud of *you*, Miss Blaxland. He spoke of you many times – it is Cambridge you're planning for, is it not? The young ladies of my acquaintance speak very highly of Newnham,' he added, rather giving the impression that the young ladies of his acquaintance were numerous. He flashed her another smile and said: 'If there is anything I can do for you, Miss Blaxland, please do consider me at your service.'

Sophie had to repress the desire to grin. This was exactly what she had hoped for. Evidently Dr Bernard was far more accustomed to independent young ladies than the elderly M. Dupont.

'I believe my uncle had an office here – would it be possible to see it?'

'Of course,' said Dr Bernard at once. 'Please, come this way.'

He showed her along a corridor and into a small office – a wood-panelled room with a desk beside the window overlooking a courtyard. She had hoped he would leave her to examine the room alone, but instead he lingered as she glanced quickly around at the desk, and the sturdy bookshelf arrayed with expensive books with gilt-tooled spines. It was very orderly, although everything was covered with a thin silvering of dust. 'Professor Blaxland only used this office occasionally – he did most of his research at home,' Dr Bernard explained.

Sophie collected together a few things – a bundle of letters, a silver ink stand, a cigar case, a grand-looking leather appointment book, mostly empty but for the occasional note scribbled here and there. She left the books on the shelves where they were, remembering that the Professor's will had specified that his books were to be left to the university library. However there were a couple of books lying on his desk: a heavy Greek lexicon and beside it, rather unexpectedly a dog-eared copy of *The Riddle of the Sands*. She picked it up and leafed quickly through the pages, noticing that a postcard had been used as a bookmark. It was a vivid image of a blue-and-silver crescent moon, surrounded by a circle of colourful figures. Written in scarlet lettering across the top were the words *LA LUNE BLEUE.*

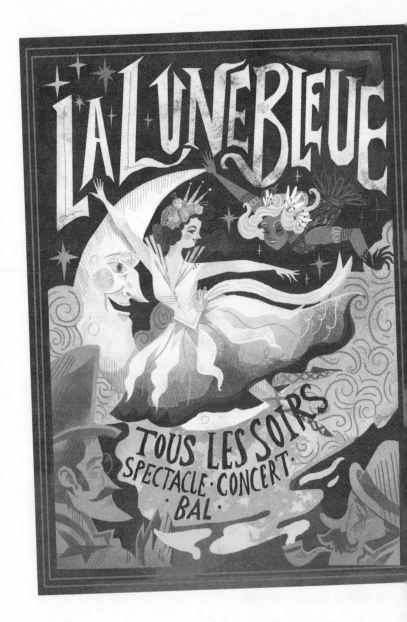

'What's *La Lune Bleue*?' she asked.

Dr Bernard glanced at the postcard and laughed, sounding a little embarrassed. 'Oh, it is a dance hall in Montmartre. The bohemian quarter of Paris. Can-can girls, cabaret. Not really the kind of place you would find a distinguished Professor! I expect this was simply a convenient bookmark.'

Sophie had turned the postcard over. On the back was scribbled a short message, reading *Café Monique, 2pm*.

'Café Monique,' she read aloud. Where had she heard that name before? 'Where's that?' she asked.

Dr Bernard glanced briefly at the message. 'Hmmm . . . certainly not anywhere around the university. Though of course there are so many cafés in Paris. Now, is this everything? I will have it all packed up and sent to you, Miss Blaxland. Where are you staying?'

'Thank you, that's very kind. I'm at the Grand Hotel Continental.'

'Very pleasant. And is this your first visit to Paris?'

'Yes,' said Sophie, still examining the postcard, but remembering a moment too late that Miss Blaxland was very well-travelled. 'I mean, that is to say, it's my first visit here *alone*,' she amended hurriedly. 'And I don't know it half as well as I should like. It's a wonderful city,' she added, thinking for a moment of how her mother had described it in her diaries.

'Indeed it is,' agreed Dr Bernard. 'Though of course

it becomes quieter over the summer months. The *Grand Saison* is coming to an end, and *tout Paris* are beginning to think of leaving for the Riviera. But there will still be plenty for you to see, Miss Blaxland, if you are not too busy with your uncle's affairs. There are galleries and museums and the theatre. And of course you must see the launch of the Grand Aerial Tour, they say it will be quite a spectacle. We have some of the pilots staying with us here at the university, you know – Charlton, a British fellow, and Captain Nakamura, an officer of the Japanese Army. As a matter of fact, there is to be a dinner to celebrate the launch of the tour tomorrow night.' His charming smile became even more charming. 'Perhaps you might care to attend, as my guest?' he suggested. 'Since you are here alone and I, well –' He gestured around him rather mournfully at the empty room, as if to suggest that bookshelves and dusty desks were the only other companions he had.

Sophie looked up, surprised. How would a young lady like Miss Blaxland respond to such an invitation, she wondered? Would she be affronted? Would she think it inappropriate to go to the launch of an air race so soon after the death of her uncle? Would she give a cool, polite refusal? But Sophie couldn't bring herself to say 'no'. Somehow she didn't think Dr Bernard looked like someone with designs on an heiress, but rather a fellow who couldn't resist the opportunity to try and charm any passing young lady. Besides, she reasoned, he might well be able to help her learn more about Professor Blaxland.

She accepted the invitation, and Dr Bernard looked pleased: 'It's to be at the *Palais Antoine*, not far from where you're saying,' he explained as they strolled together back towards the office. 'Sir Chester Norton is hosting it. He is the backer for the whole race, you know. He's the owner of newspapers all over Europe – *Paris-Soir* here in France, *The Daily Picture* in London, and so on.'

After they'd made all the arrangements, and Sophie had said a polite farewell to Dr Bernard, she stepped back into the square, where she'd agreed to meet Tilly by the fountain. There, rather to her surprise, she found her friend talking very excitedly to a young man dressed in a trim blue uniform, her prim maid's persona all but forgotten.

'. . . and a three-cylinder engine?' Tilly was saying.

'Indeed yes, and a propeller in the new style, with two blades.'

'Of course, so much more efficient than the old four-paddled kind.' Seeing Sophie approach, Tilly turned to her with bright eyes: 'Do come and meet Captain Nakamura, He's one of the pilots flying in the air race, and he's come all the way from Japan to compete. He's got a brand-new two-seater Blériot XI and he's been telling me all about it – isn't it thrilling? Captain Nakamura, may I introduce S— Miss Celia Blaxland,' she corrected hurriedly as Sophie gave her a warning glance.

'I am very pleased to make your acquaintance,' said

the captain in careful English, bowing to her rather stiffly. 'Your friend knows a great deal about aeroplanes,' he added, sounding somewhat surprised.

Sophie grinned and agreed that she did, before explaining that she'd just met Dr Bernard who had been kind enough to invite her to accompany him to the air-race dinner the following evening. 'It will be a great pleasure to see you there,' said the captain, with an old-fashioned formal courtesy that seemed quite at odds with a daredevil young pilot. 'And of course, you must both come and see the launch of the air race,' he added, with a little bow in Tilly's direction.

'Oh yes, I should *love* to,' said Tilly enthusiastically. 'All those marvellous planes!'

'If you come I will show you over the Blériot,' Captain Nakamura promised her.

Tilly looked more excited than ever, and began badgering him at once with more questions about his plane. Soon they were busily discussing things like *horsepower* and *rotary engines* and *three-axis control*, which were so mysterious to Sophie that they might as well have been talking in Japanese for all she could understand them. But she did not really mind – whilst Tilly talked to Captain Nakamura, she was thinking hard.

The air-race dinner would be the perfect opportunity to find out more about Professor Blaxland from Dr Bernard, she decided. But there was more she could investigate too. Dr Bernard had made it sound like the postcard she had found in the Professor's book was merely there by coincidence, but Sophie felt certain it was a useful clue. She would track down the *Café Monique*, and visit *La Lune Bleue* too, if she possibly could. But first, she wanted to get inside the Professor's apartment, and she made up her mind that they should try that night.

CHAPTER FOURTEEN

The Train to Zurich

Hundreds of miles south-east of Paris, a train was making its slow way through the Swiss countryside, and inside it was Princess Anna of Arnovia. She'd never felt less like a member of the Royal House of Wilderstein than she did just then, leaning back against the hard wooden seat, hot and dirty and tired.

She and Alex had never gone anywhere without carriages and guards and maids to accompany them. They'd certainly never travelled in a train. And yet here they were, in a perfectly ordinary second-class compartment, on their way to Zurich, with no one to look after them but Miss Carter and a cowherd.

Of course, the man with them wasn't really a cowherd at all. He had turned out to be another British agent in disguise, and had introduced himself to the children as Captain Harry Forsyth. At that very moment Captain Forsyth was standing with one foot up on the seat, relating

134

a thrilling tale about the time he had single-handedly outwitted a nest of German spies in the Scottish highlands. He was a good storyteller, and Alex was listening, enthralled, but Anna somehow couldn't pay attention. Her ears were too full of the jangle of unfamiliar sounds: the rattle and hiss of the train carriage, the long blast of the whistle, the clamour of feet and luggage barrows when they pulled into stations, the distant clang of a bell.

Everything looked so different too. Colours seemed brighter: the intense green fields outside the windows; the rich blue lake; even the red and white of the checked cotton frock she wore. She smoothed the skirts and stretched out her legs, still aching from the long walk over the mountain pass. Neither of them had ever walked so far before: Alex had wheezed and coughed, and she'd got such dreadful blisters that she had begun to limp, but at last Miss Carter had said: 'There, now we're over the border. There's a train station in another two miles.'

During the last part of the walk, there had been a good deal of discussion between the captain and Miss Carter about what they should do next, but at last Miss Carter had seemed to win the debate, and had bought them all tickets for the train to Zurich. Alex had slept for the first few hours of the journey, exhausted by everything that had happened, but even curled up under the old velvet curtain that still smelled of Wilderstein Castle, Anna had been unable to close her eyes. Her heart had pounded when the

Swiss train guard had come into their compartment, but he'd just grunted when Captain Forsyth had shown him their tickets, and gone on his way.

She felt very grateful for the clothes that Captain Forsyth had brought for them in his knapsack. They were quite different from those they usually wore – shorts and a shirt for Alex, and a simple cotton frock and pinafore for herself. She was even wearing her hair in two plaits – just think of that! She'd never been allowed to plait her hair before. 'If anyone asks, you're at school in Paris. Miss Carter here is your schoolmistress, and I'm the stern schoolmaster,' Captain Forsyth had said to them with a wink. Alex had got into the spirit of things at once, coming up with new names for them all. Imagining what the school was like, and making up stories about it had kept them busy and helped to take Alex's mind off wheezing as they'd traipsed on up the mountain. But now, they really *could* have been ordinary schoolchildren, Anna thought, staring at Alex who was munching a thick ham sandwich as he listened to Captain Forsyth's story. She couldn't even begin to imagine what the Countess would have said to a Crown Prince eating *sandwiches* in the second-class carriage of a train.

The thought of the Countess made her feel sick, but then Miss Carter leaned over and interrupted her thoughts. 'Not long until we get to Zurich,' she said.

In her mind, Anna seemed to see the coloured pages of

the big schoolroom atlas. The European map Miss Carter had made them copy just a few days before, their train moving across the spaces she'd carefully outlined with her pencil, towards the red dot that marked Zurich. 'What will happen when we get there?' she asked nervously.

'We'll change trains. Don't worry, Anna. Everything is going to be quite all right.'

But Anna could only shake her head. Grandfather had told them *don't worry*, and look what had happened. Nothing could ever be *all right* again. Their whole world had tipped upside down, like a picture in a kaleidoscope.

She couldn't stop thinking about what she'd heard the Countess say. Her cold voice echoing along the passageway: are a couple of children really more important than the fate of your country? *A couple of children.* As if they were anyone, not Alex and Anna. Her own relations, who she'd helped to bring safely away from Elffburg all those years ago, when they'd been in danger, who had sat opposite her at the breakfast table each morning, who she'd taught about traditions and history as if it all really mattered, as if she really wanted them to learn. *Fetch the prince* she heard the Countess say again. *Restrain him if you must.*

'What were they going to do with us?' she dared to ask.

'They'd have smuggled us out of the country,' Alex said quietly. He had stopped wheezing now, but he still looked very tired, with dark shadows smudged under his

137

eyes. 'Probably to some hidden place, where we wouldn't be found.'

'But *why*?' asked Anna. 'What were they planning to do with us then?'

'They would have used us as leverage. To threaten Grandfather, and persuade him to do whatever they asked. Maybe even to give up the throne.'

'But Grandfather would never have done that!' exclaimed Anna in disbelief.

'He might have done if he thought something was going to happen to us,' said Alex.

There was a nasty silence for a moment, and then Anna broke it. 'I just can't believe that the *Countess* would do this! She talks so much about the House of Wilderstein and . . . and . . . protecting royal traditions. If she really believes that royalty is so important, how could she *possibly* help to plot against the King?'

Miss Carter looked thoughtful. 'People will do very strange things for money . . . or power. We heard her ourselves. She said that if they handed you over, the Count would become King. That's probably what they had been promised. If the Kaiser gained control of Arnovia, he'd put the Count in charge.'

Anna shook her head limply. She felt perilously close to tears, but Alex's face was calm and thoughtful. 'Maybe she really believed it would be better for Arnovia. After all, Grandfather is a very progressive King. He's introduced reforms; done away with traditions. He's trying to make things fairer for people. But not everyone in Arnovia wants that. Some people would rather keep to the old ways of doing things.'

Anna stared at him. How did her little brother know so much more about all this than she did? How could he talk about it so intelligently? The Countess had spent so much time explaining royal traditions and telling her about what princesses should and shouldn't do, but she knew next to nothing about what Grandfather actually did, and what being royal really *meant*. It was just another thing that was considered *unsuitable for princesses*, she thought bitterly. 'Is that what he talked to you about when he came to the castle?' she asked, unable to keep a resentful note from creeping into her voice.

'Partly that. But mostly he wanted to tell me what to do if . . . well, if anything were to happen to him.'

'*Happen to him?*' The train gave a sudden lurch, and Anna's stomach lurched with it. 'What do you mean?'

'Well, it's rather a rocky sort of position to be in, isn't it?' said the captain airily, swallowing his last bite of sandwich and joining in the conversation. 'Country under threat from invaders. Risk of assassination.'

Assassination. The cold fingers trailing over her skin. Her head spun: they couldn't, surely they *couldn't* – not Grandfather . . .

Miss Carter frowned at the captain. 'All Captain Forsyth

means is that the situation is obviously a difficult one,' she said hurriedly. 'There's bound to be a certain amount of danger to your grandfather. But remember he has lots of loyal allies – the British government, for one. There are lots of people working hard to keep him safe.'

'If the kidnap plot had succeeded, it would have been much worse,' said Alex. 'If they had us – *me* – they could have done whatever they liked. But now we've escaped – and we're being protected – well, there's no sense in them trying to assassinate Grandfather. I'm next in line, so I'd have a claim to the throne ahead of the Count.'

It was like a play, Anna thought. The villainous King Richard III, imprisoning the young princes in the Tower of London; or Prospero, the Duke of Milan, cast away on a distant island so his brother could steal his title and wealth.

But the captain had picked up an apple and was polishing it on his sleeve. 'Yes, if their plot had succeeded, who knows what might've happened. Monarch assassinated, instability, perhaps even civil war. Perfect excuse for the German Empire to swoop in and take control, all under the pretence of keeping the peace, of course. And then if Britain were to step in as Arnovia's protector, it might just have been the spark needed to blow up war in Europe.' He shrugged. 'Of course, Arnovia isn't out of the woods yet, but you see why it's a jolly good thing for everyone that you're safely out of the country.'

His voice was casual and light, but Anna felt as

though she was sinking into the ground. 'But what about Grandfather? What will happen now?' she asked. Her voice sounded high and peculiar. How could Alex talk about it so calmly? How could the captain just sit there eating his apple, as though this was all perfectly ordinary?

It was only Miss Carter who seemed to understand how she was feeling. She put out a steady hand to touch Anna's shoulder. 'I know it's awful, but try not to think about it too much,' she said gently. 'We're doing all we can to help your grandfather, by making sure you are both safe.'

Looking up at her, Anna thought how different she was away from Wilderstein Castle, in the bright light of the juddering, bumping train carriage. No longer the schoolroom governess, nor the sinister, stealthy figure creeping about the castle at night. Now her hair seemed to have sprung loose from its tight pins, her spectacles had long since been forgotten, and as she accepted an apple from Captain Forsyth and crunched a big bite, Anna thought she no longer really looked like a grown-up. Instead she seemed not much older than they were – more like a big sister than a governess.

'I *knew* you weren't really a governess,' she said suddenly.

Miss Carter looked rather abashed. 'I don't think I did a very good job of pretending. It was a rotten idea, really. I never did care much for lessons.'

'*I* think you did a good job,' said Alex, loyally. He turned to Anna triumphantly. 'And I was right too, you know.

141

I *told* you she could be trusted and that she was on our side, didn't I?' he gloated.

Anna felt her cheeks reddening, but Miss Carter said, 'You can hardly blame Anna for not being sure about me. After all, she was quite right that I wasn't what I was pretending to be.'

'You're an actress, aren't you?' Anna said.

Miss Carter grinned. 'You could say that. I've been on the stage before. But now . . . well, I'm working for the British government. Just like Captain Forsyth here.'

'But infinitely lovelier,' said Captain Forsyth, with a gallant bow.

Miss Carter looked rather irritated by this remark, but went on: 'I'm sure you know that Britain is an old ally of Arnovia. Our networks suggested that someone high up in Arnovian royal circles might be conspiring with your country's enemies to plot against the King. A number of British agents have been working in Arnovia to try and find out who that is, and to help protect your grandfather. The captain and I were stationed at Wilderstein Castle specifically to help protect you. What we didn't realise at first was that the Countess was one of the ring-leaders of the plot.'

'What will happen to them now – the Countess and the Count?' asked Alex.

'Oh, the game's up for them,' said Forsyth breezily. 'You can't go round plotting to kidnap a Crown Prince. High treason, you know! No doubt they'll try to run, but our chaps will soon find them and see them arrested, don't you worry.'

Miss Carter patted the little attaché case at her side. 'I've got evidence that proves their involvement,' she explained. 'That's awfully important. We can pass it back to your government and they can use it to convict them for their crimes.'

'The photographs I saw you taking, with the little camera!' exclaimed Anna. 'Is that the evidence you mean?'

'I say, you do have sharp eyes. Yes, when I was first sent to the castle, my assignment was to watch over the two of you. But I was also supposed to gather any information I could. That's why they gave me the camera, so I could take pictures of anything that might help us find out what was going on. We call it *surveillance*. But once we discovered that the Countess was involved in the plot . . . well! Things began happening awfully quickly. We realised you were in danger, and we had to act fast.'

'Jolly fortunate you had an experienced field-agent like myself on hand,' cut in Captain Forsyth cheerfully. 'Could have all gone terribly wrong.'

But Anna was thinking about something else. 'If you aren't really a governess, does that mean your name isn't really Miss Carter?' she asked suddenly. 'What's your real name? I mean, what should we call you now?'

'My name's Lilian Rose. My friends call me Lil – you

143

can too, if you like. And we – Captain Forsyth and I – we're going to call you Anna and Alex. I know that's not really the *done thing*, but I'm afraid that saying *Your Highness* might draw unwanted attention our way. We'll have to forget about all the royal traditions – for now, at any rate.'

Anna shivered. The words *royal traditions* had taken her straight back to the Countess's sitting room. She felt again the hard back-board, and the prickle of the horse-hair sofa where she had sat embroidering coats-of-arms, longing to run or jump or shout or do anything but sit still. She heard the Countess's crisp voice: *This is simply not the kind of behaviour that is acceptable for a princess . . . You must never forget that.* And then, in the dark of the castle at night: *Are a couple of children really more important than the fate of your country?*

As though he was thinking the same thing, Alex blew out a long breath and answered for both of them: 'That's quite all right. I think we've had enough of royal traditions for a while.'

CHAPTER FIFTEEN

Rue Baudelaire, Paris

Sophie buttoned up the shirt, and confronted her reflection in the looking-glass in her hotel bedroom. She thought she looked rather silly. She was still not really used to dressing as a young man, although in her line of work, it was sometimes necessary. Young ladies did not promenade about the city streets by themselves late at night and she knew that, on this occasion, she certainly would not be able to secretly make her way inside the Professor's apartment dressed in Miss Blaxland's constraining hobble-skirts. That was why she and Billy had made sure to include in one of her trunks, beneath the travelling suits and tea dresses and satin evening gowns, a set of clothes that a boy might wear – shirt, trousers, braces and a cap to cover her hair.

Beside her, with the aid of a dozen hair-pins, Tilly had managed to fit a similar cap over her own abundant curls. 'There,' she said finally, looking for happier in her boy's clothes than she did in her frilly cap and apron.

'Are you sure you want to come with me?' Sophie asked her one last time. After all, masquerading as a maid was one thing, but breaking and entering was quite another.

Tilly looked at her as if she were quite mad. 'Of course I'm coming!' she said indignantly. 'You can't go breaking into the Professor's apartment by yourself. We'll just have to be careful that's all.'

'I always am,' said Sophie, as she shrugged into her jacket, turned out the lights, and then opened the door to the balcony.

It was true, too, she thought, as she cautiously looked around, then nodded to Tilly to follow her. She *was* careful. Perhaps she hadn't always been – there was no doubt that some of the things she had done when the Baron and the *Fraternitas Draconum* had been involved had been rather rash. But things were different now. This was her job: she was methodical and sensible. Tonight, for example, she had worked out the right time to leave the hotel, when they would be under cover of twilight. She had checked the map, pinpointing the exact location of the Professor's apartment, and working out the best route to take. The inside pocket of her jacket had been stocked with things she might need from Billy's supplies: a lock-pick, a pair of gloves, a small magnifying glass. Now, she and Tilly crept through the darkened garden, careful to keep to the shadows; slipped through a gate; and then they were out in the street and away.

It felt very pleasant to be free from the constraints of Miss Blaxland's cumbersome gowns and hobble-skirts, and to step out boldly into the city. Sophie enjoyed taking in deep breaths of air and lengthening her stride. As they walked together in the direction of Blaxland's apartment, she found herself thinking, not for the first time, of how unfair it was that Miss Blaxland and her maid must only drive primly down these cobbled streets – whilst, as boys, they were free to stroll and look about them, hands in pockets, sniffing the air.

She felt as if she were really seeing the city for the first time, and as they crossed the river, they paused to lean on the parapet, staring down at the water, Tilly pointing out the the pleasure-boats lit up with little blue-and-red lamps. They went on past restaurants and theatres and a brightly lit picture palace, past a concert hall with strains of stirring music coming from within, and she thought again of her mother's diary as they peeped into dark cafés, full of the sound of music and voices. Was this the Paris that her mother had seen, as she'd walked around the city years ago?

Her mother's diary – that was it! 'I've got it!' she exclaimed aloud to Tilly. 'Mother's diary is where I've seen *Café Monique* mentioned before. How could I have forgotten? I'm sure it's one of the cafés she wrote about. I'll look for it when we get back to the hotel.'

But Tilly hushed her, pointing to a street sign. 'Look – isn't this it? I think we're here – this is Rue Baudelaire.'

For a little while, they stood in a dark corner of the quiet street, contemplating the apartment building where the Professor had lived. Set back from the road behind an iron gate, it was a large, elegant edifice, built of yellow stone, with tall windows and elaborately twirled balconies. 'How will we get in?' Tilly murmured in a low voice, but Sophie just shook her head. She was watching, and thinking. It would be easy enough to get over the gate, but once there, how would they get through the big door and into the building? In London, she'd have known where to look for the servants' entrance or the coal-hole, but Paris was different.

Just then, a motor-taxi pulled up outside the gate, and a lady and gentleman clambered out. To her delight, Sophie realised they were going inside. She nudged Tilly, and together, as the motor rumbled away, they darted swiftly across the road, managing to slip through the gate and into the shadows of the cobbled courtyard just before the gate clanged shut behind them.

From there, they watched unseen as the gentleman unlocked the big door. Once he and his companion had gone inside, she sprang forward and caught hold of the door handle, to prevent the door swinging shut behind them. After waiting for a few careful moments she pushed the heavy door quietly open. 'Come on,' she whispered to

Tilly, and the two of them slipped stealthily inside.

She'd judged it well. The hallway was empty. Ahead of them, a tightly twisting stairway curved upwards and she hurried up it, Tilly following close behind. The Professor's door was locked of course, but Sophie had long ago learned how to pick a lock – she could do it with a couple of hair-pins if necessary – and with the help of the tools in her jacket pocket, it was quick and easy work to unlock the door. A moment or two later, they had stepped into the Professor's apartment.

Inside, it was empty and shadowy. Sophie saw a large sitting room with big windows, and leading off it, a bedroom, a small bathroom and a room that looked like it must have been the Professor's study. Everything was luxurious – thick fabrics, soft cushions, silver candlesticks, Indian rugs on the polished floor. But here and there amongst the rich comfort were some clues to what had happened: a lamp with a broken shade and a shattered vase.

'Look at this,' said Tilly, pointing to an ominous dark-coloured stain in the centre of the rug. 'I think it's blood,' she whispered.

Sophie bent down to examine it more closely. Tilly was right: this was clearly where Professor Blaxland had been shot by the burglars. No wonder M. Dupont had not wanted the delicate Miss Blaxland to visit the apartment, she thought.

'I want to know what the "burglars" who broke in here were supposed to have taken,' she said to Tilly, keeping her voice low. 'Why don't you take a look around here – and in the bedroom – and see if you can see any signs of the burglary. I'm going to look in the study: I want to see if I can find that safe Dupont talked about.'

Tilly nodded at once and tiptoed in the direction of the bedroom, the polished wooden floor creaking gently beneath her feet.

Sophie went into the study, and saw at once that this room was different. It was in a state of violent disorder: papers and notebooks were scattered across the desk as though a whirlwind had rushed through it; books were ranged in tottering piles across the floor; and broken glass crunched beneath her feet. In a corner by the desk was the small metal safe – the door gaping open, with nothing inside. Sophie bent down to look at it more closely. What could the burglars have taken from the Professor's safe? Had they caused all this chaos, or was this the work of the police, searching the scene?

She decided to risk turning on a lamp in a dark green silk shade, which stood on the Professor's desk. In the patch of light, she began to look through the Professor's papers, her gloved hands moving quickly and deftly. She flicked through notebooks containing the Professor's flowing handwriting – not grand leather notebooks this time, but stacks and stacks of quite ordinary battered composition

I am the true green and Golden Lion without Cares. In me all the Secrets of the Philosophers are hidden.

books with marbled covers, of the type that any schoolchild might use. There were some student essays, some scholarly journals, and a fat sheaf of blank paper. There were dozens of books too – quite different from the smart new editions she had seen at the university. These were clearly very old, the pages age-spotted and filled with cramped dark brown print that made her eyes hurt to look at it. Their fragile bindings crumbled even beneath her gentle gloved fingers. Some of the titles appeared to be in Latin or another ancient language – she frowned over the curious diagrams, illustrations of angels and twisted serpents and five-pointed stars. Only one was in English: a thick volume with the word ALCHEMY written across the cover in richly gilded letters. She opened it, and the pages fell open to a strange image of a lion, coloured in green and holding a yellow sun in its mouth, with what appeared to be crimson blood trickling from its jaws. A scrap of paper had been tucked inside the page, scribbled with a few words.

The green lion. Sophie stopped still. The words chimed like a bell, and she had a sudden, instinctive feeling that they were important. Acting on impulse, she grabbed one of the blank sheets of paper from the Professor's desk. She did not want to take the little note, just in case the police noticed it was missing, but she could at least scribble down the words. She picked up the Professor's fountain pen from where it was lying amidst the scattered paper, but the pen wouldn't work.

She frowned and shook it cautiously, then tried again. The pen moved quite smoothly over the paper, as though the ink was flowing, but no words appeared on the page. She gently lifted the paper and examined it under the light: tilting it, she could see now that it was wet, but the ink appeared to be completely colourless. There was a curious smell in the air – light, sharp and fragrant.

She put down the pen, and turned to the sheaf of what she had thought was blank paper, lifting a sheet into the light and sniffing it experimentally. Sure enough, there was the same peculiar scent.

Tilly appeared in the study doorway. 'I can't find anything,' she reported. 'No drawers or cupboard opened and looted, no paintings torn out of frames – nothing that seems at all like a burglary. What about you? Did you find the safe?'

Sophie was still frowning at the Professor's pen. 'Come and look at this –' she began.

But before she could even finish the sentence, there was a sound outside in the corridor. Rapid footsteps were approaching the Professor's door. As quick as blinking, Sophie turned out the lamp, stuffing the sheaf of blank papers into the pocket of her jacket. She knew they must not be caught here, and her heart began to beat faster, but at the same time she was curious. Who could be coming to the Professor's apartment? Surely it could not be the police at this time of the night?

She darted out of the study; Tilly was already gesturing frantically towards a hiding place she had found, behind a big bookcase in the sitting room. There came the sound of the door handle turning and then a stifled exclamation of surprise. They had not locked the door after themselves, and now whoever was coming in had not expected to find it open.

Sophie could feel Tilly's fingers gripping her arm, but they both stood still behind the bookcase, as the door creaked quietly open. She heard one step of footsteps pad cautiously inside, and then another. She guessed from the way they walked that they were two men, and that they too did not want to be heard. The door closed softly behind them: one set of footsteps went forward into the room, murmuring something to the other in a low voice. She had been right: it *was* a man and, what was more, he was talking German. She couldn't understand the words but she recognised the sound at once. Then there was another noise she recognised too, and this one made her turn cold all at once. It was the distinct metallic *click* of a revolver.

In the dark corner of the room, Sophie thought quickly. She did not want them to be caught by the French police, but being caught by stealthy German intruders with revolvers would be far worse. They would have to get out of here, and quickly. She held up a hand to Tilly, meaning *wait*, and then risked peering around the edge of the bookcase, and saw the silhouetted figures of two men examining the stain on the rug exactly as they had done themselves, though they had an electric torch that they were shining down on it.

Following almost precisely in her own footsteps, she saw the first man go towards the study and turn on the lamp in the green shade. But where was the second man? Had he followed his companion in the study, or was he looking in the Professor's bedroom? Sophie could not be sure, but she knew they could not afford to hesitate. They'd have to grasp the opportunity to make their escape.

'Now!' she hissed to Tilly, and together they darted out from behind the bookcase, and made a swift dash for the door. Fast and long-legged, Tilly was there first and through the door in a minute: Sophie could hear her feet on the stairs. But before she could catch up, the second man seemed to materialise out of nowhere, flashing the electric torch in her eyes. He yelled out to his companion even as he struck out at her; dancing away, Sophie dodged the blow and the torch crashed to the floor, illuminating the man's face for a moment with a bright beam of light, before it rolled under a table and went out.

In the dark she made another desperate leap for the door, but the man grabbed for her again. This time his fingers closed on her shoulder, wrenching her back. Yelping in pain, she reached desperately for something – anything – she could use as a weapon. Her grasping fingers closed over something cold and heavy on a side table, and without thinking twice, she grabbed it, and smashed it as hard as she could over the man's head.

There was the splintering of glass and the slosh of liquid, and all at once everything seemed to be dark and wet. For one horrible moment, Sophie thought it was blood, but then a rich smell of fruit and spice filled the air, and she realised she had hit the man with a bottle of wine. He gasped and spluttered and scrabbled for her again blindly, but she spun away towards the door, and as she did so the cap came loose, slipping sideways, revealing the thick plait of fair hair she had tucked so carefully underneath it. As she did so, the first man had stormed out of the study towards them, the revolver clenched in his hand.

Time seemed to slow down. Sophie knew she should already be through the door and away down the stairs, but for a split second, she stopped short and stared.

She *knew* the man standing in front of her. The last time she'd seen him, he'd been in London, standing on the pavement outside Victoria station, wearing a grey jacket and a grey hat, staring after her cab. Ziegler's spy – the grey man – was in Paris, and he was here, in Professor Blaxland's apartment.

'Sophie!' Tilly shrieked from the stairwell.

One quick, flashing glimpse of the grey man, and then she was away again, down the stairs with Tilly beside her. She heard doors opening: the Professor's former neighbours must have heard the crash, the yell, the running feet; there was no time to lose. They ran together, helter-skelter through the door, out into the courtyard, through the gate and out into the street again. Sophie clutched at her cap as she ran after Tilly towards the river, vanishing into the shadows like phantoms in the summer night.

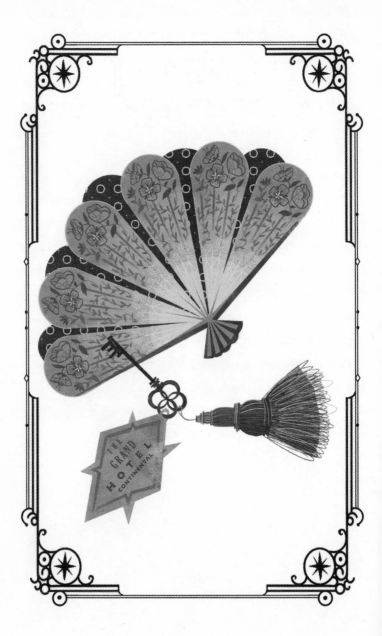

PART IV

'Papa and I have been exploring Paris – and what a delightful place it seems to be! We have seen everything – from the wonderful galleries of the Louvre to the banks of the Seine. We have dined in marvellous restaurants, walked in beautiful parks, visited theatres, and even explored the cobbled streets of Montmartre, where we sat outside the Café Monique watching all the people pass by for hours. My French is getting better every day, and I am beginning to feel that I am quite a Parisian lady. Really, I think I shall never want to leave!'

– From the diary of Alice Grayson

CHAPTER SIXTEEN

Montmartre, Paris

'There it is,' murmured Sophie, bent over the pages of her mother's diary. 'The *Café Monique*. I knew I'd seen it in here somewhere!'

Sitting in the hotel suite over a breakfast of baguette and coffee, dressed in Miss Blaxland's pale blue quilted satin dressing gown, she felt quite different from the girl who had run through the streets of Paris the night before. This morning, the only sign of her misadventure was her aching shoulder – still throbbing from where the grey man's accomplice had wrenched it. Now she stretched out her arm, thinking that a hot bath would help her painful muscles, but she knew there wasn't time for that. Seeing Ziegler's spy at the Professor's apartment had filled her with a new urgency. 'I'll go to Montmartre this morning,' she declared.

But she might as well have spoken to the empty air. Tilly was paying her no attention whatsoever. Instead, she was carefully scrutinising the papers that Sophie had taken from the Professor's apartment. Now she pushed the jam and butter aside, and spread the papers out on the table. 'Well, it's perfectly obvious what this is,' she announced. 'It's invisible ink.'

'*Invisible ink?*' repeated Sophie in astonishment.

'You said that the Professor's pen was full of a transparent liquid. I think it must have been an invisible ink he was using to keep his notes secret.' Tilly lifted a sheet of paper and sniffed thoughtfully. 'It's sweet-ish and almost floral, like a perfume. I wonder what he could have used?'

'I didn't know such a thing as invisible ink existed,' said Sophie in surprise.

'It was the Ancient Greeks who first invented it,' Tilly recalled. 'They used a liquid made from the leaves of a particular plant. It looked colourless, but when you sprinkled ashes over the paper, the message would appear. There was another kind of ink they used too, made of crushed nuts. In that case, they used ferrous sulphate to reveal the message.'

'Do you think the Professor might have used one of those inks?' asked Sophie, remembering the book on Ancient Greek she'd seen in his office. 'He probably knew all about them, given that his specialism was ancient languages.'

'It's certainly possible,' said Tilly, without taking her eyes from the paper, which she was studying so closely it was barely an inch from the end of her nose. 'But there are all kind of things it could be. I'll need to test it to know for sure. It's a shame you didn't get the pen. It'd be much easier if there was a proper sample of the ink I could work with.'

'I barely got out with the papers,' said Sophie ruefully, rubbing her painful shoulder again.

Tilly got to her feet. 'Well, I'm going to get to work,' she said. 'If I can work out what the ink was that the Professor used, we might be able to reveal the message, and see what the papers say.' She began rummaging in the trunk for books, looking as though she was rather enjoying herself. 'Why don't you . . . er . . . go out and investigate something?'

Sophie grinned and took the hint. Half an hour later, wearing one of Miss Blaxland's morning dresses, she was driving through the city once more, heading towards the eighteenth *arrondissement*. Leaving the grand tree-lined boulevards behind, the motor chugged heavily up narrow cobbled streets: past bakeries and bookshops, past a cheese shop and a *parfumerie*, its window glittering with tempting little glass bottles.

As they went, Sophie found her thoughts drifting back towards the grey man. One thing was certain, she thought: he and his companion had been as surprised to find them at the Professor's apartment as she herself had been to see him. Could he have recognised her as the girl with the parasol at Victoria station? She could not be absolutely sure, but she thought not. If only her cap hadn't slipped loose like that, and if only Tilly hadn't called out her name! She hoped that in the chaos they would not have heard her, and even if they had, they would surely not associate a girl dressed in boy's clothes named 'Sophie' with Miss Celia Blaxland, resident at the Grand Continental Hotel.

They drove along a steep little street snaking up the hill, past a confectioner's with a gilded sign advertising CHOCOLATS, BON-BONS, CARAMELS, past a woman pushing a bicycle, past a *pomme-frites* seller, and onwards, towards the great dome of the Sacré Coeur basilica on the horizon, very white against a bright blue sky. The Chief had suspected that their enemies might be responsible for the Professor's death, she remembered. After seeing Ziegler's spy at the Professor's apartment, she felt sure that he had been right. The motor stopped to let a tumult of schoolchildren cross the road, calling out to each other like a flock of noisy birds. *If you do find evidence that Blaxland was murdered, you will likely be in danger . . . you must leave Paris,* she remembered the Chief saying. But she had no definite evidence at all, did she? All she had was the rising suspicion that Ziegler's men must be behind the Professor's death, for why else would they have been creeping about secretly in his apartment?

The question was *why* Ziegler would want the Professor dead, she thought. Did he know the Professor was working for the Secret Service Bureau? That alone could not be enough reason to murder him, could it? And if the grey man and his companion had been responsible for the Professor's death, why would they return to the scene of the crime? To try to cover their tracks, or perhaps to find something important that had been left behind? Perhaps they had been after the secret papers that Sophie had taken and given to Tilly to decipher? The thought of it made her shiver in spite of the pleasant sunshine.

The chauffeur had pulled to a halt beside the funicular railway that went up to Montmartre. She asked him to wait, and then joined the crowd of waiting people; but as the little train made its slow way up the hill, she found herself casting suspicious and uncertain glances over her shoulder at the people standing around her.

Dr Bernard had said Montmartre was 'bohemian' and Sophie had heard her art student friends say it was the artists' quarter of Paris – home to painters, writers, musicians and poets. Her mother had described it in her diary as something like a country village on the edge of the city, but although Sophie could see traces of the place she had described – the windmills and vineyards – she soon realised it must have changed a great deal since her mother's visit. Now it seemed to be a haunt for tourists, crowded with little restaurants, and *ateliers* where paintings of Paris scenes were available for sale. It was true that there were artists at work here and there on the narrow streets, but they looked more like enthusiastic amateurs with paintboxes than the dashing, unconventional painters

Sophie had imagined. She passed two English ladies in straw hats, seated on camp-stools with sketchbooks in their laps, who would not have been in the least bit out of place in the Sinclair's Ladies' Lounge. A little further on, a tour group were exclaiming over the picturesque sight of a pink-and-white house thick with vines, whilst street-sellers offered photographs of famous Paris landmarks.

She looked at each café carefully as she walked, but saw no sign of the *Café Monique* anywhere. The day was growing warmer now, and with it Montmartre seemed to be coming slowly into life. She could hear a door slamming, the rattle of a bucket, the twittering of birds in a treetop, and the distant trill of someone singing. There was a delicious smell of onion soup and hot coffee. She went on, past a merchant pushing a barrow, past a curious little bric-a-brac shop and then a tiny art gallery, exhibiting bold paintings in shades of cobalt and violet, turquoise and vermillion, yellow and crimson pink. It was all so different from London, she thought. Even the air felt different: clear and golden and very warm on her back as she walked on, leaving the crowds behind her.

In a quiet square lined with chestnut trees, an old woman rested on a green bench, whilst sparrows pecked in the dirt at her feet. A man in a felt hat came up the hill towards her, leading a donkey: Sophie paused to ask him, *'Où est la Café Monique, s'il vous plaît?'* and was rewarded by a vague gesture of a hand along another winding cobbled street.

166

Following it, she came at last to an old-fashioned house with peeling shutters, a wooden fence and a sun-bleached green awning. A few rustic tables had been arranged outside, under the shade of a tree. She looked around her, feeling rather surprised. She'd expected somewhere lively, where there would be lots of people to watch – or even to ask about the Professor – but this place seemed deserted, although the door stood open, and she could make out the words *Café Monique* painted in crude lettering on a whitewashed wall. Was this really the place that her mother had written about sitting outside, 'watching all the people', and the place that the urbane Professor had spent so much of his time?

Just then, a man came out of the door of the café, whistling a little tune. His shirt-sleeves were rolled up, and a checked cloth was thrown over his shoulder, ready to polish glasses and wipe plates. '*Bonjour, mademoiselle,*' he said cheerfully to Sophie. '*Asseyez-vous, s'il vous plaît. Qu'est-ce que vous voulez? Un café? Une tisane?*'

Unsure of quite what to do, Sophie took a seat in the dappled shade and ordered a lemonade. It felt very strange to be sitting there, all by herself in such a quiet corner of Paris, with no one else there but a black cat walking along a sun-warmed wall, swishing its long tail.

The waiter must have noticed her staring around her curiously. 'It is quiet now, but it will be busy later,' he said with a knowing smile, as he presented her lemonade with a flourish. 'You come back, you will see. All the artists come here. And the writers. We are famous for it!' He puffed out his chest with pride. 'M. Matisse. M. Picasso. Mme Laurencin. M. Modigliani. All of them come to *Café Monique!*'

Seeing an opportunity, Sophie spoke up: 'Did you know an Englishman who used to come here?' she asked him, as she dropped a few *centimes* into the saucer to pay the bill. 'A Professor at the Sorbonne – Professor Blaxland?'

The waiter's cheerful face suddenly fell. 'Ah, the Professor, but of course! It was terrible, truly terrible, what happened to him. The times that we live in! He was a friend of yours, *mademoiselle?*'

'A relative,' she explained.

The waiter shook his head. 'It is most sad. Why the Professor was here just last week with his friends!'

Sophie's heart leaped. 'I'd very much like to talk to his friends – to someone who knew him well. Is there anyone I might speak to?'

The waiter frowned. 'It is hard to know,' he said slowly. 'The Professor had many friends. But I suppose you might talk to Madame Delacroix? They were very often together.'

'Madame Delacroix,' repeated Sophie eagerly. 'Can you tell me where she lives?'

But the waiter just shrugged. 'I don't know where she is now. Sometimes a studio. She moves around a good deal.' Seeing Sophie's disappointed face, he added: 'But she is often here, or at *La Lune Bleue* of course. Ah, how the poor Professor loved to go to *La Lune Bleue!* Not for the cabaret you understand, nor the food – he said the food here was much better – but for *les jeux d'argent.*' He winked, and then seeing that Sophie did not understand, he rubbed his thumb and finger together to signify money and tapped his nose.

Jeux d'argent? Sophie knew that 'jeux' was the French word for games, and 'argent' meant money. Was he talking about *gambling*, she wondered? But surely gambling was illegal in France. What had a scholarly man like the Professor been doing, mixed up in illegal gambling at a night club?

'If you are looking for Madame Delacroix, you will surely find her at *La Lune Bleue* tonight,' said the waiter.

Sophie thanked him, and got up to go. As she made her way back along the cobbled streets, she was thinking furiously. She walked past a poster for *La Lune Bleue* pasted on the wall – the same scene of ballet girls and pierrots she'd seen on the postcard, with the slogan *TOUS LES SOIRS – SPECTACLE, CONCERT, BAL.* From everything that Dr Bernard and the waiter had told her, it didn't seem at all like the kind of place that a young lady like Miss Blaxland would generally visit; but if she wanted to meet this Madame Delacroix, and find out more about the Professor, she would have to find some way to go there herself.

CHAPTER SEVENTEEN

Le Palais Antoine, Paris

When Sophie returned to the Grand Hotel Continental, she found the suite looked rather different to the elegant place she had left earlier that morning. The table, now cleared of their breakfast things, was spread with sheets of paper, some of which were scribbled with Tilly's bold handwriting. Amongst them was scattered a strange array of objects: the ends of several candles, a glass bottle that she recognised as having previously contained Miss Blaxland's expensive scent, the bathroom soap dish, her own penknife, a box of matches and a bath sponge. Two or three books were lying open on the floor, and amongst them all was Tilly, an apron over her dress, rapidly leafing through pages.

'It must be something to do with the acid . . . the chemical reaction . . .' she was muttering to herself.

Sophie picked her way carefully between the books. She very much hoped that none of the hotel staff had been in the room because, sitting on the floor with ink stains on her fingers and her hair skewered up with a pencil, Tilly had never looked less like a lady's maid in her life.

'I found the *Café Monique*,' she began. 'The waiter there knew the Professor!'

'Mmmm?' said Tilly, clearly not listening to a word that she was saying.

'It turns out that he spent rather a lot of time at *La Lune Bleue* – that cabaret place I told you about. It sounds like he might have had rather a gambling habit! If he'd been involved in illicit gaming . . . well, it would go a long way to explaining all those debts, wouldn't it?'

'Mmmm,' said Tilly, with about as much interest as if Sophie had been reciting what she had eaten for breakfast. Sophie sighed and gave up. She knew Tilly well enough to know that there was simply no point in trying to make her think about anything else when she was engrossed in her work. Besides, the faster she worked, the sooner they might know what the Professor's papers said. For a moment, Sophie watched her, feverishly leafing through pages and then scribbling something with her pencil in her spiky, illegible writing. What it must be like to study something you were so passionate about, to immerse yourself in a subject like that? For a moment she felt a sharp flash of envy – for Tilly, and for Miss Blaxland too. In another world, a world in which Papa and

Mama were still alive, in which the Baron and the *Fraternitas Draconum* had never existed, perhaps she herself would have been making plans to go to university. Her thoughts would be full of entrance exams and subjects she would study, the books she would need and the friends she would make. But instead, she was here, her thoughts a jumble of a murdered British agent, secret papers and German spies.

It was a strange kind of thought, and to distract herself, she wandered through into her bedroom to look for a gown to wear for the dinner to launch the Grand Aerial Tour that evening. She knew it would be a very grand occasion and she wanted to be sure that she looked the part, but none of the frocks she had brought seemed quite right. That ruffled white dress was simply too frilly – she'd look like she was dressed from head to toe in meringue. The violet gown was certainly fashionable, but had a hobble, skirt so tight she'd barely be able to take a step. And as for the black silk, surely that was far too severe for such a glamorous celebration?

She did not dare ask Tilly what she thought – she was far too immersed in her task, and besides, Sophie had promised her she wouldn't need to think about even so much as a petticoat. She suddenly wished more than ever that Lil was there with them. She knew that Lil would understand how much being here in Paris made her think of her mother and the other life that could have been;

and she knew too that her friend would have entered enthusiastically into a discussion about which frock Miss Blaxland ought to wear to a grand dinner. Lil would be bubbling over with thoughts and ideas and theories about the Blaxland investigation, and Sophie could barely even imagine the wild schemes she would conjure up to get them inside *La Lune Bleue*! She'd probably have them disguised as can-can girls or circus performers, she thought, grinning to herself.

With Billy's words about Miss Blaxland ringing in her ears ('She's bound to have the very latest thing!') she finally settled on a stylish evening dress of rich blue silk overlaid with lace. It was expensive-looking and elegant, but not too showy, and she'd be able to move more comfortably in the draped skirt. Besides, it would hardly be appropriate for Miss Blaxland to wear anything too eye-catching: even if she had barely known him, she must not forget that Miss Blaxland was here in Paris because of her uncle's death. Sophie completed the outfit with long gloves, a lacy fan and the pearl earrings, and after a good deal of wrangling with hair-pins and combs, she finally managed to skewer her hair into the fashionable arrangement that Miss Blaxland favoured, securing it with a blue silk bandeau that she knew Lil would have loved. Satisfied with her reflection at last, she sat down gingerly in a chair by the window, too fearful of rumpling her gown or disarranging her hair to do anything else.

Besides, it would give her time to organise her thoughts, she decided, looking out on the view of the street and the park below. There was much to try to consider: the discovery that the Professor might have been taking part in illegal gambling with his bohemian friends at *La Lune Bleue*, the papers written in invisible ink, the empty safe. But most of all, her thoughts kept drawing her back to the book about alchemy with the illustration of the green lion. *I am the green lion without cares . . .* why did that phrase 'green lion' seem so meaningful to her? Thinking of it now, she felt as if she was catching at the fragile edge of a memory, like pulling at a loose thread, but even as she grasped for it, it slipped out of her reach and disappeared altogether. It was all a fearful muddle, and she wished all over again that Lil was there to chew it over with her, and make her feel as though she was equal to the task of unravelling it.

At seven o'clock, she went down to the hotel foyer to meet Dr Bernard, very dapper in black-and-white evening dress, with a fresh carnation *boutonnière* and his little moustache even more neatly waxed than before. He greeted her warmly, with an extravagant flood of compliments upon her appearance – 'You look most beautiful, Miss Blaxland – most elegant, most charming!' – before offering her his arm.

Sophie accepted it graciously. She was rather looking forward to seeing what Dr Bernard could tell her about

Professor Blaxland – perhaps he might even be able to answer some of the questions that were troubling her. Attending a grand dinner on the arm of an admiring young man was rather outside the scope of her usual detective duties, and certainly a contrast to the previous night's activities, she reflected, as he handed her carefully into a waiting carriage.

The *Palais Antoine* proved to be an elegant building, set in pretty formal gardens. It had been built for the Paris *Exposition* in 1900, and now housed a fine art collection. Sophie's silk skirts swished across the marble floor as they made their way into the *Salon,* where dinner was to be served. The spacious room, hung with paintings in ornate frames, was already full of people: Sophie saw gentlemen in evening dress, and ladies bedecked with jewels. At a table in the middle of the room, she observed Captain Nakamura now wearing a splendid dress-uniform with gold epaulettes on the shoulders. When he caught sight of her, he nodded, and flashed her a quick smile.

It was nice to see a friendly face, but all the same, Sophie felt relieved when they were directed away from him to one end of a much less prominent table in a corner of the room. From there, they would be a little more out of sight, whilst still being able to observe all the goings-on. Amongst the gathered people, Sophie spotted the fashion designer César Chevalier, and felt more relieved than ever that they were in a quiet corner. She certainly did not want to risk

M. Chevalier recognising her from London, and sweeping over to talk about Sinclair's.

A string quartet played a sedate waltz while they nibbled their first course – delicate mouthfuls of pâté served on slices of toasted brioche, little quail's eggs and tiny stuffed mushrooms that seemed almost too pretty to eat. After some carefully general conversation and several more flowery compliments from Dr Bernard, Sophie steered the conversation towards Professor Blaxland's research: 'Do tell me a little more about his work,' she began.

'It is hard to know where to start,' said Dr Bernard, as their fish dishes were placed in front of them with a flourish. 'Professor Blaxland had a very wide field of study. He seemed to know about everything. Old English, Medieval French, Greek . . . He is a great loss to the university.'

'Do you know if he had any particular interest in alchemy?' she asked. Dr Bernard looked surprised by the question, so she explained: 'I noticed he had some books on the subject and I was curious about it. I must confess I don't exactly know what alchemy *is*.'

'It is not something I know a great deal about myself, but it is certainly most interesting,' said Dr Bernard readily. 'Alchemy is a forerunner of our modern chemistry, dating back to ancient times. The alchemists were interested in learning how to turn ordinary metals, like lead, into gold.

They also believed in the existence of an elixir which granted immortality – the power to defeat death.'

The power to defeat death? Sophie listened, intrigued, as Dr Bernard went on: 'Whilst, of course, such an elixir could not possibly have existed, the alchemists did have an important influence on shaping early science. Our chemists today still use some of their methods. They were very secretive about their discoveries, and hid their knowledge in books full of cryptic symbols. They had their own systems of secret signs and ciphers – I imagine that is what interested your uncle.'

Sophie pricked up her ears at once. 'Oh, was he interested in that sort of thing?' she asked innocently. Was there any chance that Dr Bernard might know about the Professor's secret work for the Bureau?

'Yes, very much so,' said Dr Bernard. 'He was quite an expert in that field. He did some very interesting research on Ancient Greek ciphers and medieval cryptography.'

'I had no idea,' said Sophie, careful to keep her voice light and casual. 'So, what kind of ciphers and symbols did the alchemists use?'

'Often quite simple things. A crescent moon might denote silver, for example, or a triangle could represent a flame. But they also used more complex imagery – symbolic illustrations of animals or mythical creatures. If you're interested in alchemy, there are a number of places in the city you could visit,' he went on, as the waiter brought them their next course – duck served with red wine and potatoes *dauphinoise*. 'Nicholas Flamel was one of the most important alchemists – I believe you can see his tombstone, carved all over with alchemical symbols, at the Musée de Cluny. Then of course there was the Comte de Saint-Germain: a rather interesting character from the court of King Louis XV, who was believed to possess the elixir of life . . .'

But just then, a sudden hush fell over the crowded room, and Dr Bernard fell silent. A gentleman had risen to speak, and even before he had introduced himself, Sophie knew that he must be their host for the evening – Sir Chester Norton. She'd never seen the newspaper magnate in person before, although she'd heard his name plenty of times: he was one of the most successful businessmen in Europe. He was an intelligent-looking man, in his fifties, with greying hair parted neatly and smoothly to one side. When he spoke it was brisk and brief: Sophie thought how different his no-nonsense manner was from Mr Sinclair's flair and showmanship.

'Ladies and gentleman,' began Sir Chester, getting straight to the point. 'I am pleased to welcome you here today to celebrate the Grand Aerial Tour of Europe. Norton Newspapers are proud to be launching this, the longest air race to date, and to be offering a grand prize of £10,000 for the first pilot to complete the full circuit of Europe.' There was an appreciative burst of applause before Sir Chester cleared his throat and went on: 'Our pilots will be making stops in nine different countries, each of which I am delighted to say has pledged their support for our endeavour. They will allow our pilots to pass across their borders without hold-ups, and at each stage, will provide the fullest technical assistance.'

There was another smattering of applause, and Sir Chester continued: 'As some of you will be aware, there has been some suggestion in *certain* corners of the press that this is merely a stunt to sell newspapers.' He paused and lifted his eyebrows ironically to a burst of laughter from the audience. 'However, those of you who know me personally will already be aware of my sincere commitment to promoting aviation, which I consider to be the most significant area of technological advancement of this century, and which could soon allow all of us to travel across Europe more swiftly and easily than we have ever dreamed.' He paused again to allow for another flutter of applause. 'I hope you will join me tomorrow for the start of the race, commencing at twelve noon, and for now, I invite you to join me in a toast to the good health and success of the twelve intrepid young pilots who will be setting out for the skies tomorrow,' he concluded, gesturing to Captain Nakamura and the gentlemen sitting with him at the most prominent table.

They did so, and then there was more applause as Sir Chester returned to his seat.

'It is quite incredible, imagining that we could soon be able to travel across the world by air,' said Dr Bernard, with an astonished shake of the head.

'I think aeroplanes will need to become a great deal safer before that happens,' said Sophie. She'd read so many stories about unpleasant aviation accidents in the newspaper and she couldn't imagine anything much more terrifying than being propelled up into the sky, with nothing to support you but a flimsy contraption of wood and canvas and wire. But she spoke a little absently: she was still watching Sir Chester, who had turned to say something rapid to a young woman who had been standing on the sidelines during his speech, scribbling vigorously in a notebook. She was simply dressed, making her stand out at once in a room full of rich satin gowns and the glitter of jewels.

'Do you know who that is?' she asked Dr Bernard, but he only shook his head.

The waiters had appeared once again, this time with ice cream garnished with rich chocolate sauce and black cherries. Realising that dinner was coming to an end, Sophie decided the time had come to ask Dr Bernard again about the Professor's gambling.

'I found the *Café Monique* today,' she began, as she picked up a spoon. 'It's in Montmartre. Rather a famous place, as it turns out. It sounds like my uncle spent rather a lot of time there, and at *La Lune Bleue* too.' She paused as Dr Bernard turned a delicate shade of pink.

'Ah,' he said awkwardly, twitching his moustache. 'I am very sorry, Miss Blaxland. Please believe me when I say that I did not mean to deceive you. It is simply that, well, places like *La Lune Bleue* are not very respectable. Full of artists and models and dancers, and so on. I thought you might be shocked to learn that your uncle spent time there.'

'Not at all, Dr Bernard. Though I might have preferred to learn that he had a taste for illegal gambling from someone *other* than a waiter in a café.'

Dr Bernard's cheeks flushed more than ever. 'I do beg your pardon, Miss Blaxland. I did not wish to cause you any more distress,' he said sincerely.

The only thing that was likely to cause her distress, thought Sophie in annoyance, was people's constant attempts to keep her wrapped up in cotton wool, as if she was not a real girl at all, but a fragile porcelain doll that could be shattered at any moment. She knew that Dr Bernard meant well, but all the same she felt a stab of irritation that threatened to spoil her enjoyment of her ice. It seemed that Miss Blaxland could be as *independent* and *modern* and educated as she liked, but everyone she met was still trying to tell her what to do and what to think. She wouldn't swap places with her for the world,

Sophie thought suddenly: not even all her wealth, and her beautiful clothes, and her expensive hotel suites would be worth that.

Dr Bernard looked acutely uncomfortable, and she took pity on him. 'Never mind about it now. The thing is, it turns out he was in rather a lot of debt; I daresay he had lost money at the card table. Did he ever talk to you about anything like that?'

Dr Bernard looked shocked. 'Oh no, nothing like that! I had no idea. He always seemed perfectly comfortable.'

'He even took on some additional work to help cover his debts. Did he ever tell you about it?'

'Tutoring students, do you mean, or something of that kind?' But before Dr Bernard could finish what he was saying, Sophie saw that some of the people around them had risen to their feet. Sir Chester himself had appeared beside them – he was greeting everyone personally, nodding and shaking hands. Just behind him came the young woman with the notebook.

'I am Dr Emil Bernard, sir, from the Sorbonne,' said the young scholar, getting to his feet in a hurry. 'And this is Miss Blaxland, who is currently visiting from London.'

'How do you do?' said Sir Chester, shaking their hands cordially. 'I must say, it's a pleasure to see some young faces here tonight. Apart from the pilots, everyone seems

182

rather aged – myself included, I regret! Are you interested in aviation, Dr Bernard?'

Whilst Dr Bernard answered, Sophie found the young woman with the notebook at her elbow. 'Did he say your name was Blaxland?' she demanded.

'That's right. I'm Celia Blaxland – how do you do?' replied Sophie, holding out a hand, while at the same time feeling a stab of trepidation. She didn't at all like the searching way this young woman was looking at her.

'Roberta Russell, of *The Daily Picture*. I work for Sir Chester – I'm here to cover the air race,' replied the young woman, giving her hand a firm shake. Sophie recognised the name at once of course: after all, she read Miss Russell's articles almost every day in the newspaper. Her stomach flipped over as she realised that she was standing in front of one of the smartest young journalists in London. Was there any way that her pose as Celia Blaxland, with her grand dress and elaborate hairstyle, would deceive Miss Russell? Or would she recognise Sophie at once as one of the young lady detectives of Taylor & Rose?

'I must say, you look awfully familiar, Miss Blaxland. Have we met somewhere before?' said the journalist sharply, almost as if she could hear her thoughts.

Feeling increasingly anxious, Sophie tried to smile vaguely. 'I don't believe so. Though I did have my photograph in one or two of the magazines when I made my debut. Perhaps you might have seen one of them?'

'Hmmm,' said Miss Russell sceptically. She did not look in the least like the sort of girl who spent much time poring over the society pages. 'Any relation to Professor James Blaxland? The fellow killed by burglars in his Paris apartment?' she asked suddenly.

'Yes, I'm afraid so. Professor Blaxland was my uncle,' Sophie replied carefully.

'My condolences, Miss Blaxland.' But Miss Russell was still looking at her, as though weighing her up. 'That was a strange affair. Would've been on the front pages, if it wasn't for everything else happening just now – all this business in Arnovia. Tell me –'

But to Sophie's enormous relief, Sir Chester interjected: 'Miss Blaxland, Dr Bernard, let me introduce you to some of the young pilots. I'm sure they'd be delighted to have the opportunity to meet some young people after putting up with an evening's conversation with us old bores.' He ushered them over to Captain Nakamura's table, Miss Russell following close at their heels.

A group of men turned to greet them as they approached. 'Miss Blaxland, Dr Bernard, may I present Signor Rossi of Milan? And this is Monsieur Claude Laurent. He's the winner of last year's Paris to Madrid race, you know, so he'll be the man to beat.' The tall, grave-faced Frenchman nodded coolly, while beside him the Italian pilot performed a low bow, with much flourishing. 'And this is Captain Nakamura, of the Japanese Army,'

'We met yesterday at the Sorbonne,' said Nakamura with a solemn smile. 'It's a pleasure to see you again, Miss Blaxland. But where is your friend, who is so enthusiastic about aeroplanes?'

Sophie smiled back and made a quick, evasive reply. She hoped Nakamura wouldn't ask too many awkward questions about Tilly: Miss Blaxland was, after all, supposed to be travelling with a lady's maid, and she didn't imagine they typically had such an in-depth knowledge of aviation. But Sir Chester had already turned to a suave-looking fair man. 'Then Mr Charlton – he's one of the British pilots who'll be flying the Union Jack for us tomorrow. Daring fellow, used to be a racing-car driver, before we persuaded him to turn his talents to flight. You'll have to watch out for him in the air, eh, Laurent? And this is Herr Grün of Berlin. He'll be flying the Farman monoplane tomorrow – a very fine machine'

Sophie smiled at the young Englishman as he shook her hand, but when Sir Chester indicated the fifth man, Herr Grün, it was all she could do to keep her face fixed into a courteous expression. The German pilot bowed politely, evidently not recognising her, but she knew him at once. Herr Grün was the man whose face she had seen illuminated in the sudden bright beam of torchlight the previous night. He had been in the Professor's apartment with the grey man. He wasn't just a pilot: he was a spy.

CHAPTER EIGHTEEN

La Lune Bleue, Paris

Sophie knew she mustn't show her alarm. She tried to fix her attention on the conversation, nodding and smiling as Sir Chester exchanged a few pleasantries with the pilots. She was fairly sure that Herr Grün would not connect the elegant young lady in the blue evening gown with the intruder in the rough cap who had broken a bottle of wine over his head the previous night, but she could not be absolutely certain of it.

'Well, I shall leave you young people to continue the celebrations' said Sir Chester at last, strolling away from them towards another waiting group. 'Enjoy yourselves tonight.'

'Yes , tomorrow we shall be competitors, but tonight we should celebrate as friends!' declared Signor Rossi enthusiastically, clapping the nearest pilot – M. Laurent – on the back. The Frenchman looked slightly disgusted and took a small sidestep away.

But Charlton nodded approvingly. 'Yes, I call that a

splendid idea,' he agreed. 'Raising a glass and toasting one another's success, as gentlemen. Quite right too. Good show, Rossi. And you must join us, Dr Bernard and Miss Blaxland – and Miss Russell too, of course.'

'Where shall we go?' asked Captain Nakamura.

'Ah, but there is only one choice!' exclaimed Rossi at once. 'It must be *La Lune Bleue* – they say it is the best night-spot in Paris! The finest dancing – the best champagne and cognac – the music –'

'Oh, I say,' interrupted Charlton, in a hurry. 'But I'm not sure that it's quite the sort of place to take *ladies*.'

But Miss Russell was not to be put off that easily. 'Don't worry your head about us, Mr Charlton,' she said with a smirk. 'I'm quite sure we can cope, can't we, Miss Blaxland?'

Dr Bernard looked rather uncertain about the idea, but Sophie nodded at once, thrilled by this unexpected opportunity. This would be her chance to see *La Lune Bleue!* The waiter at the *Café Monique* had said that Madame Delacroix would be there tonight – perhaps she could find her and speak to her! And what was more, if Herr Grün joined them, she might have the opportunity to discover more about the German spy.

She knew she was taking a risk. The more time she spent with Grün, the greater the danger that he might recognise her from the Professor's apartment. Then there was Miss Russell, who was still watching her intently. But she felt a burst of reckless excitement as they came out of *Le Palais*

Antoine, and she found herself clambering into a cab with Captain Nakamura, Dr Bernard and Miss Russell. Just ahead of them, she saw that Grün was getting into a second, along with Rossi, Charlton and Laurent. As she watched, he glanced quickly back over his shoulder, and she hurriedly turned her face away.

Miss Russell leaned towards Sophie as they settled into the carriage. 'You know, I'm *sure* we've met before, Miss Blaxland,' she murmured. 'And I'm certain it isn't because I've seen you in *Tatler*.' Sophie just shrugged and smiled, but Miss Russell gave a little bubbling laugh. 'Mark my words, Miss Blaxland, I'll find out your secret. It's my job – I always do.'

It was rather a relief when the cab pulled up outside *La Lune Bleue* and Miss Russell's attention was distracted. Montmartre seemed very different in the dark: the cobbled streets she'd seen in daylight were now a blur of coloured lights and illuminated signs and shadows. They were whisked at once through an entrance, the blue velvet curtains swinging back to admit them.

Inside there was music and darkness, broken only by the greenish-golden glow of electric lights filtered through a smoky haze. Circular tables were arranged in a semi-circle around an immense stage, draped with curtains and decorated with gold-and-silver lights. Here, a line of dancers kicked and whirled, their skirts flying in a vivid splash of colour – scarlet and yellow, emerald-green and pink.

Their party was directed towards a mezzanine where a number of tables had been laid ready for them, but Sophie hung back. She did not want to spend any more time than she needed with the sharp-eyed Roberta Russell – what she wanted was to try to track down the Professor's friend, Madame Delacroix.

Slipping quietly away from their group before Dr Bernard noticed she was gone, she began to look keenly around her. Most of the tables were occupied by parties of rowdy gentlemen, though here and there she noticed a lady in evening dress. Waiters in white coats moved between them, pouring champagne. Archways led out of the main hall into several smaller rooms: here, she saw three gentlemen in silk hats smoking cigars; there, two ladies reclining on a chaise, laughing behind their fans at some unheard joke. Peeping through a curtain, Sophie thought she saw a card game taking place – a quick glimpse of a green baize tablecloth and playing cards – but as she tried to step through, a waiter appeared and pulled the curtain carefully into place, blocking her view. 'I am sorry, *mademoiselle*. This is a private party.'

'I'm looking for Madame Delacroix,' Sophie tried. 'I wondered if she was inside? Do you know where I might find her? My name is Blaxland – Celia Blaxland.'

'One moment, *mademoiselle*.' The waiter disappeared between the curtains, returning a moment later. 'Yes, she will speak with you. Please, follow me.'

Sophie followed the waiter under another archway;

through an empty salon, sumptuously furnished; and then into another small room, swathed entirely in rich blue fabric, the carpeted floor scattered with heaps of silk and velvet cushions. It was like stepping into a tent. Dimly, Sophie could hear the hum of the music, but it was fainter now, far away as though muffled by the rich draperies.

'*Voilà, Madame Delacroix*,' said the waiter, bowing before he departed.

In the centre of the little room, a woman uncurled herself from where she was sitting on a large cushion. She had a frizz of hair into which a large crimson rose had been pinned; and her lips were lacquered a daring crimson to match it. She was smoking a cigarette in a long holder, and she wore long, glittering earrings, which tinkled as she tilted her head and looked at Sophie appraisingly. She said nothing.

Sophie stepped forward. 'My name is Celia Blaxland,' she began. 'I believe that my uncle, Professor Blaxland, was a friend of yours?'

The woman put down her cigarette abruptly. Then she muttered something to herself in French, too low and rapid for Sophie to hear.

'At the *Café Monique*, the waiter told me that I might find you here,' she continued, a little desperately. 'I want to talk to some of the people who knew him, you see. May I sit?'

The woman still did not speak, and Sophie boldly took a seat beside her. 'I'm trying to find out more about what happened to him,' she explained.

'*What happened to him . . .*' the woman whispered. She looked away from Sophie for a moment, and when she looked back, her face was fierce and unhappy. 'How can I be sure that you are who you say you are?' she demanded. She shook her head, and then took a swig from the glass of cloudy liquid on the table in front of her. 'No. I can't say anything. I can't. I mustn't.'

'Say anything about what?' asked Sophie, leaning forward.

'That's the mistake *he* made. Saying too much. It was all because of the money. So stupid. It got him mixed up with the wrong people.' She lowered her voice. '*He was working for them, you know. He was working for them both.*'

'Working for who?' asked Sophie breathlessly. Was this strange woman talking about the Bureau? Did she know about the Professor's secret work?

'He knew that someone was coming. When I last saw him he was terribly afraid . . . *I think he was afraid for his life.*'

Sophie stared at her, fascinated. By *someone*, did she mean Ziegler's spies? Had the Professor known that the Germans were on his trail? 'You know that it wasn't an ordinary burglary that killed the Professor, don't you?' she said gently, trying to encourage the woman to say more. 'It was something else.'

But the woman remained silent. All of Sophie's persuasive questions came to nothing. At last she spat out: 'I don't know you. I won't talk to you. You should go!'

When Sophie did not move she hissed at her like a cat:

'Go away! Leave me alone!'

Alarmed, Sophie sprang to her feet. But then suddenly, the woman reached out a long thin hand and grabbed her sleeve, pulling her back. 'If you are who you say you are, you shouldn't stay here,' she said in a low, furtive voice. 'Go back to England. Do not ask these questions. Forget about what happened to him. *It isn't safe.*'

As soon as the words were out of her mouth, she flung a long crimson shawl about her shoulders and then abruptly rose up and departed. Sophie was on her feet and after her at once, but as soon as she had ducked through the curtain, she could see no sign of Madame Delacroix anywhere. She seemed to have vanished into the crowd.

After a minute or two, she gave up and walked swiftly back towards the group of pilots. The strange encounter had prompted more questions than it had answered. What had Madame Delacroix meant when she'd talked about the Professor *saying too much?* Could it be that he'd become indiscreet about his secret work for the British government? Was that how Ziegler's agents had tracked him down? Could the Professor really have known he was in danger? Should Sophie even believe a single word that Madame Delacroix had said?

As she approached the two tables where the pilots were sitting, drinking champagne, Dr Bernard jumped to his feet. 'Miss Blaxland! I was worried!' he exclaimed. 'Where have you been?'

Beside him, Miss Russell rolled her eyes. 'Come and sit by me,' she said, pulling out a chair beside her and patting it. 'And for goodness' sake, I hope you've got something to talk about besides aeroplanes. I'm as fascinated by flight as anyone, but I'm afraid I've quite run of conversation about engines.'

Sophie took the chair, trying to set aside her extraordinary encounter with Madame Delacroix for the time being. There was still Grün to watch, sitting at the next table, listening to Rossi telling some wild story. It was warm and she was glad of the excuse to open her fan, which she hoped would keep her face at least partly concealed.

'Tell me about *your* work,' she said swiftly to Miss Russell. She was always interested in other young women who were earning their own living, but what was more, she felt that if she could encourage the journalist to talk about herself, there was less danger of her asking difficult questions. 'How long have you been working for Sir Chester Norton?'

'Almost two years,' said Miss Russell. 'It's not a bad job. Plenty of travel, which I've always wanted. Lots of papers won't hire women, or if they do, it's only to write about fashions or society news and that sort of rot. But Norton's not like that. He sees people's potential – he's smart that way. Somehow he always manages to be two steps ahead of everyone else.' Seeing that Sophie was listening with interest, she leaned a little forward across the table. 'Take this flying business, for example,' she said, lowering her voice so the

194

others around them wouldn't hear. 'He might say the air race is about supporting technical innovation, or collaborating with nations across Europe, or even about selling papers. But the truth is, he's thinking about the big picture. Really, it's all about making sure that *they* don't get an advantage over *us*.' She flicked a quick finger at the pilots at the next table – Laurent, Rossi and Grün.

'Whatever do you mean?' asked Sophie.

'*Aviation*. The French are miles ahead of us, you know, and the Americans and the Germans aren't far behind. D'you know, in Germany, Prince Heinrich himself has learned to fly a plane, and he's the Kaiser's brother and an admiral in the German Navy. The German military are taking aeroplanes very seriously, and the Japanese too – that's why Nakamura was sent here to train as a pilot, and to learn about aviation from the French. If Britain doesn't keep up, we'll be frightfully vulnerable. At the moment, our government aren't investing in aviation, and Norton wants to make them sit up and take notice. That's what all this is really about.' She lowered her voice even further: 'You didn't hear this from me, but he's offered Charlton a bonus as well as the prize money if he can beat Laurent and the others. You know – to show the world what British pilots can do.'

But Sophie was still thinking about what Miss Russell had said about the German military. 'D'you mean that aeroplanes could be used if a war broke out?' she asked.

Miss Russell nodded. 'Of course they could. Just think of

the possibilities. The Americans are already experimenting with dropping bombs out of planes you know. And then there's surveillance.'

Sophie's eyes widened. Her work for the Secret Service Bureau made her only too aware of what the possibilities of aeroplanes might mean for spies. 'You could fly a plane right over enemy lines, and spy on them from the air,' she said slowly. 'See exactly what they were doing.'

'And if you had a camera, you could even take photographs,' agreed Miss Russell. 'Just imagine that.'

Her glass was empty and she waved a hand impatiently to attract a waiter's attention. As a waiter moved forward to fill her glass, Sophie saw that at the next table, Herr Grün had been joined by a companion. As he turned his head, everything Miss Russell had been saying seemed to fall away, and to her horror she realised that sitting beside Grün, only a few feet away from her, was the grey man himself. He looked quite different now, smart in evening dress, but she knew him at once.

Beside her, Miss Russell was watching her, a triumphant look on her face. 'I've been trying to place you all evening but I've got it now,' she announced. 'I know who you are. You aren't *Miss Celia Blaxland*. No debutante would go wandering off by themselves in a place like this, nor want to talk about *aeroplanes spying between enemy lines*. You're one of those young lady detectives, aren't you? Miss Sophie Taylor from Taylor & Rose – that's it, isn't it? Oh, how perfect!

Do tell me, Miss Taylor, what are you investigating here in Paris?' She burst into a sudden peal of laughter. Then her eyes widened: 'I say – it's Blaxland, isn't it? You're here to investigate his murder!'

Sophie's heart was pounding in her chest. 'Very amusing!' she said, forcing herself to give a light-hearted giggle. 'Me, a lady detective. My goodness, what a funny idea!'

Miss Russell smirked at her, but Sophie knew that it was already took late. Across from them, Captain Nakamura and Mr Charlton were having an involved discussion about flying while Dr Bernard sipped champagne and watched the dancers, all three of them quite oblivious, but at the next table, Herr Grün had stiffened. *He'd heard her*, Sophie realised. He leaned forward and said something to the grey man in a low voice. The grey man turned to look, and she saw a look of furious recognition flash over the grey man's face. In that moment, she knew he had recognised her as the girl from Victoria station.

'Excuse me for a moment – so warm in here – I must get some air,' she murmured to Miss Russell, and without waiting a moment, she darted away across the room.

The orchestra had struck up a new tune: they seemed to be playing faster and faster, as she pushed her way as quickly as she could between the tables, dodging a crowd of gentlemen, then a waitress with a tray of glasses. She dared not stop to so much as glance over her shoulder to see if Grün and the grey man were following her. She felt intensely frustrated. The game was up: the grey man had recognised her and, thanks to Miss Russell, he now knew exactly who she was. As if he was whispering it in her ear, she heard the Chief say: *You'll have to be discreet . . . Stay on your guard . . . Whatever you do, don't reveal who you really are.* She had ruined everything, she realised, a sick feeling rising up in her stomach. Her assignment was a failure.

Just the same, she was not going to give the grey man the chance to catch her. She speeded up, slipping between tables. Everything seemed to swirl around her, a hot blur of colour: crimson and gold and rich purple and silver. She went through another set of velvet curtains, and found herself emerging outside, on to a roof terrace where people sat beneath strings of coloured lights and paper lanterns. Behind her, she heard a yell: she ran faster, pushing past a young Englishman with a glass of wine who called out indignantly: 'I say! Watch where you're going!' She dived through another door, darting along a high balcony. Down below her, the musicians played faster and faster; she caught the bright gleam of flutes and trumpets; she glimpsed the whirling skirts of the dancers on stage; and then she was racing through another door marked *Privé* and down a set of stairs. She was in a kind of backstage area now, though she could still hear the rapid thud of the music: the dizzy crescendo of the strings, the fanfare of the trumpets, the audience's wild bursts of applause. She opened a door and found herself speeding through a dressing room, where can-can girls were powdering their noses and combing their hair; and a clown was carefully painting his face; then through a storeroom piled with exotic props; and then at last she emerged, breathless, out into the street, with the music still shrilling in her ears.

Even then she dared not pause. She raced off as quickly as she could into the Montmartre night. It was a long time before she decided she'd gone far enough to risk stopping to flag down a cab. The cab driver looked a little uncertain as she climbed aboard, and she realised what a sight she must look: a girl alone, breathless from running, her elaborate hairstyle in disarray. She sat back against the seat of the cab, shivering and trying to catch her breath.

She felt simply furious with herself. She'd thought she was being so clever, finding a way to go to *La Lune Bleue*, tracking down Madame Delacroix, working out that the grey man's companion was the pilot, Herr Grün. Now, she saw that, instead, her investigation was in tatters. She'd done exactly what the Chief had told her not to – she'd allowed their enemies to discover her identity. She was supposed to be a *secret agent*, she thought bitterly. Yet Miss Russell had seen through her disguise almost at once. *Why* had she gone babbling on about surveillance like that? Now she and Tilly would have to leave Paris, and quickly. After all, it wouldn't be at all difficult for the grey man to discover where Miss Blaxland was staying. What if he came after her at the hotel?

Worst of all, she still wasn't even close to solving the investigation. Although she was almost certain now that the Germans were behind the Professor's death, she still had no idea *why*. Even if they had discovered he was working for the Secret Service Bureau, then surely that wasn't enough to justify his murder? And what were Ziegler's spies doing mixed up in an air race? Could it be anything to do with what Miss Russell had said – about aeroplanes and surveillance and war?

She felt self-conscious and flustered as she hurried into the Grand Hotel Continental, and through the lobby, which was alive with activity. Although it was almost midnight, guests were still drinking coffee in the lounge, the lady with the lorgnette was sitting in an armchair sipping cognac, and a station cab was pulling up at the door. She ran up the stairs, keen to get away from everyone and think.

As the door of their suite closed behind her, she began to peel off her gloves and unhook her earrings, shaking down her hair as if to shake away her Celia Blaxland identity altogether. 'Tilly –' she began, half of her wanting to pour out everything that had happened, half of her dreading admitting to her failure.

But Tilly's voice, when it answered her, was tense and full of nervous excitement. 'Come here and look at this,' she called out from her bedroom. 'I've done it – I've worked out how to read the invisible ink. Just wait until you see what the Professor's letter says.'

Sophie hurried through to the bedroom. Tilly had three sheets of paper spread across a wooden table: a flat-iron stood close by, and there was a hot, singed smell in the air. As Sophie leaned over the table, she saw that the pages, previously bare and white, now showed a message written in brownish handwriting.

'He used lemon juice!' Tilly explained, rubbing her forehead wearily. 'The simplest thing – a solution of lemon juice. But the clever part was that he knew the smell would give it away, so he mixed in a perfume to mask it. I don't know why it took me so long to work it out. But of course, once I realised it was lemon juice, I knew straight away how to read it.' Seeing Sophie staring at her blankly, she explained as though to a small child: 'You *heat it*, of course. Heat makes the sugar caramelise and turn brown. So I asked the hotel if I could use an iron – of course no one thought twice about a lady's maid asking for one of those – and I *ironed* the pages, and now we can see – just look.'

Sophie gazed at the paper Tilly was pushing towards her. Two words, written in bold capitals, immediately jumped out at her from the top of the paper. They were two words that she hadn't seen for some time, and which she certainly hadn't expected to see here in Paris. Two words that shocked and disturbed her more than anything else that had happened that evening:

FRATERNITAS DRACONUM.

CHAPTER NINETEEN

The Grand Hotel Continental, Paris

When Anna awoke the next morning, she couldn't think where she was. She seemed to be nestled amongst white linen sheets, fluffy pillows and a velvety-soft eiderdown. Warm golden light was filtering through white curtains.

As she lay there, surfacing from sleep, the events of the previous evening began to trickle back. The hotel foyer, all crimson and gilt and sparkling. The music and the voices, the people like pictures come to life – gentlemen in tall silk hats, a lady with a lorgnette sitting in a high-backed armchair sipping a drink from a crystal glass, porters in rich red-and-gold uniforms, a young lady running up the stairs in a beautiful blue gown.

It had been almost midnight when they'd finally arrived. Alex had been yawning and blinking and staring around them and, for a brief moment, Anna had thought how strange and out of place they must look here. She felt very small in her cotton frock, covered in smuts from the train. But they did not have long to linger: suddenly brisk and practical, Lil had bundled them both upstairs. 'Well, here we are at last. Come on. There are rooms ready for us, and you'll feel much better after a hot bath and a good long sleep.'

It had felt like a very a long time since Anna had been in a real bedroom, in a proper bed. She'd wondered if she'd lie awake, thinking about everything that had happened since they left Wilderstein Castle; or whether she'd dream of being woken up suddenly in the middle of the night, a dark figure looming over her. But instead she'd fallen almost at once into a deep, dreamless sleep. Now it was morning and she realised with a sudden thrill that they were in Paris.

Without even waiting to put on the dressing gown and slippers that had been carefully laid ready for her, she got out of bed and rushed over to push back the curtains and open the window. Down below her was the Paris street: broad and graceful, and already beginning to rumble with activity. There were motor cars and prim horse-drawn carriages, lumbering omnibuses and bicycles. There were people: doormen greeting newly arrived hotel guests; a waiter laying tables outside a restaurant across the way; a woman going by with a basket of flowers; a boy whistling, with a bundle of long, thin loaves of bread tucked under his arm. In the tall elegant building across from the hotel, she could see more people in the windows: a maid in a white cap shaking out a checked tablecloth; a lady reading a newspaper and drinking a cup of coffee; a gentleman watering a window-box of scarlet geraniums.

She could have stood there watching for hours, feeling the sun against her face and breathing in gulps of warm, smoky Parisian air. But soon she began to hear voices in the sitting room and to smell a most delicious breakfast.

Lil grinned at the look on Anna's face as she stared, delighted, at the breakfast table. She'd told M. Martin that the children would be hungry and he'd certainly provided them with a jolly good spread. The snowy tablecloth was laden with heaps of delicious-looking pastries topped with apricots or apple slices, gleaming with sweet glaze. There were purple grapes and a bowl of sun-warmed peaches; sparkling glass dishes of jam; new bread and a yellow pat of butter; and a steaming silver pot of hot chocolate.

Alex was already tucking in hungrily, all thoughts of proper royal behaviour long forgotten. 'Morning!' he said happily, his mouth stuffed full.

'My word! You'd think they'd never seen food before,' said Forsyth, chuckling. He'd only just reappeared, having muttered mysteriously about urgent business to attend to on their arrival in Paris, and then disappearing into the night.

'I'm not sure they have – not food like this, anyway.

They certainly didn't get anything like it at Wilderstein Castle,' said Lil, thinking without regret of the sausages and potatoes that they'd been served almost every day. Beyond the King's boxes of chocolates, the most the children had ever had as a treat was an occasional spoonful of jam to go with their tea-time bread and butter. It had been nothing at all like what she'd imagined the life of a prince and princess to be.

'Huh! I suppose that frightful old Countess was probably squirrelling away the money she ought to have been spending to give these kids a decent feed,' Forsyth said. He yawned and stretched out in his chair. 'I say, old girl, I'm just about ready to drop. Pour me some coffee would you?'

Lil was about to inform him that she was not a waitress and he could jolly well fetch it himself, but Forsyth did look tired – his bronzed face was paler than usual, and his eyes were red-rimmed. If he had been working while she had been asleep at the hotel, then she supposed she could probably manage to pour some coffee. 'Where've you been?' she asked him, as she did so.

'Oh, I had to telephone a report through to HQ. Got to keep the Chief up to date, of course. He said the Arnovian delegation will be with us by this evening, so all we have to do is sit tight here and keep our heads down. Unfortunately the kidnap plot is all over the papers and the kids' pictures are on the front pages. But thanks to Martin, no one knows we're here. He's one of the Chief's contacts, you know – that's why he sent us here. We can trust him to keep the press at bay.'

'Any leads on the Countess?' asked Lil as she poured them both a cup of coffee.

'Nothing yet. She and the Count have left the castle, but no one seems to know where they are or what they're up to. I'll bet they've gone over the German border, though I don't suppose they'll be very popular in Berlin now that their little scheme has gone to the wall. Dashed embarrassing situation for the Kaiser. The Germans are distancing themselves from the whole thing. They say they've never worked with the Countess, and they'd never stoop to get involved in anything like kidnapping a child. The latest word is that they may pull back from the Arnovian border. They don't want to be associated with the likes of this.

'The Chief is no end bucked with us. Though of course with all my experience in the field, he knows he can count on *me* to deliver the goods. But he's pretty pleased with you too, old thing. He said you'd really done quite well! You are something: really, you've almost proved *me* wrong, when I said that letting girls into the Bureau was an idiotic idea.' He gave a merry laugh.

'Do be careful, Forsyth,' said Lil in her sweetest voice, as she stirred a heaped spoon of salt into his coffee. 'Before you know it you'll be suggesting that female agents can do as good a job as men.'

Forsyth hooted as if she'd said something very amusing. 'Ha! Good show!' He took a great gulp of coffee and made a face. 'Ugh! I thought the French were supposed to make good coffee? I'd take a good old British cup of tea any day. Well, I'm off for a bath and a shave and a proper feed. After I'd got my call through, I met up with an old pal of mine who took me to a rather amusing night-spot. A little place called *La Lune Bleue*. We had quite an evening, except that some fool of a girl managed to spill mine all over my shirt! I'd better go and smarten up before the big-wigs turn up later, what?' He winked and added: 'You'll stay here and look after the kids, won't you?'

He strolled off without bothering to wait for a response, and Lil resisted the urge to throw her cup of coffee at his departing head. Although, really, she oughtn't to have expected any better from Forsyth. She knew that he saw himself as an intrepid hero of the kind that you might read about in a sixpenny novel. He was convinced he was the backbone of the Secret Service Bureau and the Chief's right-hand man, whilst she was little more than a nursemaid, along to look after the children. That was in spite of the fact that *she* was the one who'd been working undercover at Wilderstein Castle for weeks, doing all the hard work and taking most of the risk, whilst Forsyth sunned himself on the mountains, enjoying the local beer and the company of pretty Arnovian maidens. And now, no doubt, he had claimed all the credit for her work.

It was all terrifically frustrating, but the main thing was that Anna and Alex were safe, she told herself, as she munched an apricot pastry appreciatively. When she'd first been given this assignment by the Chief she'd feared the worst, imagining herself as the hopeless governess to two spoilt monsters. What she hadn't expected was how much she'd like the prince and princess, nor that she'd end up feeling sorry for them. Now she thought how jolly nice it was to see them enjoying themselves, wolfing down their breakfasts and chattering happily, hundreds of miles away from the Countess and the Count and awful old Wilderstein Castle.

She'd be sad to say farewell to them, she realised. But with the Arnovian delegation arriving that evening, she knew that her assignment was almost at an end. She'd soon be back in London, in the cosy, familiar surroundings of Taylor & Rose. It would be awfully nice to be home again. She lingered over the thought of seeing her brother, and all her friends, and wearing her *own* clothes instead of these frightful governessy tweeds. And best of all, Sophie would be there, and she'd be able to tell her all about this strange adventure.

She'd been thinking of Sophie even more than usual since they'd arrived in Paris. She knew Sophie had always wanted to come here: she'd told Lil about the diaries in which her mother had written all her impressions of visiting the city for the first time, when she was a young girl herself. Perhaps one day they could come back here together. Anyway, she'd describe it all for Sophie when she was back in London. They'd go to Lyons for tea and buns, and she'd tell Sophie about everything that had happened since she'd left London – about Arnovia, and Wilderstein Castle, and the horrid Countess, and what it had been like taking a train right across Europe, and how much Forsyth made her want to throw things at him – she knew Sophie would understand that. Most of all, she'd tell her what it had been like arriving in Paris at midnight, and how jolly peculiar it seemed to be here, in a grand hotel in the heart of Paris, giving a Crown Prince and Princess their breakfast.

Anna and Alex had gone back to the windows. 'Look – I think I can see the Eiffel Tower!'

'And there's the ferris wheel!'

Lil came over to join them. The street was already busy: a parade of motor cars was passing by the hotel – some pulling up at the entrance to allow passengers to disembark, before driving away again. Ladies in the latest Paris fashions were taking a morning *promenade* under their parasols; and just along the street from the hotel were the gates to a park. Beyond, she could glimpse trees and fountains and a carousel: children in sailor hats were playing with hoops, and nursemaids were pushing babies in big perambulators, and a girl of about Anna's age in a white frock was taking four tiny dogs for a walk. Above it all, a large red air-balloon was soaring slowly across the wide blue sky, printed with a message in tall white letters.

'Grand Aerial Tour of Europe . . .' read out Alex, craning his neck.

'That's the big air race, isn't it?' said Anna, remembering. 'There were posters for it at the station. Oh, couldn't we go and see it?'

Lil hated to disappoint them, but she knew they'd have to stay in the hotel room. 'I'm afraid not,' she said regretfully. 'We're under strict instructions to stay here.'

They nodded, disappointed, but not really surprised. 'I suppose we couldn't go to the park, at least?' tried Anna tentatively. 'Or even just to that *pâtisserie* down there?' She gestured to a shop with a striped awning, where a group of girls were peering into the window, pointing at cakes fluffy with cream and drizzled with chocolate.

'I'd like to go *there*,' said Alex wistfully, indicating an illuminated sign which read CINÉMA in large letters. Alex was as fascinated by moving pictures as he was by the theatre, but there was no picture palace in Elffburg, so he'd never had the chance to see any for himself. Now there was a real cinema just a short distance from their hotel: he leaned out a little further, trying to make out the names of the pictures that were showing and Anna grabbed the back of his jersey as though she were afraid he'd fall out.

'I'm awfully sorry, but we can't,' said Lil, gazing out at the trees, and the fountains, at the girls now emerging from the *pâtisserie* with candy-striped boxes of cakes. The morning sun gleamed gold on the distant carousel, and there was the faint tinkle of music. They only had one day in Paris – it seemed so dreadful that they had to spend it shut up in a hotel room. She'd have loved nothing more than to take Anna and Alex on a jolly day's sight-seeing. But she had her instructions, and she meant to follow them.

'At least we can watch from up here,' she said, trying to console them. 'And look – M. Martin has sent up some books, and a game and a jigsaw. That ought to be plenty to keep us entertained until luncheon. Then we'll order something really splendid to eat.' Even if she couldn't give them a day out, she could at least make sure they were well fed. Perhaps she would see if someone could go out to that little *pâtisserie* Anna had seen, and fetch them some cakes?

Just then, there was a tap on the door. Lil went to answer it, careful to open the door only the merest crack. If the children's faces were all over the newspapers, she didn't want any passing hotel guests to catch a glimpse of them. 'Yes?'

One of the hotel bell-boys in a red-and-gold uniform was waiting outside. 'Excuse me, *mademoiselle*, there's a telephone call for you downstairs.'

'A telephone call?'

'Yes – from London. Very urgent, *mademoiselle*.'

Lil's first thought was Sophie. What if something was wrong? But of course, neither Sophie, nor her brother

Jack, nor anyone else had the first idea she was here, at the Grand Hotel Continental in Paris. A call from London could surely only mean one person: the Chief.

She turned to Alex and Anna. 'I'll be back in a moment. I'll lock the door behind me – don't open it to anyone but me or Captain Forsyth,' she instructed them.

A moment later, the bell-boy had ushered her down to the grand reception desk, where the telephone was waiting for her. But when she picked up the receiver, there was nothing but a strange buzzing at the other end of the line. 'Hello? *Hello?*' she asked. 'Operator?' But there was no answer and after a moment or two, she hung up the receiver, frowning.

'Did the caller give a name?' she asked the smart gentleman on duty at the desk.

'I'm afraid not, *mademoiselle*. But I would advise you to wait a minute or two, Perhaps it was a bad line – if so, they may telephone again.'

But the telephone did not ring, and Lil began to feel a prickle of apprehension. The Chief was always so careful about keeping their missions a strict secret, so why would he risk telephoning her at the hotel? With a sinking heart she wondered if something had happened in Arnovia. For a minute or two she hesitated by the telephone, wondering if she should place a call to HQ. But what if it had not been a genuine telephone call at all, but some sort of trick to make her give herself away? Her chest squeezed tight, and then coming to a sudden decision, she hurried as fast as she could back to the suite, fumbling with the tasselled room key.

The sitting room was empty. The books and games lay untouched on the table. Her heart was pounding, but she was being silly – surely Alex and Anna must be in their bedrooms. She opened the nearest bedroom door – Anna's – and found it deserted.

'Hello? Where are you? Are you playing a game?' she called out, hoping to hear muffled laughter coming from behind the curtains or under the bed.

But there was no answer. She opened one bedroom door, then another; she pushed back the curtains; she looked behind the chairs. But there was no one there.

To her growing horror, she realised that the hotel suite was completely empty.

The royal children were gone.

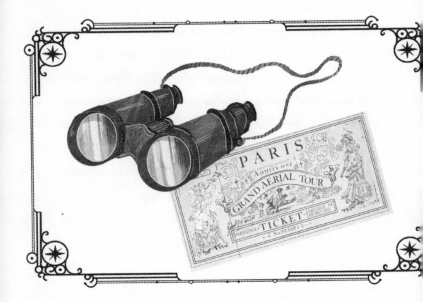

PART V

'Today Papa says he will take me to see an exhibition by the famous "Flying Man". They say he can fly through the air in a machine of his own construction – a glider with propellers! That such a phenomenon should be possible is quite incredible to me – I shall not believe it until I have seen it with my own eyes.'

– From the diary of Alice Grayson

CHAPTER TWENTY

The Grand Hotel Continental, Paris

From the window of the hotel suite, Anna gazed down at the street below. Behind her, on the table, lay two brand-new school stories she'd never read before, but neither *The Bravest Girl in the Fifth* nor *Two Schoolgirl Chums* held any appeal for her now. Instead, she stared at the girl in the white frock as she strolled on, into the park and past the fountains. She wondered what it must feel like to walk in a park alone, with the breeze blowing in your hair. The thought of it seemed as light and carefree as the red air-balloon drifting lazily across the blue sky.

'I do wish we could go down,' she said again.

'Well, we can't, so there's no sense going on about it,' said Alex, rather grumpily, not taking his eyes off the sign for the *cinéma*. But it was all right for *him*, Anna thought. Even after everything that had happened, she supposed that Alex would still be going away to boarding school. He'd soon be playing cricket, and making new friends, and he'd

217

probably become the hero of the Fourth Form . . . well, of course he would. Everyone was bound to like Alex – people always did. He'd be able to travel and meet new people, and stay in grand hotels like this one. He'd go to all those places she'd gazed at in the schoolroom atlas: London and St Petersburg and Vienna and New York. Meanwhile, she'd be back in Arnovia, perhaps even back at Wilderstein Castle, no doubt under the care of another elderly relative or a boring governess, practising her deportment. All this – the train journey, Paris, the park, the red air-balloon, would seem like a story she'd read in a book once, rather than something real that had actually happened to her.

The thought of being at Wilderstein Castle, without either Alex or Lil, was almost too much to bear. She opened her mouth to ask Alex whether he thought she'd be sent back there, but before she could speak, there came another quick tap at the door.

Anna frowned, remembering what Lil had said. Alex looked at her uncertainly and neither of them moved, but then the voice of a bell-boy called out, '*Pardon, mademoiselle?* Some refreshments for you?' and they scrambled to their feet at once.

'Ooh, I'll bet Lil sent out for some of those cakes from the shop we saw,' said Alex gladly.

Anna was first to the door, and opened it a little way as she'd seen Lil do. But before she even had the chance to cry out, the door was forced open and she was pushed back into the room.

In a jagged shock of terror, she heard Alex yell. Her hands were forced behind her back; a gloved hand was pressed over her mouth. But this time it was not Lil muffling her screams for help. 'Hello, Princess,' said a voice, very close to her ear, and fear crashed over her as she realised that the man holding her was the footman from Wilderstein Castle.

Another yell and a scuffle. She realised that two other men were seizing Alex, and once again she tried to scream, but the footman's hand pressed harder, half-choking her. It *can't be real*, she thought, as they were carried out of the room, the suite door swinging shut. They had left Arnovia behind them. They were hundreds of miles away from Wilderstein Castle. This was Paris; they were *safe*.

She caught a horrible flashing glimpse of Alex, slung like a shapeless old bundle in the arms of another big, square-shouldered man. His eyes wide and wild, and one struggled desperately to free herself from the footman's grasp, but she could not. Her vision seemed to twist and blur, but all the same she made out the figure of a woman standing in the corridor, watching them through a lorgnette. She was one of the hotel guests – Anna had seen her in the lobby the night before! Surely she would help them?

'Help! Help! We're being kidnapped!' she tried to cry out, but muffled by the footman's glove, the only sound she could make was a dreadful groan. The woman simply stood and watched her, a cold expression on her face.

'Better for you if you do not try to fight, Your Highness,' she said. Then to the footman: 'Get the princess out of here quickly, before she causes a fuss.'

Anna heard a door bang open. There were steep dark stairs looming below her – this must be a service staircase that the hotel staff used. The footman bundled her down them as though she were no more than a sack of laundry. Then another door was opening and they were outside in the sunlight, where an enormous black motor car stood waiting for them, the engine already running, and Alex was already being shoved inside.

Sitting watching from the front seat, Anna saw the Count was sitting with Würstchen on his lap, and worse still, in the back, sitting very stiff and upright as Alex was pushed in beside her, was the Countess.

In spite of the hot sun, Anna felt a shock of cold rush over her like icy water. They had found them. She didn't know how they had done it, but somehow the Countess had traced them to Paris and the hotel. She had tricked Lil into leaving them alone in their room; and they had come to take them away. In the doorway, the lady with the lorgnette was watching coolly: she gave the Countess a swift nod, then turned away and went back into the hotel, closing the door securely behind her.

The footman pushed Anna roughly towards the car.

But in one flashing moment, she remembered how she'd fought back against Lil in her bedroom at Wilderstein Castle, and how Lil had looked at her almost admiringly. *I didn't think you had it in you . . . You aren't going to make this easy for me, are you?* No, she was not going to make it easy. Something seemed to awaken inside her that made her want to fight.

Summoning all her strength, she made a desperate effort to claw her way free of the footman's grip. All thoughts of *what princesses ought to do* were quite forgotten. She was no princess now, but a wild creature, kicking and biting and scratching. She clawed for the footman's face and he gave a yell of pain: excited by the commotion, she heard Würstchen let out a few frenzied barks.

'For heaven's sake! Get her in the car! And shut that dog up!' she heard the Countess say. But almost as if he was deliberately disobeying her, Würstchen wriggled free of the Count's arms, and dived into the fray, jumping up and barking, snapping his jaws at the footman.

The footman kicked out at him, and in that moment, Anna had the chance to wriggle free. She darted away, feeling a surge of triumph, but her victory was short-lived.

'Leave her,' came the Countess's harsh voice. 'We have the prince, we don't need her. Get in the car and drive!'

Aiming one final kick at Würstchen, the footman did as she said, leaping into the driver's seat. The door slammed shut behind him, and then the motor car disappeared out in a cloud of smoke, leaving Anna staring horrified after it. She ran behind it into the street, but it had already sped off, flashing by the park until it had disappeared, and Alex had vanished away with it.

CHAPTER TWENTY ONE

The Grand Hotel Continental, Paris

Somewhere high above, Sophie sat in her dressing gown by the window of Miss Blaxland's suite. She was dimly aware that down below, a car was roaring along the street and a dog was barking, but she didn't really hear them. Her whole attention was fixed on Professor Blaxland's letter, which lay in her lap. She'd already read it at least a dozen times, but now, even though she was beginning to feel that she knew it by heart, she looked down at it once more. The first two pages had been written in the flowing handwriting she had recognised immediately from the other papers she had seen on the Professor's desk:

25 May 1911

Dear Sir,

Please find outlined here a brief summary of my research concerning the FRATERNITAS DRACONUM

References to the Fraternitas appear in a number of medieval texts – though these are often ambiguous and contradictory. Two in particular give more detail: one of these describes a great treasure (Magnum thesaurum) said to be in their possession, described as a powerful weapon (Maximum telem). Whilst the nature of this weapon is never specified, it is implied that it holds mysterious – perhaps even legendary – power.

The weapon is supposed to have been hidden for safekeeping after the Fraternitas had dissolved into a number of warring faction. Its location was kept secret, identified only by clues in a series of seven symbolic paintings, which were divided between Fraternitas members. The idea was that future generations would be able to reunite the painting and locate the hidden weapon.

They would then be able to use this weapon to herald in a new Age of the Dragon in which the Fraternitas would reign supreme.

Whilst it is not specified in the text, it seems likely that the paintings mentioned are Benedetto Casselli's 'Dragon Sequence'.

Throughout this and other texts, alchemical symbolism is frequently used in reference to the Fraternitas - which may even have counted some alchemists amongst its members. This is very much in line with the message concealed in the painting: the green lion consuming the sun is thought to represent Mercury, or green vitriol - though arguably it may also represent a process of spiritual transformation.

The image of the black sun also appears

The third page of the letter was very different. Sophie couldn't be sure whether there were pages missing, or whether the Professor had simply broken off part-way through writing his report. Either way, on the final page his handwriting had become wilder and more ragged. There were only a few disjointed sentences, but they seemed to burn off the page with importance.

The weapon is more dangerous than I dreamed You Must prevent them from Possessing it at _all Costs_ I have been unwise and now I fear I May be in danger.

As I write this, the Book containing My research is under lock and Key in my Safe, and Will remain so Until I can place it into Your hands and your hands _ONLy_

As an additional precaution I have Made my notes in Code — For Whatever Happens we _Must_ prevent this information from getting _into_ the hands of the drangons.

The letter was unsigned, but Sophie knew it had been written by Professor Blaxland. She guessed it must have been intended for the Chief himself.

Now, she sat with her chin in her hands, pondering over all that she had discovered. It was beginning to make sense to her now: a picture emerging from all the scattered fragments. The Professor had taken on undercover work for the Secret Service Bureau, and the Chief had given him the task of researching the *Fraternitas Draconum*. He'd written his notes in code, and his reports in invisible ink to prevent anyone intercepting them and stealing the information they contained. It had been a wise precaution: after all, she herself had spent enough time intercepting secret letters on behalf of the Bureau to guess that Ziegler's spies would do the same.

The discovery that the Professor had been researching the *Fraternitas* was surprising enough, but what was even more startling to her was the fact that he had been investigating the dragon paintings by Benedetto Casselli. They were paintings that Sophie knew very well indeed: after all, she and Lil had been the ones who had saved them after they were stolen by the crooked art collector Raymond Lyle, on behalf of the Baron and the *Fraternitas Draconum*. It had later been discovered that one of the paintings concealed a mysterious secret message reading *green lion, black sun. That* was where Sophie had come across the image of the green lion before.

Thinking back on that case, she remembered that the government had planned to continue examining the paintings to see what else they could learn from them. She supposed the Bureau had taken on the enquiries, and the Professor had been given the task of working out what the cryptic message might mean. It sounded as though he had discovered that the message was one of a series of clues to the location of some kind of weapon. She lingered again over his description of it: *a powerful weapon* which held *mysterious, perhaps even legendary, powers.*

The words made her think immediately of her old adversary, the Baron. He'd been desperate to get his hands on the dragon paintings: he'd even murdered her father's old friend, Colonel Fairley, to obtain one of them. Surely he must have known about the secret clues they held? And the phrase *Age of the Dragon* – she knew she'd heard the Baron himself say it, once before.

He had always been fixated on new and powerful weapons, she remembered – naval warships, explosives, rifles, infernal machines – and no doubt aeroplanes had interested him too. He'd been obsessed with trying to kick start a war in Europe, planning to profit from selling weapons to warring nations at high prices. She knew that there was nothing he would have loved more than a mysterious secret weapon that was supposed to have legendary powers.

The Baron was long gone now, of course. But what

if the other members of the *Fraternitas Draconum* had shared his ideas, and were still working to find the secret weapon? Without the clue in the painting – now safely in the possession of the British government – they would be unable to locate it. But if they had somehow learned that the Professor was investigating the paintings, they would have known exactly where to find the information they needed to get their hands on the weapon.

That was why they had broken into the Professor's apartment, Sophie concluded. They had stolen the notebook containing his research; and then they had killed him. Sophie knew enough about the *Fraternitas Draconum* to be certain that they would let nothing stand in the way of what they wanted; certainly they would not think twice about murdering a British agent if it would help them reach their goals.

Now, at last, she began to understand what the grey man and Herr Grün had been doing in the Professor's apartment. She knew the *Fraternitas Draconum* had had dealings with the German Empire in the past – what if they were now working hand in glove with Ziegler? Could they have secured the services of the spymaster and his agents to go after Blaxland and get the information they needed? Might they even have promised the German government the use of this secret weapon, the very idea of which had so horrified the Professor? The thought of it made her heart beat a little faster, especially when she thought of how close she'd come to being caught by Ziegler's spies at *La Lune Bleue* the previous night. Now, she glanced quickly out of the window, down at the park below. It would be such easy work for a professional like the grey man to track 'Miss Blaxland' back to her hotel. For all she knew he could be down there now, lying in wait for her, planning to pounce the very moment they appeared.

As though she was reading her mind, Tilly spoke up from across the room: 'It's not safe here any more. We've got to *go*, Sophie. We can't risk staying here any longer, not now Ziegler's spies know who you really are.' She was already beginning to toss their things – a chemistry book, the blue dress Sophie had worn the previous night, her boy's cap – hastily and untidily into one of the big trunks. 'Besides, we've done it. We've solved the case. We know who killed the Professor, and we know *why*.'

'Yes. It was Ziegler's spies, on behalf of the *Fraternitas Draconum*. Perhaps even the grey man himself – or Herr Grün – or both of them together,' said Sophie. She'd sat up very late the previous evening thinking it all out: now, as she often used to do in the Taylor & Rose office, she got up from her chair, and began walking up and down the room. The motion was calming: it helped her to think.

'I suppose they must have forced the Professor to open the safe and hand over his research, and then they killed him,' said Tilly, even as she bundled more things into the trunk. She gave a little shiver. 'It's horrible.'

Sophie nodded gravely. 'They probably only left this letter behind because it was written in invisible ink. They must have thought it was just blank paper. But perhaps they realised there might be more information in the apartment, and that was why they came back.'

She fell silent again, wondering why C hadn't given her even an inkling that the Professor had been researching the *Fraternitas Draconum*. Of course, it was possible that it hadn't been his only assignment, or that C did not think it had any connection to his death. But he knew *her* own history. He knew that the *Fraternitas Draconum* had been responsible for her parents' death. He no doubt knew too that she and her friends were members of the Loyal Order of Lions, sworn to oppose the *Fraternitas Draconum*. After all, the Chief always knew everything about everybody. But then, she reasoned, perhaps that was exactly why he hadn't told her. He might have guessed she'd find it hard to be cool and logical and cautious if she knew the *Fraternitas* were involved. Anyway, that was the way the Chief worked, wasn't it? Each case kept so carefully neat and separate. In just the same way that he had kept her from knowing anything about Lil's assignment, he'd made sure she did not know any more than she needed to about the Professor's work.

'All the more reason for us to leave – now,' said Tilly briskly. 'If Ziegler's spies have guessed we've got these documents, they might try and take them from us. We need to get them back to London and back to the Chief, so hurry up and get dressed and help me pack,' she went on, rather tartly. 'If we hurry we can catch the twelve noon express from the Gare Du Nord.'

But Sophie ignored her, and paused, gazing out of the window. Her eyes were following the red air-balloon as it cruised across the sky. There was something about it that was bothering her.

'What about the air race . . .?' she murmured aloud.

'The air race?' Tilly stared at her incredulously. 'What are you talking about? I know I said I'd love to see it – and I jolly well would have done too – but it's hardly important now, is it? We have to go and report all this to the Chief!'

'I know that, but I can't stop thinking about *this*.' Sophie jabbed a finger at the the third sheet of paper, with its wild scribbled message. 'If the German spies – Grün and the grey man – have the Professor's notebook, then they'll need to get it back to Ziegler and the *Fraternitas Draconum*, won't they? And once they have it, they'll have all the missing information they need to get hold of this weapon the Professor writes about.'

'If they can crack the Professor's code that is,' Tilly reminded her.

'Yes. But first, they'll need to get it back to Berlin, and I think I know how they'll do it. Grün is one of the pilots in the air race – what if he's planning to use that as cover to fly the Professor's research secretly out of the country?'

232

Thinking of it now, Sophie remembered how the French authorities had searched their trunks on their arrival at the Gare Du Nord, and then thought of Sir Chester saying: *They will allow our pilots to pass across their borders without hold-ups.* The air race would offer the perfect way to smuggle a secret notebook over the border without any risk of discovery.

Tilly groaned, realising what Sophie was getting at. 'But you can't possibly know that,' she protested. 'What if he's already packaged it up and sent it to Ziegler in Berlin by post, or something like that?'

'But I don't believe they'd risk that. The information is too important. Look – I *know* Ziegler's spies. I know how they operate. I've been working to try and intercept their messages and telegrams and parcels for months! They're clever, and using the air race as cover would be a jolly clever way of smuggling some highly important secret information out of the country. It's exactly the kind of thing they would think of.' She took up the newspaper, flicking quickly past the front-page stories about the attempted kidnap of the royal children in Arnovia and the upcoming coronation of George V to find the information about the Aerial Tour. 'The first stage of the tour goes to Liège . . . and yes, *from there they go on into Germany.* I'll bet you *anything* that's how Grün is planning to deliver the Professor's notebook back to Ziegler.'

'But even if that's true, what are you proposing? Going

to the air race and somehow . . . getting the notebook away from Grün?' Tilly crossed her arms and furrowed her brow. 'It sounds jolly well impossible.'

'It would be *difficult*, but not impossible,' Sophie said. 'He'd only need to put it down for a second. I've managed something like that heaps of times before after all – getting parcels or documents away from Ziegler's spies.'

'But Sophie, this time he knows who you are, and so does the grey man. If they see you again, who knows what might happen. These are terribly dangerous people!' Tilly stared at her for a moment and then said rather bluntly: 'If they killed the Professor, you may be sure they wouldn't even hesitate to harm you, especially if this research is as important as we think it must be. Going after them would be idiotic. We have to go back to London. Let's take the Professor's letter back to the Bureau and let the Chief decide what to do next.'

But Sophie shook her head. She knew that Tilly was right, of course. Taking the letter back to the Bureau was the sensible thing, the rational thing, the *careful* thing to do. But this was the *Fraternitas Draconum*, and she could not afford to be careful any longer. She was a member of the Loyal Order of Lions, sworn to do whatever she could to oppose the *Fraternitas Draconum*. These were the people who had murdered her parents – her mother, who had once been an innocent young girl, exploring Paris for the first time.

All of a sudden, she found herself thinking of what her own first visit to Paris could have been like, had her mother been with her. In a rush, she saw them together: sitting outside pavement cafés sharing a strawberry tart, choosing books from the book stalls on the Left Bank, looking at hats in the windows of the *grands magasins* or poring over a map outside Notre Dame. Perhaps they'd sit with sketchbooks on the streets of Montmartre like the English ladies she'd seen, or drink *citron pressé* at the *Café Monique*, or they'd walk in the park below, arm in arm, under the shade of the trees. The *Fraternitas Draconum* had taken all that away from her. She was not about to sit back and let them take the Professor's research. She would not wait for the Chief and risk that information falling into their hands for good.

'If this powerful weapon does exist and the *Fraternitas* get hold of it, who knows what they might do with it,' she said aloud. She picked up her mother's diary from where it lay on the table nearby, and grasped it like a talisman. 'I have to go to the air race. If there's even the smallest chance that I can stop them getting their hands on this weapon, then I simply must try.'

Tilly let out a long breath, and then let the trunk fall shut. 'Very well,' she said, getting to her feet. 'I must say, I think it's completely mad. But if you're doing this, I'm jolly well coming to help you.'

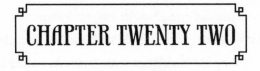

CHAPTER TWENTY TWO

The Grand Hotel Continental, Paris

Anna threw herself down on the grass. Tears rushed into her eyes, hot and terrible.

She'd longed to come down and explore the park, but now she was here, the light and brightness was overwhelming. From close by came the jingling, creaky old tune of the carousel, whirling on and on in a dizzying circle, pink-and-white as an iced birthday cake. Children in sailor hats sat aboard the painted horses, their faces sticky with sweets. The air smelled of box hedge and cut grass, and the sun beat down on her head, and the music went on, a relentless jangle.

She'd run out, through the rush and rumble of the traffic, and straight into the park, desperately trying to catch up with the motor car that had sped away in a cloud of smoke, with Alex inside it. She'd run and run, until her sides ached, and her feet were skidding on the hot gravel. Spots had burned before her eyes and one or two elegant

Parisian ladies had turned to look at her disapprovingly, and she'd fallen back onto the grass, defeated. She was too late. The car was gone, and Alex was gone with it.

What was she to do? They'd come so far – escaping the castle, walking through the mountains, travelling halfway across Europe – and it had all been for nothing. It was all her own fault for opening the door – Lil had told her not to – how could she have been so stupid? Now the Countess had Alex and who knew what she planned to do with him? The terrible word whispered in her ears again, soft and slithering, twining itself close about her. *Assassination*. She let out a ghastly sob.

Just then she felt something damp and cold pushing against her hand, and then a kind of snuffling sound. Surprised, she pushed back her plaits and looked down. Something was nosing against her – something small and furry and very familiar.

'*Würstchen!*' she gasped. The dog gave a short yap, as though he was answering her. 'Würstchen, you followed me!'

The feeling of the dog's silky fur was very comforting as she picked him up and cuddled him close, trying to blink away the hot tears. At last, she found the strength to scramble to her feet. She knew she must not sit here any longer: she had to let them all know what had happened.

As she approached the hotel, she saw Lil running towards her, looking around wildly. 'Anna . . . Anna . . . oh, thank goodness!' she burst out. 'Where's Alex?'

237

Anna hardly knew how to begin to tell her, but in painful gasps, somehow she managed to relate the story. As she listened, Lil's face turned deathly white. 'Are you sure? Are you absolutely sure?' she kept saying. 'Did you see what kind of car? Did you see the number plate? Who was the woman who helped them?' The questions came so fast that Anna could hardly answer her, and then there was a horrible silence in which she said nothing at all.

Anna clung to her arm. 'I'm sorry,' she whispered.

Lil looked up at her sharply. 'This isn't your fault, Anna. If it's anyone's at all, it's mine.' But all at once, she seemed to be burning with a new energy. 'Come inside. We have to get a message to your grandfather.' She pulled Anna into a quick, fierce hug. 'Buck up. I'm not giving up on Alex. We can still rescue him, but we'll have to move fast.'

They rushed back into the hotel, where Lil made a dash for the reception desk, pushing in front of a fashionable young gentlemen who gave an outraged *tut* at her bad manners. But Lil did not give him so much as a second glance. 'Get me Monsieur Martin, the hotel manager, at once,' she demanded of the man behind the desk. 'It's extremely urgent!'

A moment later, the manager appeared, and then things began to happen. They were rushed into an office: M. Martin sent a bell-boy to summon Captain Forsyth, but he was not in his room. 'Probably off enjoying the bright lights of Paris again,' muttered Lil crossly. 'Blow! Why is he never here when I need him?'

But she didn't really seem to need the captain at all, Anna thought, as Lil made several rapid telephone calls, her face growing graver and graver.

'That's right . . . No, we don't know for sure . . . M. Martin has identified the woman who helped them. We think it was the Countess von Stubenberg – yes, she's a distant relation of the Countess's. She was staying here at the hotel – she could have alerted them . . .'

A moment later she had set down the receiver. 'I've got an idea,' she said to Anna, who had been sitting nervously watching and listening, holding Würstchen in her lap. 'I think the Count and Countess must have been somewhere nearby – watching and waiting for the right moment to sweep in and grab Alex. If Würstchen was with them, there's an outside chance that he might be able to lead us to their hideout.' She bent down to the little dog. 'Now you listen, Würstchen,' she said sternly. 'Can you take us to the Count and Countess, and Alex? Because if you do, I promise you can jolly well have bacon for breakfast for the rest of your life.'

She wanted Anna to stay behind at the hotel while she and M. Martin went out with Würstchen, but Anna had no intention of being left behind, and Lil did not take much persuading. 'I don't feel I want to let you out of my sight ever again,' she declared. 'But stay close beside me, just in case.'

Anna did as she was told, her heart thumping. Not that she felt that she herself was in any danger. The Countess had made it perfectly clear that she was of no importance to them. After all, princesses could not inherit the Arnovian throne – Alex was the only one who mattered.

Just the same, she found herself gripping Lil's arm rather tightly as the two of them walked down the street with M. Martin. Allowed to make his own way, Würstchen trotted briskly forward, past the park, around a corner. He stopped for a moment to sniff a lamp-post, but then went on, down another street and then into a narrow cobbled alleyway between two tall houses. Anna's heart began to pound harder, but they soon saw that there was nothing there but an old shed. Würstchen raced towards it, barking happily, but Anna felt confused – surely this dark back alley was not somewhere that the Countess would ever go?

Lil was peering through the dusty window of the little shed. 'I say, there's a motor in there!' she exclaimed. 'Anna, is that the car you saw?'

Anna stood on tiptoes to look. Behind the dirty windows, she could see an enormous black motor car. 'That's it!' she gasped. 'I'm sure of it!'

Lil darted to the door and shook it. It was locked fast, but the wood was old and rotten.

'Let me fetch some of the men from the hotel – they will

break it down,' said the hotel manager. But Lil shook her head. 'There's no time for that. Stand back, both of you.'

To Anna's amazement, she hiked up the hem of her skirt and gave the door a swift firm kick, just below the handle. The wood splintered at once, and the door gave way.

M. Martin looked astonished, and perhaps a little shocked, but Lil was already inside the shed. Anna scrambled quickly after her, half hoping that they'd find Alex shut inside, a prisoner waiting to be rescued. But instead there was only darkness. The motor car was empty.

'They must have changed cars to prevent anyone recognising them,' said Lil, examining the vehicle. 'Well, it's a clue at least. We can find out who this shed belongs to, and we can trace the car registration number. I say – what's that?'

Anna followed her gaze. On the back seat of the car was something small and white. It was a handkerchief and Anna recognised it at once. She saw her own embroidery – the slightly wonky crest of the Royal House of Wilderstein. 'It's Alex's!' she cried out at once.

'Look – there is something else here,' said M. Martin, who had picked his way after them, careful not to dirty his immaculate trousers. In a patch of dust at the back of the car, a message had been written as though with a fingertip. They all stared at it: the shape of a letter T followed by six numbers.

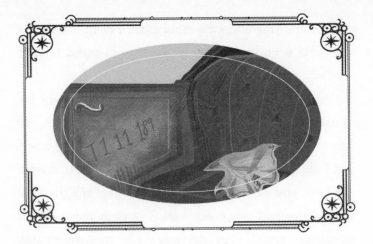

'It must be a message!' exclaimed Lil. 'Oh, well done, Alex! He's left us a clue to follow!'

'But what does it mean?' murmured M. Martin.

'He must have thought it would help us find him,' said Lil. 'Could it be a clue to where they were taking him? A house number . . . or a car registration?'

'Or I wonder – could it be perhaps a telephone number?' suggested M. Martin tentatively.

Lil clapped her hands together in excitement. 'Of course! T must stand for telephone! Gosh, it must be a number that he overheard while he was in the car. Perhaps if we find out who it belongs to, we could learn who is helping them, or even where Alex is being hidden! M. Martin, you're a genius. Do you have a telephone directory? Can you find me a car, and spare one of your men to drive me there?'

'I will come with you myself,' said the hotel manager,

carefully copying down the number on a piece of paper he produced from his pocket, before they hastened back to the hotel.

'Anna, you really *must* stay here this time,' said Lil, whilst M. Martin swiftly identified the address and summoned a motor. 'I don't want to leave you by yourself, but I certainly won't risk putting you in any more danger. Go back up to the suite with Würstchen. Lock the door behind you and don't let *anyone* in except me – anyone at all, no matter what happens – do you understand? We're leaving a message at the reception desk for Captain Forsyth.'

'But –' Anna began hopelessly. The thought of being left alone to worry in the hotel room while Lil raced across Paris in a desperate attempt to rescue Alex was almost more than she could bear. Lil paused and gave Anna another quick hug. 'I'll do everything I can to find him – I promise.'

And then she was gone, and Anna was alone again in the window of the suite, still holding the paper with the number on it. She watched Lil and M. Martin drive away at top speed in a motor. She watched two other young ladies, who also seemed to be in a terrific hurry, come out of the hotel and climb into another. She watched carriages and omnibuses going up and down the street, just as if nothing unusual was happening; she watched people promenading arm in arm; and children going to play in the park, carrying balls or hoops or toy boats to sail on the lake. She watched a black crow on a roof opposite, and she thought again of Alex's wild eyes. She looked down again at the paper she was holding, scribbled with his message in M. Martin's French handwriting:

Anna had not used a telephone very often, but there had been one in the Count and Countess's private sitting room, and sometimes they had been allowed to put through a call to Grandfather in Elffburg. If this was a telephone number, it was a funny-looking one, she thought. There was something not quite right about the spaces in between the numbers. Really it wasn't quite like a telephone number at all, but more like something else she'd seen recently, back in the schoolroom at Wilderstein Castle. She searched her memory: black-and-white print danced before her eyes; she heard Alex's voice. The velvet cloak with its tarnished paper stars was lying on the arm of the chair beside her: she reached out and slid the edge of it between her fingers thoughtfully.

It wasn't a telephone number, she realised. It was a *line reference*. Alex didn't mean *111189*. He meant *I.II.189*. The line reference for a Shakespeare play, and surely *T* could only mean *The Tempest*, the play they'd performed together before they left Wilderstein Castle. *The Tempest*: Act I, Scene II, Line 189. Anna's thoughts raced: it was the scene they'd acted out together: Alex as Prospero the magician and exiled Duke of Milan had summoned Anna as Ariel, his servant. Line 189: *Approach, my Ariel, come.*

Even as she murmured the line aloud, she saw the bright red air-balloon moving slowly across the blue sky printed with the words *GRAND AERIAL TOUR OF EUROPE*.

She gasped aloud. Lil had been wrong, she saw at once.

Alex's message had not been a telephone number at all. He'd been trying to send them somewhere else altogether – to the *Aerial Tour*. But if his kidnappers were taking Alex to an airfield then they could be planning to fly him out of the country, she realised in a sickening flash. And meanwhile Lil was on a wild goose chase, following up a telephone number that had nothing to do with anything; Captain Forsyth was nowhere to be found; and Anna was here all alone, and time was running out.

Her knees felt weak. There was nothing she could do, she thought desperately. There was no way that she could help. She was quite alone, and Lil had told her to stay in the hotel suite, and under no circumstances to open the door to anyone, no matter what. But then she saw the red balloon soaring overhead, and she thought of Alex's message: *Ariel, come*. It wasn't just a clue to the Aerial Tour – it was an instruction to herself. *Come*, Alex had said. He'd left a message asking for *her* help. She was his sister; she would not let him down.

She turned away from the window. The books M. Martin had left for them were still lying on the table: the title *The Bravest Girl in the Fifth* seemed to sing out to her. She had to try, she thought, growing more and more resolute by the minute. If she could even find out where Alex was, or learn who the Countess was working with, or where they planned to take him! If she could even get some of the *evidence* that she remembered Lil had said

246

was so important! That gave her an idea, and she sprinted through into Lil's room, Würstchen following at her heels, obviously considering this part of a very good game. The attaché case was lying unlocked on a table and she grabbed it, pausing only to scribble a quick message to Lil, which she left lying on the bed. Swiftly, she fastened her pocket handkerchief to Würstchen's collar as a makeshift lead.

'Hang on, Alex,' she murmured under her breath. 'We're coming!'

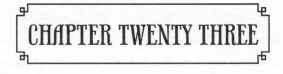

CHAPTER TWENTY THREE

Issy-les-Moulineux Airfield, Paris

'Ladies and gentlemen, we are delighted to welcome you to the first Grand Aerial Tour of Europe! *Mesdames et messieurs, bienvenus . . .*'

The music rang in Anna's ears, growing louder and louder, as she pushed her way with difficulty through the crowds. She'd never been among so many people in her life before: even on her visits to Elffburg, she'd been standing apart, waving down at the crowd from the palace balcony or the window of the royal carriage. Now she was amongst them, they were no longer a pleasant blur of smiling faces, but a jostling mass of elbows and shoulders. People jumped out at her from the crowd for a moment – a group of aviation enthusiasts with field-glasses and notebooks; a photographer wielding a large camera and tripod; an exasperated nursemaid dragging a small wailing child by the hand. There was a festival atmosphere in the air: red, white and blue bunting was strung up everywhere; a band

248

was playing a jolly tune; the planes themselves had been gaily decorated with their nations' flags; and a great banner reading *GRAND AERIAL TOUR* could be seen fluttering high against the blue sky.

It seemed the last place that she could imagine the Countess would take Alex, and as she staggered through the throng, she began to wonder if she'd got it all horribly wrong, but just the same she fought onwards. She couldn't give up now.

The cab journey had been difficult enough: she'd barely been able to understand the driver's accent, and she hadn't even been sure exactly where the air race was taking place. Thankfully he'd seemed to understand when she said she wanted to see the launch of the air race, and had brought her straight here, and now that she saw the crowds, she understood why. Clearly half of Paris had turned out to see the planes set off.

She was very glad that she'd brought Lil's attaché case with her. She'd forgotten all about money to pay for the cab – after all, she'd never had to carry money before – but just in time she'd remembered the roll of bank notes she'd seen inside. She had hardly known how to pay, fumbling with the notes, but the cab driver had picked out what he wanted, and now – here she was.

She'd had to steel herself to plunge into the crowd, picking up Würstchen and tucking him under her arm, so he wouldn't be trampled underfoot. Now, a wave of panic rushed over her. The airfield seemed so vast and hot and crowded, and if Alex was here, then he could be almost anywhere. A crowd of schoolboys pushed past, almost knocking her over, and she felt suddenly very lost and frightened. Where should she go? What should she do?

Strangely it was the Countess's voice that suddenly came to her, though this time her words were rather different. *A princess should not be afraid*, Anna thought to herself. *You are an ambassador for your country wherever you go. You must never forget that.* Then Grandfather saying: *Look after each other.*

Anna pulled herself taller. She remembered the green-and-white flag of Arnovia, flying from the turrets of Wilderstein Castle, and the snowy peaks of the mountains in the distance. She thought of the oil paintings of her ancestors, and the Countess's stories about the brave Arnovian kings of the past. This was not the time to be weak and helpless. This was the time to fight.

She could see no Arnovian flags here, but there was a German flag flying high above one of the sheds, beside an open expanse where an aeroplane was already being pushed across the grass. The Countess had been working with the Germans, hadn't she? Filling herself with thoughts of King Otto the Wise, leading his people bravely into battle, Anna tucked Würstchen more securely under her arm, and set out towards it.

Sophie made her way swiftly through the crowds, Tilly

close behind her. They'd left the hotel without any trouble, but she felt nervous and keyed up, looking all around her. The whole airfield was alive with people waiting to see the start of the race, and they had to swerve to avoid a group of rowdy boys, and then again to avoid colliding with a girl carrying a little dog. Thank heavens she'd left the fancy gowns and hats behind in the hotel suite, choosing instead a simple blouse and skirt in which she could move quickly and easily. She was not Miss Celia Blaxland any longer. Her cover might be blown, but at least now she could be herself again – Sophie Taylor, detective and secret agent.

Now, she took in the grassy field where the aircraft would take off, and beside it a row of hangars where the final preparations to the machines were being made. Standing tall above everything was a platform for the race officials, strung with coloured flags and bedecked with a banner bearing the words *GRAND AERIAL TOUR*. She could just make out the figure of Sir Chester Norton alongside several other gentlemen, surveying the field below and consulting their pocket watches, and not far away from them, the ever-present Roberta Russell, with notebook ready in hand. Sophie ducked quickly away behind a refreshment tent before Miss Russell's sharp eyes picked her out in the crowd.

The race was clearly about to begin: the first plane was already being wheeled out on to the flat expanse of grass by a team of mechanics in greasy overalls. It was the Italian plane, Sophie saw, recognising the flag fluttering from its tail. From inside, Signor Rossi grinned and waved at the crowd. It seemed quite impossible that such a frail, spidery contraption of wires and struts could go anywhere, never mind up into the sky. Its wings looked impossibly fragile, made only of linen fabric stretched over a delicate wooden frame. And yet, all at once, it was roaring into life – the propeller was spinning – and the pilot was waving – and the men were pushing it forward – and it was away, teetering slowly but surely over the ground and then rising up into the air, the flag flickering wildly. The watching crowd burst into wild applause, and to delight them still more, Rossi performed a bold swoop towards the race officials, turning in the nick of time to gasps from the crowds, and then sailed down over the spectators, low enough to make the plumes on the ladies' hats flutter. The crowd cheered louder, waving flags and handkerchiefs joyfully in the air.

But Sophie was staring through a gap in the crowds to someone else, someone who was standing at the door of one of the hangars. It was the grey man – Ziegler's spy. His grey jacket and grey hat were gone now; and so was his smart evening attire. He was wearing mechanic's overalls, wiping his hands on a dirty rag. Dr Muller's vague, polite expression was gone too: now the man's gaze was piercing as he looked disdainfully over the crowds gathering to watch the planes take off, the band playing, the striped refreshment tents serving ices and lemonade.

'I'm going after him – he might have the notebook. You stay here and watch for Herr Grün and his plane,' she said to Tilly, but before she had been able to take a step towards the grey man, she heard a voice calling out: 'Miss Blaxland! Good day to you, Miss Blaxland!'

Dr Bernard was making his way towards them through the crowd, dressed in a straw boater and neat white flannels, his moustache more beautifully waxed than ever. 'What happened to you last night? You disappeared! I was terribly worried! Miss Russell said –' he began and then faltered, looking at her, clearly confused.

Sophie realised how very different she must look from the girl he had dined with the previous night, in her ordinary blouse and skirt, her hair twisted up into a simple knot. But there was no time to explain it now. The grey man was already disappearing down the side of the hangar. She couldn't lose him: she *must* follow.

'I'm sorry, Dr Bernard, but I have to go,' she said, and before he could reply, she sprinted away through the crowds.

Anna watched from the shadows as the mechanic disappeared from the doorway, down the side of the German hangar. This was her chance: now, she dared to creep in through the open door, into the big lofty space full of rattling sounds, the air thick with a pungent chemical smell of engine oil and smoke.

Another mechanic caught sight of her and yelled out in German: 'Hey, you – no children here! Get out!'

She darted quickly out of his sightline. She was shaking – no one had ever yelled at her like that in her life – but she did not leave the hangar. She had to find out if Alex was here. Peering from behind an oil drum, she saw that the plane seemed to be ready: the pilot was climbing up into the front seat.

'It's time! Open the doors!'

Anna heard the music outside swell, and the crowd cheering. One of the mechanics pulled the big door wide, letting light flood in. The others were helping to push the aeroplane out into the field: seated inside it, the pilot smiled and waved to the crowd. Anna craned her neck to look, but there was no passenger. The plane had only one seat. The German pilot was alone, and there was no sign of Alex anywhere.

Sophie darted down the narrow passage between two of the big hangars. She'd been certain she saw the grey man go this way, but it soon turned out to be a dead end, leading her only to a space behind the hangars where a few empty crates had been stacked. She paused to catch her breath, and then a voice spoke:

'You shouldn't have come here.'

He appeared as if out of nowhere, standing before her, blocking her exit. She stepped back, the sudden movement knocking a couple of crates to the ground. It was the grey man, and he was holding a heavy spanner in his hand.

'Oh, my goodness, I'm so terribly sorry! I just wanted to have a closer look at the aeroplanes. I think I must have taken a wrong turn,' she fluttered, opening her eyes very wide as though she was no more than an innocent young lady who had wandered mistakenly away from the crowds.

But the grey man only laughed. 'That won't work on me now. You may have taken me in once but not again. *Once bitten, twice shy* – that's the English expression, isn't it?' He took a step forward. 'I know who you are. I know who you work for. I know you're the one who tricked me out of those code books at Victoria station.'

Sophie glanced around her, desperately hoping for a way out, or at least a weapon. She might know how to throw a punch, but she knew she would be no match for the grey man – at least not with that big spanner held menacingly in his hand.

'Those code books were the property of the British Navy!' she flashed back, stalling for time. 'And they aren't the only *secret codes* you and your bosses are trying to get your hands on, are they? I saw you and Grün snooping at Blaxland's apartment. I know what you were looking for.'

The grey man stepped back and stared at her for a moment. 'That was *you*?' he demanded. Then he gave a short laugh. 'So! The British were behind it after all. Well, Blaxland must have known he was taking a risk, working for the other side. But I cannot believe your Bureau would send the likes of *you* to kill him.'

It was Sophie's turn to stare. 'Me? Kill the Professor?' she asked in astonishment. 'What do you mean? *You* were the ones who killed him. You murdered him – and took his research notebook – and now your pilot is going to fly it out of the country to hand it over to the *Fraternitas Draconum*. I know that's who you and Ziegler are working for.'

'The *Fraternitas*?' the grey man spat out in disgust. 'We do not work for the *Fraternitas*! What ridiculous new scheme is this? As if it was not enough that your people are trying to smear us by associating us with this preposterous kidnap plot, now you say we are working for the dragons too? *We* do not have the notebook. It was not *us* who killed the Professor. Your own people killed him, no doubt because you learned that he was also working for *us*.'

Sophie's eyes widened. So the Professor had been working for Ziegler! She heard Mme Delacroix's voice again: *It was all because of the money . . . It got him mixed up with the wrong people . . . He was working for them both.* Suddenly in a rush of understanding, it all made sense – the Professor's debts, the money left behind in the cash-box at his apartment. The Professor's love of gambling had got him into financial trouble. His work for the Secret Service Bureau hadn't been enough to cover his debts, so he'd offered his special skills to the German secret service too.

Perhaps he'd even been passing on British secrets to Ziegler behind the Bureau's back! She knew the Germans would pay him well for that, which explained the stack of cash in his apartment. But if all that was true, then why would Ziegler have sent his men to kill him? *Because he hadn't*, she realised with a gasp.

'You were at the apartment to *investigate the Professor's murder*,' she said.

'Of course we were! And who did we find at the scene of the crime – *you*. No doubt covering your own agency's tracks.'

'No,' said Sophie incredulously. 'No. I was doing exactly the same thing that you were. I was investigating his murder too. *We were both there for the same reason*. The Bureau had no idea that he was also working for you. *It wasn't us who killed him.*'

'This is ridiculous!' the grey man snapped back. 'If it wasn't the Bureau who killed him and took his secret notes, then who was it?'

'It was the *Fraternitas Draconum*,' said Sophie. Dimly she was aware of the whir of an engine and the roar of the crowd, as the next plane made ready for take-off. She could see it quite clearly now. Professor Blaxland might have been working for Ziegler, but the Germans had no more to do with his murder than the British Secret Service Bureau. It was the *Fraternitas Draconum* who had murdered the Professor, knowing he had the information they wanted so badly. Just as they'd murdered her father and her mother, all those years ago.

Above them, the announcer's voice boomed out: 'Good luck to Herr Grün of Berlin! *Bonne chance, Herr Grün!*' She could hear the sound of the German plane rising into the air, but that did not matter now – she knew that Grün did not have the Professor's precious notebook.

The grey man was frowning at her, still holding the spanner. 'The *Fraternitas* . . .' he repeated, almost disbelievingly. 'Could it be?' He stared at Sophie. 'We already suspect they are behind the Arnovian kidnap plot – the ones who are pulling the strings . . . but this too?' He muttered a few angry words in German under his breath.

Now it was Sophie's turn to stare. The *Fraternitas Draconum* were behind the attempted kidnap of the Arnovian prince and princess that had been all over the newspapers? But of course – that made sense too – it was so like one of the Baron's schemes to stir up trouble in Europe!

'You believe they are the ones who have the Professor's research?' demanded the grey man.

'I know they are – they must be,' said Sophie. She had no idea whether the grey man knew anything about the Professor's research – about the dragon paintings and the secret papers and the hidden powerful weapon – but she knew from his furious face that he was no friend to the *Fraternitas Draconum*.

258

As they stood there, the announcer's voice rang out again: 'The next pilot to take off . . . Oh . . . er . . . I see here we have a new, late entry to the race, representing the nation of Arnovia. Please welcome to the field Arnovian pilot Herr Wild!'

There was another thunder of applause from the crowd, but the grey man stiffened. 'What? An Arnovian plane?' he exclaimed.

Their eyes met and with a jolt, Sophie knew exactly what he was thinking. As one they turned, and then they were both running across the grass.

CHAPTER TWENTY FOUR

Issy-les-Moulineux Airfield, Paris

'What an almighty shambles,' muttered Forsyth as he and Lil pushed their way through the crowds. 'How on earth are we going to tell the Chief that not only have we lost the Crown Prince, now we've lost the princess as well?' His voice rose to a fretful note. 'I was in line for a promotion, you know. I was going to be made Major! I might have got a *medal* out of this. All that's jolly well out of the window now.'

'Shut up about your stupid promotion!' hissed Lil. 'If you hadn't gone off, the children would never have been left on their own in the first place!' She felt furious with him, and with herself too, for leaving Anna alone, for being such an idiot as to mistake Alex's message for a telephone number, for letting any of this happen. 'We have to find them! Anna's here all by herself, and if she's right, then Alex is here too. We've still got a chance to save him! Come *on*, Forsyth.'

But even as she dragged him forward, there was the roar

of a plane taking to the air. Lil could see the German flag fluttering from its tail: '*No!*' she cried out, imagining the worst and Alex already aboard.

But Forsyth had grabbed for his field-glasses. 'It's all right,' he said. 'It's a one-man plane. There's only the pilot aboard. No room for a passenger.' He shook his head. 'Look, I'm certain the princess got this wrong – all that gibberish about Shakespeare plays! The prince is only eleven, for heaven's sake! He'd never have been able to come up with something like that.'

'You don't know Alex,' Lil flashed back. 'He's smart. He's got an imagination. Being *eleven* hasn't got a thing to do with it. In any case, Anna must be here somewhere. Anna! *Anna!*' she called out desperately.

'*Ssshhhh!*' Forsyth hushed her at once. 'You know the kidnap attempt has been in the newspapers. We have to stop them finding out about the prince being missing, and there are journalists everywhere! Why, there's the frightful Russell girl who writes for *The Daily Picture* up there. We have to be *discreet!*'

'I don't care a bit about newspapers, or about being discreet,' answered Lil hotly. 'All I care about is that Anna and Alex are safe.'

Before she could say any more, the announcer's voice boomed out again: 'We have a new, late entry to the race, representing the nation of Arnovia. Please welcome pilot Herr Wild!'

'An *Arnovian* plane?' murmured Forsyth. 'And who the devil is Herr Wild?'

But Lil had already grabbed the field-glasses out of his hand and was training them on the plane bumping out of the hangar and on to the field. The taller man in the front seat in overalls, cap and goggles could have been almost anyone, but the smaller figure behind him, even disguised in a muffler and a big leather flying coat, was someone she would recognised anywhere.

'Forsyth – *look!*' she exclaimed. 'I can see him! It's Alex!'

Anna watched as the German plane roared up into the sky, becoming smaller and smaller until it disappeared altogether. She felt desperate. There was no passenger – Alex had not been on the German plane. Had she got the clue completely wrong? What if Alex wasn't here after all?

Tears blurred her eyes again but she wiped them roughly away with her sleeve. She couldn't cry now. She had to *think*. What would Beryl or Mops or Jean, or any of those Heroines of the Fourth Form have done now?

Würstchen was yapping and struggling in her arms. '*Shush!*' she scolded him sharply, even as she tried to work out what to do next. But he wriggled so much that she had to set him down on the floor, at which point he began to tug on his makeshift lead, pulling her in the direction of another one of the hangars, giving a volley of little excited yaps.

As he jerked her towards the door, she realised why. The word *Arnovia* had been scribbled on a piece of paper and pinned to the hangar door; and as she came closer, she realised she could hear someone speaking inside:

'Make sure His Highness stays strapped in tightly. I don't trust him not to struggle.'

She dared to creep forward into the hangar. From behind a pile of crates she stared as the Countess stood instructing the pilot in a sharp voice. She was dressed in an elaborate gown and grand plumed hat that were quite unsuitable for an airfield, and even from here, Anna could see that her face was made up with its usual heavy rouge and powder.

'Hurry up!' she was snapping at the pilot. 'You're next. Are you certain you really know how to operate this machine?'

There was something about the way she was speaking to him that seemed familiar, and with a sudden shock of recognition, Anna realised that the man clambering into the cockpit was not merely a pilot – he was the Count. His shiny domed head had been hidden by a leather flying cap, and goggles covered most of his face, obscuring his bristling moustache, but now he pushed them aside to reply. 'Of course I do!'

'Well you'd better take care. This is our only chance to get the prince out of France,' retorted the Countess sharply. As she spoke, she stepped back, and then Anna

263

saw that beyond her, in the passenger seat of the plane, was Alex. He was dressed in a big leather coat and cap, with goggles and a muffler wound tightly over his face, and he was struggling to free himself.

'Stop that!' demanded the Countess. 'You'll only endanger yourself.'

Anna's heart seemed to stop still. Alex was there, only a few feet away from her, but what was she supposed to do? She knew that one girl and one little dog had no chance at rescuing him – not with the Count and Countess there.

Evidence, she thought desperately, grabbing for the attaché case with shaking fingers. If she could do nothing else she could get *evidence*. Her hands fumbled clumsily for the watch-camera, and she tried to steady them. Remembering what she had seen Lil do, she carefully positioned it, and then pressed the button just as the Countess handed something to the Count. It looked like an exercise book: as Anna watched, he tucked it carefully inside his flying jacket.

'Be careful with it!' she said strictly. 'They care even more about *that* than they do about the prince. We mustn't let them down now, Rudolf. Things are bad enough as it is. This is our last chance and heaven knows we don't want *them* as our enemies. So be sure you take care.'

With shaking fingers, Anna dropped the camera carefully into her skirt pocket. The hangar door was opening: the Countess was saying goodbye. 'I'll see you at the *rendez-vous*, just as we agreed. Good luck.'

She stepped back from the plane, and the mechanics stepped forward, ready to roll it outside. From her corner, Anna could clearly see Alex struggling in the back seat and shouting something, but whatever it was, it was quite lost in the loud roaring of the crowd. The Countess gave a little nod of satisfaction. Anna could have screamed aloud.

'Here's Herr Wild, coming on to the field now,' came the announcer's voice, amplified by the loud-hailer so it could be heard even above the roar of the crowd. 'Herr Wild will be flying this fine aeroplane, a new top-of-the-line two-seater Farman . . .'

But there was something strange happening, and a little murmur of surprise flickered through the crowd. Across the airfield from where Anna stood, two people had detached themselves from the crowd and vaulted the fence. One was an athletic young man, and with him was a tall young woman with dark hair. They were racing across the field towards the plane, as though determined to reach it before take-off.

'What's happening?' murmured the people in the crowd. 'Is something wrong?'

Up on the platform, Miss Russell shaded her eyes with her hands to get a better look.

'Can the persons on the field please return behind the fence immediately!' called out the announcer. 'Members of

265

the public are not permitted on the airfield. Please go back at once or you will be removed by the police!'

But Lil had no intention of going back. She knew that Alex was in that plane, and she was going to do whatever it took to save him. She lengthened her stride, pulling ahead of Forsyth, and as she did so, she saw to her amazement that across the airfield, two other figures had broken away from the crowd and were running towards the plane, like their own mirror images. It was a tall man in overalls, and a little way behind him, the smaller figure of a girl with fair hair. For a moment, she looked almost like . . . but of course, it couldn't possibly be . . .

Forsyth was close behind her; they were gaining on the plane now; Lil could hear the announcer shouting at them even more furiously. She *must* catch the plane, she had promised Anna, she *must*.

She put on an extra burst of speed, and so did the girl running towards her. It *couldn't* be . . . it simply *couldn't* be . . . but then, unbelievably it was – it *was*!

'*SOPHIE!*' she screamed in a voice that didn't even sound like her own.

Sophie's face turned towards her – shocked and amazed, and then for one brief second, filled with delight. For a second they stared, unable to believe their eyes, and then they yelled to each other, at the very same moment: '*We have to stop the plane!*'

*

The crowd were pointing and exclaiming. Up on the platform, Sir Chester Norton was speaking in a low, rapid voice to the race official; beside him, another official had wrested the loud-hailer away from the announcer. 'Clear the airfield!' he yelled. 'Clear the airfield!'

Several policemen were running after them towards the plane. 'Get back!' they cried. 'It isn't safe!'

Miss Russell was staring more closely at the figure of the fair-haired young woman. 'Good gracious – it's *her* again,' she exclaimed, reaching quickly for her notebook. 'But whatever are they *doing*?'

Everyone on the platform was so busy staring down at what was happening on the airfield below them that not one of them noticed the figure of a girl with plaits, with a small dog under one arm and a battered attaché case in the other, who had come racing up the steps of the platform. Not a single one of the race officials even glanced in her direction, as she scrambled up to where they stood, looking down at where Lil and Captain Forsyth, and two others that Anna did not recognise, were running towards the plane. But the plane was getting away from them, Anna saw – bumping over the grass, carrying Alex away with it. The police, the officials, none of them understood what was happening. It was going to be too late.

She saw the backs of the race officials, all peering down into the field below, and then beside them, abandoned on the ground now, the loud-hailer. As she grabbed for it, the young lady with the notebook turned sharply towards her, but Anna already had the loud-hailer in her hand.

For a moment she was not sure if she could do it, but then everything the Countess had ever said to her came back in a rush. *Princesses should not raise their voices. A princess should be seen and not heard.*

Not any more, thought Anna.

She raised the loud-hailer and then shouted through it as loudly as she could: 'ARRETEZ! STOP! STOP THE PLANE!'

CHAPTER TWENTY FIVE

Issy-les-Moulineux Airfield, Paris

Sophie heard the voice scream out from somewhere above their heads. She heard the startled exclamations of the crowd, the yells of the mechanics. Her breath caught in her throat as she and Lil fell into step beside each other, running towards the plane. It was still moving, but the pilot was looking up at the platform, confused by what was happening. For the briefest of moments, the plane began to slow. His hesitation was all they needed: together they lunged forward and grabbed for the plane's tail; together they braced their feet on the grass; together they felt their muscles strain. The plane rocked to a standstill.

The pilot yelled out something that Sophie could not hear, and tried to start the engine again. His mechanics were already running towards them, but then the grey man was there, shielding them, and blocking the mechanics way. One aimed a blow at him, but he dodged smartly and in one fluid motion, tripped the man, who fell hard on to the grass.

*

Lil didn't know the man who was helping them, but this didn't really seem the time to begin asking questions. Besides, every ounce of her energy was focused on reaching Alex before the plane could begin moving again. 'We have to get him out!' she yelled to Sophie, pointing to the passenger seat, where Alex was even now fighting to free himself. 'He's the Crown Prince of Arnovia. They're trying to kidnap him!'

Sophie's eyes widened, but she seemed to understand at once. In spite of everything that was happening, Lil felt a sudden surge of joy that she was here. It seemed somehow *right* to be dashing round to the side of the plane together; *right* that Sophie was with her as she leaned forward to pull Alex free.

'Lil! Look out!' Sophie screamed, and Lil saw that a mechanic was rushing towards her, swinging a crowbar. She dodged him, and then Forsyth was there, grappling with him, wrestling the weapon away.

Together, she and Sophie managed to rip off the straps that were holding Alex into the passenger seat: a moment later, he was wriggling free, and then she had pulled him safely down on to the grass.

The grey man was still grappling with the mechanics: 'Get the notebook!' Sophie heard him shout. She made a dive towards the pilot, but he pushed her roughly away, screaming something angry in German, and she fell back on to the grass. The engine let out a howl as one of the mechanics managed to begin pushing the plane forward again, the propellers starting to spin. Sophie struggled to her feet; the grey man was hurling himself forward too; but she knew that it was already too late. The plane was bumping across the grass again, moving wildly and unsteadily now but, almost before they could reach it, it was in the air.

The plane wobbled low over the heads of the crowd, dipping and shaking, and for a moment Sophie thought that there was going to be a terrible accident. But then the nose of the plane lifted and it roared higher into the sky, dragging away a tangled length of red-and-blue bunting with it – up, up and away.

'Ladies and gentlemen, *mesdames et messieurs*,' came the flustered voice of the announcer. 'As you can see there has been a slight . . . er . . . technical hitch with the departure of Herr Wild. We apologise for the disturbance. However he is now in the air and we wish him good luck! There will now be a short intermission and then next to depart will be Captain Nakamura of Japan!'

The music started up again in a hurry. All at once, the airfield seemed to be thronged with people: angry officials hustling them all off the grass, policemen asking questions, a reporter with a notebook elbowing her way to the centre of it all.

'So much for keeping this out of the papers,' groaned Forsyth. But Lil did not hear him. Anna was racing towards them, still carrying the attaché case, with Würstchen bounding joyfully at her heels. *Princesses do not run* – but this one did. She flung herself towards Alex and Lil.

Alex was wheezing more strenuously than she'd ever heard him, even now that Lil had unfastened his heavy leather coat and cast it aside, along with the scarf and goggles, but he still managed to pant out: 'Anna, you did it! I knew that you would – I was scared that if I wrote something obvious they'd notice and *know* it was me, but I knew you'd be able to work it out.'

'Well done, Anna,' said Lil, with a delighted laugh. 'I *told* Forsyth the two of you were jolly smart.'

But Anna was pointing across the airfield. 'Look – over there! It's the Countess – she's escaping!'

Sure enough, some distance away from the throng of people, Anna could see the figure of the Countess and her footman, disappearing into a motor car. Captain Forsyth had obviously already seen them, and was running towards the motor accompanied by two of the French policeman, but it was obvious that they would not get there in time. The footman was behind the wheel, and he was going to start the engine. They were going to escape.

But as Forsyth drew closer, something unexpected happened. The motor car would not start. Anna saw the Countess's face, red with screaming, in the back seat as she yelled at the footman to make the car go. So much for *discipline* and *decorum* now.

'She can scream as much as she likes. It isn't going to work,' said a nonchalant voice. To Lil's enormous surprise, she saw that Tilly was now standing beside them. In spite of being amongst the chaos of a Paris airfield, she looked as matter-of-fact as if she was back in her workshop at Taylor & Rose. 'I've removed a few essential components from the car engine,' she explained briskly. 'When I realised what was happening, I put two and two together, and I thought I'd take a few precautions to prevent anyone using that car to make a getaway,' she explained. 'Oh, this is Dr Bernard, by the way.' She gestured to the man standing beside her, in white flannels. 'He was very helpful in passing me spanners.'

Lil stared at her, and then back to where the Countess could be seen shrieking with rage and hitting out at Forsyth and the policeman. It was all completely perfect, she thought, and grinning at Sophie in delight.

But Sophie could not share her joy. She gave Lil a quick, rueful smile, and then looked away from the chaos, to stare up at the plane, already barely more than a speck in the sky, and with it the Professor's precious notebook, containing everything the *Fraternitas Draconum* needed to find the secret weapon.

'I've lost him,' she muttered to herself. 'He's gone.'

'Not necessarily,' said someone behind her. She looked round and saw that Captain Nakamura had strolled out from his hangar, and was surveying the chaos with interest. His dress-uniform had gone, to be replaced by a neat flying outfit, and his team of mechanics were even now bringing his plane into position.

'Clear the airfield!' called one of the officials. 'Everyone out of the way!'

'You wished to catch the Arnovian plane – is that right?' asked Nakamura.

Sophie nodded desperately and gulped. 'It sounds mad, I know, but the pilot has something vitally important. Top-secret information stolen from the British government which could be terribly dangerous if it falls into the wrong hands. I wanted to get it back, but it's too late now.'

'It doesn't have to be,' said Nakamura. 'I have a spare seat in my plane. We will be only minutes behind the Arnovian plane, and I am rather a good pilot – there is every chance we may catch him up. Tell me, have you ever flown before?'

Sophie gazed from him to the plane, and back again. 'You mean, I could go with you?' she asked incredulously.

'Why not?

'But . . . I couldn't possibly!'

'Of course you could. You'll need this, though.' The pilot picked up the leather coat the prince had worn, which was now lying abandoned on the ground. 'Put it on, and then the scarf over your hair. Tuck in the ends – that's right. And now the goggles.'

Almost as though she were in a dream, Sophie found herself doing as he told her. Although she could feel her heart racing, it was rather as if she were outside her own body, watching someone else as she shrugged into the heavy jacket. Nakamura put out a hand to help her into the passenger seat of the Japanese plane, and a moment later he had clambered into the seat in front of her.

'See – quite easy. Now all you have to do is sit back and relax,' the pilot said.

'Clear the field! Clear the field!' called the race official again, and Sophie saw the others fall back. Her stomach twisted horribly and her heart pumped harder, as Nakamura's mechanics set the plane moving across the grass. What was she *doing*? She was afraid of heights; the thought of flying terrified her; she didn't really know if she could trust Nakamura; she had no idea what she'd do when she found the Arnovian pilot, and what about Lil? She'd only just found her again. Tilly was right, she thought. She must be completely mad.

'*Sophie!*' Lil screamed out suddenly, seeing what was happening. 'Sophie, what are you doing?'

But Lil herself wouldn't think twice about doing something like this, Sophie realised suddenly. 'I'm going after the plane,' she shouted back. 'I have to try and get the notebook back!' But she didn't know if Lil had any idea what the notebook was. 'Tilly can explain everything,' she shouted.

Lil was running alongside the plane now, her eyes fixed on Sophie. 'Here – take this,' she cried, and tossed something up to her – a heavy rectangular object which rattled. Sophie caught it awkwardly – a small, brown leather attaché case, stuck all over with luggage labels – and wedged it carefully in beside her.

'Good luck!' called Lil, her voice both heartening, and at once making Sophie long suddenly and powerfully for home. *London: the striped deckchairs in the park; the hats in the windows of Sinclair's; tea and buns at Lyons Corner House with Lil.* 'Goodbye. I'll see you soon!' she tried to shout back, but her voice rushed away in the wind, and she could only stretch out her hand towards Lil in a half-wave, half-reaching movement as the machine lurched away. Then the propeller was spinning and they were running over the grass, and Lil was left behind them.

She was vaguely aware that the announcer was speaking: 'Ladies and gentleman, the next to take to the air is Captain Nakamura of Japan! Good luck, Captain Nakamura. *Bonne chance!*'

The ground was moving below her; the grass rushing past. The racket in her ears was terrible and the wind stung her cheeks. They rattled forward, faster and faster, and fear rose up in her throat. The plane felt so small, so flimsy, as though it would fall to pieces at any moment; the rattling grew louder; but then, almost as she felt she couldn't bear it any more, the jarring and shuddering suddenly stopped.

She felt them swoop upwards. They were in the air, rising higher and higher. The ground was falling away from her and the red-and-white Japanese flags that decorated the plane were fluttering wildly. She gripped the sides of the plane, a terrible sickness rising within her. The airfield and the spectators were growing smaller. She saw the flags and the balloons; she saw Sir Chester Norton on the platform; and the race officials with their watches and field-glasses; and Miss Roberta Russell with her notebook, receding away from her, as though something from a disturbing dream. She saw the grey man watching, shielding his eyes with his hand; she saw Tilly, hopping from one foot to another in excitement; she saw Dr Bernard, staring after them in confusion; and last of all, she saw Lil. She was standing with the prince and princess, a small dog barking at their feet. She was gazing up at the plane, waving her arm, her hat blown off and her skirts flying out. In spite of the goggles she was wearing, Sophie's eyes burned, and she found herself blinking in the wind.

Captain Nakamura's machine climbed up and away from them, neat and sure, into the open sky. They were so high now she hardly dared look down; for a while she made herself concentrate hard on the back of Nakamura's head. But after a while, her stomach seemed to stop its

277

terrible lurching, and she dared to peek down again. Now, Paris was spread like a map beneath her: she could see the shapes of buildings and roads, the green square of a park, the river slicing through everything. It was more beautiful than she could ever have imagined, and so still. There was no sound at all but the wind, rushing in her ears. She had never known such quiet.

Captain Nakamura glanced quickly over his shoulder, giving her a little nod, and she found herself nodding back. The air rushed against her face, clean and cold, and the sun glinted on the wires and strings of the plane, as they climbed upwards and away, towards the horizon.

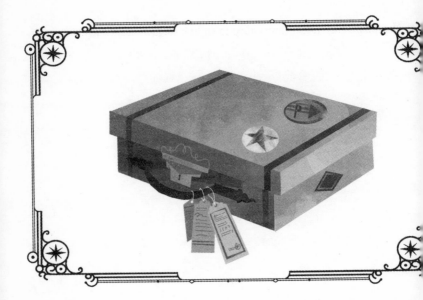

PART VI

'*I suppose even adventurers have to go home again eventually.*'

– From the diary of Alice Grayson

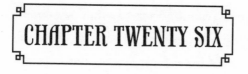

CHAPTER TWENTY SIX

Secret Service Bureau HQ, London

'Oh, it's *you*,' said a sardonic voice. Captain Carruthers was lounging in his chair by the open window, his shirt collar slightly open, his feet resting on the desk.

'Yes, it's *me*,' said Lil, bursting into the office with a theatrical flourish. She opened her eyes very wide and added dramatically: 'Why, were you expecting someone else?'

Carruthers rolled his eyes. 'Please. Spare me. It's far too hot to play the fool. You want the Chief, I suppose?'

'Oh no. I only come here to see *you*, Captain,' she trilled. 'Didn't you know that?'

'*Ha ha*, yes, very funny. He is waiting for you, you know, when you've quite finished your little comedy routine.' But Lil had already strode past Carruthers towards the Chief's office.

As she tapped on the door, Lil made up her mind to ask him for news of Sophie. After all, she'd been back from Paris for more than a week, and she still hadn't heard anything about what had happened after Sophie had climbed into the Japanese plane and soared off in pursuit of the Count.

Tilly had told her some of what had happened, and the Chief had filled in the rest of the gaps for her on her return to London. He'd shown her the blurry photograph that had been developed from the watch-camera: Princess Anna had managed to capture the Countess in the act of handing a notebook to the Count, sitting in the cockpit of the Arnovian plane. The notebook, the Chief had explained, contained highly dangerous and important information stolen from a murdered British agent, and that was what Sophie was trying so hard to get back.

'There's no doubt about it at all,' the Chief had explained. 'The Count and Countess von Wilderstein were working for the *Fraterntias Draconum* all along. Berlin have been very clear that they had nothing whatsoever to do with the plot to kidnap the prince and princess. We now believe that the entire kidnap plot was orchestrated by the *Fraternitas Draconum*. Up to their old tricks again, it would seem!'

Lil knew that the secret society had long been trying to stir up tensions in Europe. The Arnovian kidnapping had probably been intended to create conflict that would flare into a war between Britain and Germany. But instead, in an unlikely turn of events, British and German agents – for she knew now that the man who had helped them stop the plane had been one of Ziegler's spies – had ended up working together to rescue the prince. The German agent had disappeared from the airfield soon after the Japanese plane had taken off in pursuit of the Count, and no one had seen him again. How he'd ended up working with Sophie was anyone's guess – even Tilly didn't seem to understand that.

There were still an awful lot of questions to be answered. Who had broken into the British agent's apartment and stolen the notebook for the Count and Countess? Who was their contact at the *Fraternitas Draconum*, and if not to Berlin and Ziegler, then where was the Count planning to take the notebook? Lil wondered whether the Countess herself might answer any of these questions, now that she was being sent back to Arnovia to face trial. The Chief said that the evidence that Lil had gathered while she was undercover at Wilderstein Castle, together with the photograph taken by Anna, and Alex's testimony, would be quite enough to prove that the Countess had been working for the *Fraternitas Draconum* to plot against the King, and would doubtless see her sent to prison as a traitor to her country.

Meanwhile, the Count was still at large, though no one knew where. Lil had been following the air race closely, but 'Herr Wild' had vanished from the list of competitors. Some of the other pilots had left the race too, after accidents or technical problems; the Italian, Rossi had been disqualified after endangering the crowds with a particularly flamboyant display. But as the days went by, Captain Nakamura's plane continued to be listed amongst those that had completed each stage of the race safely.

The race had been all over the news, of course. If Sir Chester Norton had hoped that the race would help him sell more papers, then the attempted abduction of the Crown Prince at the airfield had only improved matters. Everyone wanted to read Miss Roberta Russell's breathless descriptions of the dramatic rescue of the young prince. Of course there was no mention of German spies, nor secret notebooks, nor the *Fraternitas Draconum*, but there was a description of 'Miss Sophie Taylor of London's Taylor & Rose Detective Agency' who had played an important part in stopping the treacherous Count and Countess von Wilderstein's second attempt to kidnap the Crown Prince of Arnovia, using the air race as a cover. Miss Russell's account implied that the scheme had been prevented by the British, German and French detectives working together, and the young journalist had praised this example of European collaboration. She had also pointed to the unexpected help of the Crown Prince's sister, Princess Anna, who had bravely helped to expose the plot, describing her as 'the young Arnovian princess, as brave as a warrior queen'. It made Lil smile: she suspected that Anna might prefer to think of herself as the 'Bravest Girl in the Fifth'.

But the newspapers weren't the only thing that kept Lil's

European adventure at the front of her mind. Everything she saw seemed to remind her of what had happened: the flags flying on the roof of Sinclair's made her think of Wilderstein Castle; that little dog she saw in the park looked a bit like Würstchen; a poster outside the Fortune Theatre informed her that they were about to open a new production of *The Tempest*. Even when she paused outside a bakery while she adjusted her hat to a more dashing angle, she couldn't help feeling a little sad looking at the array of delicious-looking confections set out in the window – rows of gleaming strawberry tarts, chocolate éclairs and iced buns, arranged on delicate paper doilies. They made her think of Anna and Alex, and how delighted they'd looked when they'd first seen that breakfast in the hotel in Paris.

She'd had a letter from Anna, sent from the Royal Palace in Elffburg, where she and her brother were now living with their grandfather. After the scandalous kidnapping attempts, the Kaiser had ordered his troops to retreat from the Arnovian border. A new peace treaty had been signed, reinforcing Arnovia's independence. Anna wrote that they would now live permanently in Elffburg:

It's wonderful to be here. Grandfather says we needn't ever go back to Wilderstein Castle again. And you won't believe what else! I told Grandfather that I don't want another governess - and he has agreed! Instead, he says we are both to be allowed to go to school in England in the autumn. He says the Countess's idea about what's suitable for princesses are fearfully outdated - and that after what happened, no one can ever say that princesses should be seen and not heard ever again! It is all very thrilling.

Could you please write and send me the address of the boarding school for girls that you went to? I think I should rather like to go there. When we come home for the holidays, we are to come back to Elffin Elffburg to be with Grandfather. He has appointed Karl as our own personal footman - he says he will be a sort of body-guard to look after us, although really we think of him as more of a friend. Grandfather has given him a medal of to honour his bravery in helping us escape from Wilderstein Castle, and he is awfully proud of it. Of course Grand father would very much like to give you a

Medal too — and Captain Forsyth of course —
although we have explained that he can't
because the whole point of the British Secret
Service is that it has to be a <u>secret</u>!
But I thought you'd like to know,
just the same.

Würstchen is also with us here at the
Royal Palace in Elffburg. He'll stay here with
Grandfather when we go to school. We do
give him bacon for breakfast, though not
every day. Karl says it would not
be good for him, especially when his tummy
is already so very tubby.

Alex is going to write to you soon. He has
been very busy writing a play in which the
hero gets abducted by an aeroplane-flying
villain, and he wants to send some of it to
you to read. He has only let me look at
the first scene so far, but I think it is
rather good. We have been looking at the
prospectus and all the papers about his new
school, and he's already decided that he's
going to join the dramatic society.

We hope that you will write to us both very
often. We are very glad indeed that you
came to Wilderstein Castle and I must say
that I agree with Alex that you are
the best governess we ever had.

With love from Anna

The letter made Lil smile a great deal. She'd written straight back with the details of her old school for Anna, already imagining the uproar that the arrival of a princess would cause for the headmistress Miss Pinker and her girls. A *Princess at Miss Pinker's* – it sounded exactly like the title of one of Anna's school stories. And how very put out Forsyth would be to hear that he had missed out on being given a medal!

But the letter made her feel a little sad too. It was wonderful to be back in London with her brother Jack, and Billy and Joe and all their friends, but it was also strange. The city seemed both familiar and oddly different. The people still surged in and out of Sinclair's department store; motors still passed by on Piccadilly; and the offices of Taylor & Rose were just the same as ever: Mei answering the telephone; clients arriving for appointments; Tilly working busily in her little workshop – after her discoveries in Paris she was now working on her own new and improved formula for a scentless invisible ink. Yet nothing seemed quite right without Sophie. Walking past Lyons Corner House gave Lil a pang; and somehow she couldn't settle down to work in the office they shared. She'd felt relieved that afternoon when Mei had come in with the message that Mr Clarke wanted to see her at Clarke & Sons Shipping Agents.

'Ah, Miss Rose,' he said now as she came into the office, hearing the strains of Tchaikovsky emanating from the gramophone. 'Delightful to see you. Do come in and sit down. Terribly hot, isn't it?' he added, as Lil sat down and took off her hat. 'Now, I suppose you'll be keen for news of Miss Taylor.'

She looked up at him in surprise. 'Is there any?' she asked eagerly. 'Where is she? Is she still trailing the Count? Has she got the notebook? Has she found out anything more about the *Fraternitas Draconum*?'

The Chief smiled at her. 'All I can tell you at present is that she is quite well, although she's unlikely to be back here with us any time soon. But you must not worry, Miss Rose. Your friend is a very resourceful young lady. This particular assignment has evolved in ways I had not expected, but I have every confidence in her.'

Lil nodded. She did too. She hoped they'd soon be back together, having tea and buns at Lyons and talking over everything, but for now she was happy just to know that Sophie was safe and well – wherever she was.

'And, of course, there is plenty we can do to help Miss Taylor,' said the Chief. 'There is a great deal about this business still to be investigated. Starting with *this*.' He pulled out a fat dossier and pushed it across the table towards her. 'Miss Rose, I believe I have a rather interesting new assignment for you . . .'

NO8934   **NORTON NEWSPAPERS**   ONE HALF PENNY

THE DAILY PICTURE
SPECIAL CORONATION EDITION

23rd JUNE 1911

LONDON CELEBRATES
CORONATION OF KING GEORGE V

Their Majesties, wearing their crowns, present themselves to the people after the Coronation ceremony at Westminster Abbey
- continued on p2.

SPECIAL REPORT
PERIL IN PARIS!

Our own correspondent, Miss R. Frost, reports on the failed plot to kidnap Crown Prince Alexander of Arnovia. Miss Russell was on the scene to witness the courageous rescue of the young Arnovian prince by a daring team of British, French and German detectives - continued on p3.

INTERNATIONAL NEWS

New treaty signed to protect Arnovian independence - p5

DIAGHILEV's Ballet Russe

DIAGHILEV brings fantastic Russian ballet to London - p15

A RELIABLE REMEDY
ELY'S CREAM BALM IS QUICKLY ABSORBED. CLEANSES AND SOOTHES HAYFEVER BE GONE!

ELY'S CREAM BALM FOR COLD IN HEAD CATARRH HAYFEVER HEADACHE ELY BROS

292

AUTHOR'S NOTE

This story is fictional – but just like the *Sinclair's Mysteries*, *Taylor & Rose: Secret Agents* takes inspiration from history. In particular, the Secret Service Bureau which appears in this story is inspired by the real-life Secret Service Bureau, which really was set up by the British government towards the end of 1909. Although it was initially very small, the organisation soon grew, and was later divided into two separate divisions, one dealing with counter-espionage at home, another gathering intelligence abroad. Today we know these two divisions as 'MI5' and 'MI6'.

The Grand Aerial Tour of Europe is based on the real-life air-races of the 1910s, such as the 1911 Circuit of Europe Race, which covered a distance of almost 1,000 miles and was sponsored by the newspaper *Le Journal*. 43 pilots took part in the race, but only nine of them managed to complete the course.

The country of Arnovia, and the Arnovian Royal Family are of course, completely imaginary. However, the adventures of Princess Anna and Crown Prince Alex were inspired by a grand tradition of stories set in fictional European countries – from the *The Prisoner of Zenda* to *The Princess of the Chalet School*, and many more.

ACKNOWLEDGEMENTS

I am so grateful to Ali Dougal and to the fantastic team at Egmont for all their support – and for helping Sophie and Lil to set out on this exciting new adventure. Special thanks to Laura Bird for the gorgeous design, and to Karl James Mountford, whose illustrations are so glorious that I simply had to name a character in this story after him.

Merci beaucoup, as always, to my agent and friend Louise Lamont for her wise advice (and the spoon of salt in Forsyth's tea). Enormous thanks to my parents, my friends, and particularly to my husband Duncan, who kept me company as I wandered about Paris imagining Sophie and Lil's adventures there.

Many thanks to the brilliant readers I met in schools in November and December 2017, who helped me to come up with the title for this new series. Thank you to all the wonderful booksellers, librarians and teachers who have supported the books; and to the readers (of all ages) who have enjoyed the *Sinclair's Mysteries* and who were so enthusiastic about wanting to know 'what happens next'.

Finally, very special thanks to my mum, for all the Paris memories.

See how it all began with Sophie and Lil's
original adventures in

The Sinclair's Mysteries

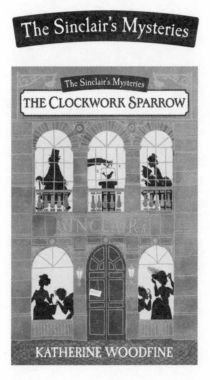

CHAPTER ONE

Sophie hung on tightly to the leather strap as the omnibus rattled forwards. Another Monday morning and, all about her, London was whirring into life: damp and steamy with last night's rain and this morning's smoke. As she stood wedged between a couple of clerks wearing bowler hats and carrying newspapers, she gazed out of the window at the grey street, wondering whether that faint fragrance of spring she'd caught on the wind had been just her imagination. She found herself thinking about the garden of Orchard House: the daffodils that must be blooming there now, the damp earth and the smell of rain in the grass.

'Piccadilly Circus!' yelled the conductor as the omnibus clattered to a halt, and Sophie pushed her thoughts away. She straightened her hat, grasped her umbrella in a neatly gloved hand, and slipped between the clerks and past an elderly lady wearing a *pince-nez*, who said 'Dear me!' as if quite scandalised at the sight of a young lady alone, recklessly jumping on and off omnibuses. Sophie paid no attention and hopped down on to the pavement. There was simply no sense in listening. After all, she wasn't that sort of young lady any more.

As the omnibus drew away, she turned and gazed for a moment at the enormous white building that towered above her. Sinclair's department store was so new that, as yet, it had not even opened its doors to customers. But already it was the most famous store in London – and therefore, some said, the whole world. With its magnificent columns and ranks of coloured flags, it wasn't like any other shop Sophie had ever seen. It was more like a classical temple that had sprung up, white and immaculate against the smog and dirt of Piccadilly. The huge plate-glass windows were shrouded with royal-blue silk curtains, making it look like the stage in a grand theatre before the performance has begun.

The owner of Sinclair's department store was Mr Edward Sinclair, who was as famous as the store itself. He was an American, a self-made man, renowned for his elegance, for the single, perfect orchid he always wore in his buttonhole, for the ever-changing string of beautiful ladies on his arm and, most of all, for his wealth. Although they had only been working for him for a few weeks, and most of them had barely set eyes on him, the staff of Sinclair's had taken to referring to him as 'the Captain', because rumour had it that he had run away to sea in his youth. There were already a great number of rumours about Edward Sinclair.

But whether the stories were true or not, it seemed an apt nickname. After all, the store itself was a little like a ship: as glittering and luxurious as an ocean liner ready to carry its customers proudly on a journey to an exotic new land.

Somewhere, Sophie could hear a clock chiming. Drawing herself up to her full height – which wasn't very tall – she lifted her chin and set off smartly round the side of the great building, the little heels of her buttoned boots clicking briskly over the cobbles. As she approached, her heart began to thump, and she put up a hand to check that her hat, with its blue-ribbon bow, was still at exactly the right angle, and that her hair was not coming down. She was part of Sinclair's department store now: a small cog in this great machine. As such, she knew she must be nothing short of perfect.

Through the doors was another world. The staff corridors were humming with activity. All about her, people were hurrying along carrying palms in pots, or stepladders and tins of paint, or stacks of the distinctive royal-blue and gold Sinclair's boxes. A smart saleswoman whisked by with an exquisitely beaded evening gown draped carefully over her arm; another hustled along with an armful of parasols, seemingly in a terrific rush; and the strict store manager, Mr Cooper, could be seen dressing down a salesman about the condition of his gloves. Sophie dived in among them and then slipped into the empty cloakroom to take off her coat and hat.

It still seemed extraordinary that she was here at all. Even a year ago, the thought of earning her own living would never have entered her imagination – and now, here she was, a fully fledged shop girl. She paused for a moment before the cloakroom looking-glass to survey her hair, and pushed a hairpin back into place. Mr Cooper was a stickler for immaculate personal appearances, but worse than that, she knew that Edith and the other girls would be only too quick to notice any shortcomings. Once upon a time she had been rather vain about her looks, carefully brushing her hair one hundred times each night and fussing Miss Pennyfeather to tie her velvet ribbon in exactly the right sort of bow, but now she only wanted to look neat and businesslike. She didn't feel in the least like the girl she had been back then. Her face in the looking glass was familiar, but strange: she looked older somehow, pale and tired and out of sorts.

Her shoulders slumped as she thought of the long week that lay ahead of her, but at once she frowned at herself sharply. Papa would have said that she ought to be thinking about how fortunate she was to be here. There were plenty of others who weren't so lucky, she reminded herself. She had seen them: girls her own age or even younger, selling apples or little posies of flowers on street corners; girls begging for pennies from passing gentlemen; girls huddled in doorways, wearing clothes that were scarcely more than rags.

Thinking this, she shook her head, squared her

shoulders and forced herself to smile. 'Buck up,' she told her reflection sternly. Whatever else happened today, she was determined that she wouldn't give Edith any more excuses to call her stuck-up.

She strode purposefully towards the door, but before she had taken more than a couple of steps, she tripped and fell forwards.

'Oh!' exclaimed a voice. As she righted herself, she glanced down to see a boy gazing up at her in alarm. He was sitting on the floor, partly hidden behind a row of coats, and she had fallen over his boots. 'Are you all right?'

'What are you *doing* down there?' demanded Sophie breathlessly, more embarrassed to have been caught pulling faces and talking to herself than actually hurt. No doubt this boy would make fun of her now, like all the rest, and he'd soon be telling all the others what he had overheard. 'You shouldn't hide in corners spying!' she burst out.

'I wasn't spying,' said the boy, scrambling to his feet. He was wearing the Sinclair's porters' uniform – trim dark-blue trousers, a matching jacket with a double row of brass buttons and a peaked hat – but the jacket looked too big for him, the trousers a bit short, and the hat was askew on his untidy, straw-coloured hair. 'I was *reading*.' For proof, he held out a crumpled story-paper, entitled *Boys of Empire*, in one grubby hand.

But before Sophie could say anything else, the door slammed open, and a cluster of shop girls pushed their way into the room, in a flurry of skirts and ribbons.

'Excuse us! Beg your pardon!'

A pretty dark-haired girl caught sight of the boy and smirked. 'Haven't you fetched that tin of elbow grease for Jim yet?' she demanded, sending a ripple of titters through the group.

'Learned to tie your bootlaces all by yourself, have you?' another girl giggled.

A third took in Sophie, and made a ridiculous curtsy in her direction. 'Forgive us, Your Ladyship. We didn't see that you were gracing us with your presence.'

'Aren't you going to introduce us to your young man?' added the dark-haired girl in an arch tone, making the others laugh even more.

The boy's cheeks flushed crimson, but Sophie tried her hardest to look indifferent. She had heard this kind of thing many times already during the two weeks of training that all the Sinclair's shop girls had undertaken. She had realised that she had started all wrong on the very first morning, arriving wearing one of her best dresses – black silk and velvet with jet buttons. She had thought she ought to be smart and make a good first impression, but when she arrived, she realised that every other girl in the room was dressed almost identically, in a plain dark skirt, and a neat white blouse. The rustle and swish of her skirts had made them all look at her, and then begin giggling behind their hands.

'Who does she think she is? The Lady of the Manor?' the dark-haired girl, Edith, had whispered.

The next morning she had come carefully dressed in a navy-blue skirt and a white blouse with a little lace collar, but it was already too late. The girls called her 'Your Ladyship', or if they wanted to be especially mean, 'Your Royal Highness' or 'Princess Sophie'. All through the training, they made game of the way she spoke, the clothes she wore, the way she did her hair, and especially whenever she was praised by Mr Cooper or Claudine, the store window-dresser.

She had tried hard to look unconcerned, and not to let her feelings show. Papa had always said that in times of war, the most important thing was never to let the enemy see that you were intimidated. Remembering this she saw his face again, almost as if he were standing right in front of her with his bright, dark eyes and neat moustache. He would have been pacing up and down on the hearth rug in his study, the walls hung with maps and treasures he had brought back from distant lands, relating one of his many stories about battles and military campaigns. *Keep calm, keep your head, keep a stiff upper lip*: those were his mottoes. But the truth was, the more she ignored the other shop girls, the worse they seemed to become. They said she was haughty and high-and-mighty, and called her the name she hated most, 'Sour-milk Sophie'. Not for the first time, she reflected that perhaps Papa's advice was not *entirely* helpful when it came to dealing with horrid shop girls.

Now, she turned away and went out into the passage, the boy trailing behind her. He looked so miserable that she felt a twinge of guilt for having assumed that he would make fun of her, when, in fact, it seemed that they were in the same boat.

'I shouldn't pay any attention to them,' she said.

The boy tried to smile. 'I really wasn't spying on you – honest, I wasn't,' he said anxiously. 'I just wanted to finish my serial. I didn't even notice you were there. It's the latest Montgomery Baxter.' Seeing that she looked blank, he went on: 'It's about a detective. He's only a boy, you see, but somehow he always solves the crime and outwits the villain, even when no one else can.' He beamed at her enthusiastically and, rather to her surprise, Sophie found herself smiling back. 'I just had to find somewhere out of sight to finish it, so Mr Cooper didn't catch me reading. Anyway, I'm sorry I tripped you up,' he finished.

'It doesn't matter,' said Sophie. She held out her hand politely, like Miss Pennyfeather had taught her. 'I'm Sophie Taylor. I'm in the Millinery Department.' She had already learned that using her full name, Taylor-Cavendish, would do her no favours here at Sinclair's. It was safer to stick to plain old Taylor.

'Billy Parker, apprentice porter,' he explained, accepting her hand and giving it a firm shake.

'Parker? Then are you –?'

'Related to Sidney Parker? Yes. He's my uncle, worse luck,' Billy said, grimacing. 'Oh cripes, and here he comes now,' he murmured in a lower voice, hastily stuffing the creased story-paper into his pocket as a man came striding towards them along the passageway.

Like everyone else at Sinclair's, Sophie already knew exactly who Sidney Parker was. He was Head Doorman, in charge of the whole team of doormen and porters, and Mr Cooper's right-hand man. Tall and handsome in a bullish sort of way, he was impossible to miss in his immaculate uniform. With his hat perfectly brushed, his buttons gleaming and his glossy black moustache always smoothed into place, he couldn't have been more different from his untidy nephew.

'Good morning, miss,' he said, sweeping off his hat with the respectful manner he used for all ladies. Then he turned to Billy. 'Where do you think you've been? Stand up straight, lad – and cheer up, can't you? You look like a wet weekend.'

He winked at Sophie as though they were sharing a joke at Billy's expense and then swung the door that led to the shop floor open for her with exaggerated politeness. Throwing a quick smile over her shoulder to Billy, she walked out of the passageway.

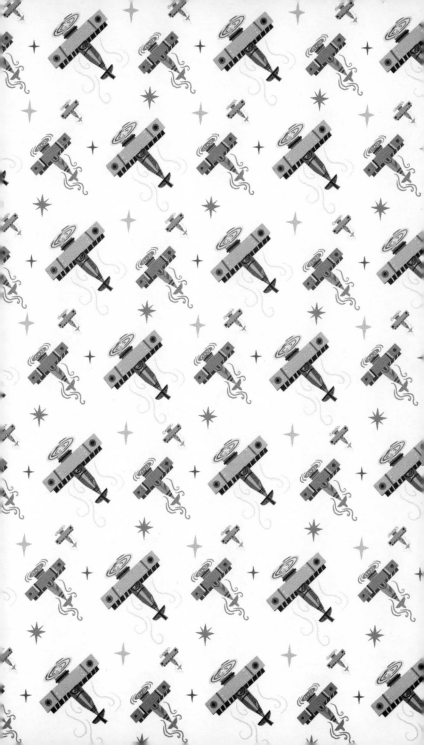